The Scarlet Key

OTHER TITLES BY DEBBIE TERRANOVA

Enemies within these Shores

Baby Farm

Mowbray Brothers

The Scarlet Key

DEBBIE TERRANOVA

This is a work of fiction. Names, characters, organizations, places and incidents either are the product of the author's imagination or are used fictitiously, and any resemblance to actual persons, living or dead, business establishments, events or locales is entirely coincidental.

Copyright © Debbie Terranova 2016

All rights reserved. Except for private study, research, criticism or reviews as permitted under the Copyright Act, no part of this book may be reproduced, or stored in a retrieval system, or transmitted in any form or by any means without prior written permission from the publisher.

First published 2016 by Terranova Publications
Revised 2018
PO Box 4144, St Lucia South, Queensland 4067 Australia
Email: terranovapublications@gmail.com

ISBN-13: 978 0 9941700 1 9 (paperback)

Cover design by Elise Terranova
Website: www.eliseterranova.com

For Sam, Elise, and Adam

My inspiration always

1

The Key Courier

Thursday 6 August

Late for work after a heavy night, Seth VerBeek locked the Jeep and ran up the fire stairs to the first floor of Newspaper House. His desk was a war-zone of papers, folders, magazines, and the odd pack of cigarettes. On the wall were a dozen yellowed news clippings, all with his name on the by-line. He swept the clutter aside and put the cardboard coffee cup down on the desk.

Propped up against his computer screen was a plain white envelope. He flipped it open, tipped out the contents. Wrapped in a crinkled scrap of paper was a house key. Anodised, scarlet in colour, flat on one edge and serrated on the other.

Holding it up, he called out across the office. 'Anyone know where this came from?'

His colleagues were all busy tapping keyboards, yabbering on phones, or scrolling the newsfeeds for stories. Cate Bradshaw in the next cubicle was the only one who answered.

'Hey, boss. Didn't hear you come in.'

Two white wires protruded from her ears. Tinny music from her phone reverberated through the bones of her skull. The volume was way too loud.

'It's a wonder you can hear at all,' he said through gritted teeth.

She pulled out an earbud. 'What?'

Seth dangled the red key over the drab office divider. 'Is this yours?'

'Nope.' Ropes of black hair coiled down her shoulders. 'Did you read my email?'

1

'Tell me; it's quicker.'

She shrugged. 'An elderly gentleman gave me the envelope this morning. He said *Seth VerBeek will know what to do.* Those were his exact words. Inside is the address. He said you should go there straight away.'

On his desk Seth smoothed out the torn notepaper. The address had been scribbled in blunt pencil, the sort a carpenter might use. The handwriting was worse than his family doctor's. He angled the paper to the florescent light but it was indecipherable.

He went around the divider to Cate. 'Can you make this out?'

As smug as a cat with feathers on its lips, she smiled. 'Yes, of course.'

With as much patience as he could muster, he waited for a proper response.

She touched the screen of her phone, held it over the page and touched the screen again. 'There. I've sent it to you.' With that, she stuffed the earbud back into its socket.

Sometimes she was intolerable, but she was also indispensable and she knew it. Without her, his ineptitude with technology would be outed. Sure he could surf the internet and send photos from his phone. But when it came to blue teeth and clouds and wonder apps that did everything from taking your blood pressure to ordering pizza, he was a Luddite.

At his desk he opened the virtual message box and found Cate's scanned image. Beneath it, the appalling scrawl had been translated into plain font.

53 Maryland Avenue, Corinda.

If that wasn't enough, there was a convenient satellite map, pinpointing the exact location and showing the quickest route from Newspaper House.

He took a sharp breath. The place in question was two blocks away from the nursing home where his elderly mother lived. For ages he'd been meaning to visit but hadn't found the courage. For his mother it probably didn't matter. Long ago she'd forgotten that he was her own flesh and blood. Mostly she called him Alec. He had no idea who Alec was but it seemed to make her happy. Often she'd rage or swear or throw things at the wall. It seemed that the kind, capable lady she once was had departed this world, leaving an evil twin that looked exactly like Lorna VerBeek.

Cate came into his cubicle. 'We should get going.'

'We?'

'Tell me you don't need me, boss.'

'Okay, okay. I acknowledge your superior intellect, Ms Bradshaw—'

'Despite the sarcasm, thank you!'

'—and your impertinence.'

Grinning, she turned and trotted down the corridor to the stairs. For a moment he stood there shaking his head. If he chose to stay with *The Morning Post* another five years, it was likely she'd be *his* boss. Would she lose that wicked sense of humour? He hoped not. Days like this, she was the only reason he came to work.

In the post-war suburb of Corinda, Seth parked outside a squat weatherboard cottage with a picket fence. Sixty years ago, all the houses in the street would have been modest timber boxes exactly the same. Now there was a salt-and-pepper mix of downtrodden originals, expensive renovations, and modern two-storey townhouses. Number 53 was definitely one of the first. Most of the paintwork had peeled away, leaving strips of silvered hardwood. The casement windows were shut and sad lace curtains sagged behind dirty glass.

A jacaranda, all limbs and bark, hung over the footpath. A tangle of shrubs concealed the gate. Outposts of sticky cobblers' pegs lay in ambush amongst the knee-high paspalum. Abandoned houses were fuel for the imagination. Seth touched the scarlet key in his pocket. Although his curiosity was whetted, a sense of foreboding moistened his palms.

Why would an *elderly gentleman* bearing a red key and a cryptic address seek him out? Didn't the old coot recognise the intermediary? Cate Bradshaw's youthful face had graced every story she'd ever written. And if she already knew what was in the envelope, why didn't she tell Seth outright?

Suspicion niggled like a toothache.

'Okay Cate, what *don't* I know?'

She raised her hands, a silent plea of innocence. 'Nothing. The old bloke came up to me in the carpark and gave me the envelope. It was over in seconds.'

'Can you describe him?'

'A bit scruffy. Grey hair, jeans, Broncos football jersey.'

'How old *was* he?'

'Oh … you know.' She frowned and tapped a finger against her chin. The corner of her lip gave an upward twitch. 'About sixty I guess.'

Seth shot her a caustic look. 'Not very old at all then.'

He lifted the gate latch and they walked up a cracked concrete path. At the front door he knocked, not expecting a response. From all appearances, the house had been empty for some time. He waited a polite twenty seconds and knocked again.

'Let's give this baby a try,' he said. In the sun the key sparkled like a ruby.

Cate's cheeks were glowing in anticipation.

He pressed the key to the slot but it wouldn't go in.

'Let's try the back.' She skipped down the steps and disappeared around the side.

Wroooo wroo wrooooooo! The eerie cry rose and fell. Whatever the breed of canine, the message was clear. *Get out or I'll bloody well rip you apart!*

Dodging rocks and clumps of long grass, Seth entered a narrow gap between the house and the fence. It was cluttered with fallen branches. Spiky undergrowth snapped at his ankles. The dog was growling with menace and scratching at the fence.

From up ahead came a crack like a bolder being dropped onto concrete.

A yelp of shock—or was it fear—and something heavy crashed to the ground.

'Cate!' He sprinted through the shrubs. A high timber gate, slightly ajar, pulled him up. The gap wasn't wide enough for him to get through. He pushed against it with his shoulder but it wouldn't budge. Looking down, he immediately saw the problem: the lower edge was partly buried in the dirt.

He called out again. 'Cate, you okay?'

No answer. The dog next door was going wild.

Seth clenched his jaw and heaved the gate up and out of the bog. Once through, he batted away vines and cobwebs as he scrambled towards the rear of the house.

A massive sinkhole was right front of him. Face-down at the bottom was Cate. Surrounded by chunks of broken concrete, her body lay at an awkward angle. Her hair splayed out, a dark halo around her head.

In horror he stared. Flashbacks to the dying days of the war flooded his memory but he pushed them aside. Cate needed help and only he was there to give it.

The sinkhole was more than a metre deep. He lowered himself in, removed a few pieces of concrete to make room, and squatted beside her. The impact had knocked her out cold. Her breathing and pulse were okay and no bones seemed to be broken. Gently he rolled her into the recovery position. A gash on her forehead was oozing profusely.

Suddenly she opened her eyes and grabbed his arm. 'Get … me … outta … here!'

'Don't move.'

'I'm … just … fine.' She pushed herself up. Her face was covered in mud. A line of red trickled over her left eyebrow.

Seth mopped it with a hanky.

'Owww!' She pushed him away.

The gash looked deep and nasty. It was clear she needed medical attention but he didn't want her to panic. 'Can you stand up?' His tone was calm, encouraging.

'I … I think so.' She raised her arms; he lifted her up. Swaying slightly, she closed her eyes and clung to the concrete wall.

To steady her, Seth grabbed her shoulders. Her hair brushed against him, as soft and sensuous as liquid silk.

Moments later she regained her composure. 'Where the hell am I?'

'In a septic tank.'

'What!' Her eyes went wide.

'You know, from the days before sewerage. The waste water from the house went into the septic tank, then into a trench where it was absorbed into the ground.'

'So this is *crap* all over me?' Her nose wrinkled.

'Once, maybe. Now it's just dirt. C'mon, let's get you out.'

Next-door's dog—a brown kelpie—was watching them through a section of chain-wire fence. Sniffing, it put its snout through a diamond of wire. With a parting growl it lifted its leg and trotted away.

Seth knelt on one knee and made a step of the other. Cate hauled herself up and rolled out onto the grass, puffing from the effort. The wound opened further. Ignoring her protests, Seth pressed his hanky to her forehead.

'Straight to the doctor with you.'

'Try the key first,' she urged.

'Not a chance.'

'It'll only take a sec.' She kicked his leg. 'Go!'

When her mind was made up, arguing was useless. He bandaged the hanky around her head and, armed with the scarlet key, hurried up the ramp to the back door.

The house was in worse condition here than the front. Banana-skins of yellow paint hung from the weatherboards. Battalions of ants marched along the woodwork. Cobwebs hung in thick blankets from the eaves.

One glance and he knew the key wouldn't fit. The old lock had an open keyhole, the sort you could spy through. The scarlet key was shaped like a saw.

'Well?' said Cate. The improvised dressing was already soaked in blood.

'Struck out. Seems your *elderly gentleman* has a touch of dementia.'

'Bummer! This had the makings of an excellent story.'

He helped her up. She was shaking so hard that her teeth were chattering. Slowly they retraced their steps through sagging gate and the overgrown bushes to the Jeep parked out the front.

Exhausted, she flopped into the passenger's seat.

As he started the ignition, he took a long last look at the dilapidated house. In his hand was the red key. Its zigzag of cut metal bit into his palm.

Was it a case of mistaken identity or a misguided prank?

One thing was certain: he needed to get Cate to a doctor. He planted his foot on the accelerator and took her to the Corinda Family Practice where they waited in a roomful of coughs and sneezes for an hour.

Later he drove her home.

2

Redundant

Twenty-one months ago: early summer

At eight-fifteen Monday morning, Isla Bright parked her white Toyota Camry in the bay reserved for the Head of Art. The best spot in the staff carpark—the only one with shade—was her reward for being the longest-serving teacher at Corella High. A giant ironbark teeming with blossoms spread its arms over the bitumen. By afternoon her car would be yellow with threadlike petals and splattered with bird poo but she didn't care. In the heat of summer, hers would be ten degrees cooler than all the rest.

For a moment she paused to gather her wits before facing the rabble of the classroom. Students in faded green-and-white uniforms were mingling on the quadrangle. Somehow they were able to talk and copy homework and eat and fiddle with their smartphones all at the same time. Every day their routine was the same. Soon the bell would ring and the daily rollercoaster ride would begin.

Isla opened the boot of the car and collected her bag, books, and a box of assignments that she'd marked at home. Hugging the carton she tramped across the quadrangle and up the stairs to the double classroom in C-Block. The art studio.

She put down the carton to get out the keys, unlocked the door. What was inside, made her gasp.

The stench alone almost knocked her off her feet. The odours of paint, glue, and solvent had combined into a toxic stink bomb. Desks were lying on their backs and chairs were scattered about the floor. The vast expanse of vinyl glistened with a glaze of acrylic paint as shiny as a technicolour skating rink.

Her previously immaculate art studio was the victim of a paint-ball attack. Everything she'd held dear was slashed and splashed with all things bright and gruesome. *Skool sux* was spray-painted on one wall and *Brite sux* was on another. In a small way it saddened her that, after a decade or so of education, the perpetrators still couldn't spell.

Never before had this happened. Not to her, not to anyone at Corella High. Never, in all her years of teaching, had her classroom been trashed. Her mouth opened in a silent scream of rage.

How dare they! A geyser of blood shot into her head.

In that room were the final assessment pieces, works destined for the end-of-year art show in a few weeks' time. As usual Isla was organising everything. The agenda was set, the refreshments were arranged, the prize categories had been advertised. The most outstanding students would win books, bought from coins collected in the 'Swear Jar'. Kids thrived on encouragement and recognition. Despite their diverse and disadvantaged backgrounds, most had risen to the challenge.

Overnight all that effort had turned to shite.

Isla stepped into the room. The rubber soles of her sandals squelched in the goop. Stooping, she picked up a sodden paper from the floor. *View from My Window* by fifteen-year-old Amber Collier. Post-impressionist style, nicely executed, good balance. The best piece she'd done all year. Now it was in tatters.

Pale yellow liquid rolled over the surface and dripped onto Isla's feet. The unmistakeable smell of urine drifted into her nose. She raced to the washbasin, rinsed her feet and sandals and scrubbed her hands with soap.

Filthy creatures! Who could have done this?

Seething, she strode out of the art room and stormed towards Principal Dean's office at the far end of the building. Every step added to the mounting head of steam. By the time she arrived, she was a pressure cooker ready to blow.

Marjorie Wippet—the white-haired receptionist who'd worked there forever—was hunched over the desk. Her head was buried in her hands; she seemed not to notice that Isla was fuming beside her.

The principal's door was shut. The raised voices of Brian Dean and an unidentified female seeped through walls as thin as cardboard.

Isla drummed her fingers on the reception desk. 'When you're free, Marjorie …'

The other woman's hands opened.

'Oh my! You gave me quite a start!' Marjorie made a show of straightening a stack of papers. She tucked a stray lock of hair behind her ear and brushed invisible crumbs from her keyboard. When she finally looked up, her blue eyes were rimmed with red.

Marjorie Wippet gave the impression of being a caring and benevolent old lady, but she was nothing of the sort. She could charm you one minute and eat you alive the next. Her moment of weakness soon passed and the steel shutters crashed down again.

'I need to see Brian urgently,' Isla said.

'He's busy. Come back at morning recess.'

'My art room has been vandalised,' Isla snapped. Every square inch of her skin was hot, even the inside of her mouth.

Showing no reaction, Marjorie reached for the phone. 'I'll call the police. In the interim, you may relocate your classes to the library.'

'School protocol requires serious incidents to be reported immediately to the principal. *In person.* Someone has broken in, trashed school property and destroyed students' work. That, in my opinion, constitutes a serious incident. Don't you agree?'

Marjorie's eyes faded to the colour of Antarctic ice. Any emotion shown earlier was now dead and buried. The two ageing war-horses glared at each other across the desk in a contest of stubbornness and nerve.

Suddenly the principal's door flew open and the music teacher, Maxine Daniels, blundered out. Her cheeks were shiny and plastered with strands of hair. Looking neither left nor right, she walked straight past them. Isla had never seen her so upset. The one-time hippie was into karma, meditation, and drumming circles. Normally she could turn rebellious fourteen-year-olds into toe-licking puppies with a single clap of her hands. Today her clogs clattered defiantly down the stairs.

Principal Brian Dean had followed Maxine out and was standing in the doorway. His over-large face and broad chest gave him the appearance of a human bull-dog. Courtesy of twenty years' service in the military, his vocal chords knew only how to bellow and he harboured an obsession for mirror-clean black leather shoes. Every lunch break he'd march around the grounds and haul out anyone who was playing up or making a nuisance of themselves. But, despite a terrifying exterior, he had a kind heart.

Today he looked as if he'd been caught in the schoolyard wearing just his underpants. Clearly, something was amiss.

Isla said, 'Brian, I need to see you.'

'I need to see you too.' He straightened his tie and stepped aside to let her pass.

The principal's den was spacious, functional and undoubtably masculine. Although flooded with morning sunlight, the temperature was as cool as a wine cellar. The northern window gave sweeping views across the rose gardens to the big ironbarks along the boundary line and the rooftops of the workers' cottages beyond. Lining the walls were bookshelves of leather-bound volumes: all literary classics probably selected for appearance rather than content. Brian, a teacher of maths and physics, would be more interested in *Science Weekly* than the works of Thomas Hardy or Joseph Conrad.

She sat in the visitor's chair, the seat still warm from Maxine. A drop of moisture glistened on the armrest.

Brian sank into an oversized swivel chair. On the wall behind him hung a faded print of Queen Elizabeth wearing a lemon dress, blue sash and diamonds. Folding his arms, he rocked forward and flashed a grin. His teeth were slightly uneven and dimples rippled about his cheeks. 'How's my favourite art teacher today?' he began.

Isla's crankiness evaporated. She'd been infatuated with him for more years than she could count. An impossible fantasy, for Brian was married and obviously loved his wife. Knowing that nothing would ever happen made it easier for her to dream.

The man was charming. No, not charming exactly. Charismatic. Of course she was the *only* art teacher at the school but his corny compliment plucked her heartstrings. Her skin was tingling and an embarrassing hormonal rash was crawling up her neck. The more she tried to control it, the more her body smouldered. For seven years it had been like this. Menopause was shaping up to be worse than adolescence.

Isla let the air flow in through her mouth and over her tongue, a yoga trick to manage melt-downs. Today it didn't help. She needed to tell him about the vandals so that he could put everything right and she could get on with her job.

Simultaneously they both began.

'Sorry ...' she said, red-faced. 'I didn't mean to interrupt.'

'No, you go first.' His tone was flat; his eyes were sunken.

She sensed something was about to happen. Something big.

All thoughts of the break-in flew from her mind. Instead of launching into a tirade she said, 'What is it, Brian?'

'Isla ...'

To her complete surprise, he reached across the desk and grasped her hand. Her heart gave a limp flutter. Ordinarily she would have been swooning. Instead, she tensed. The bottom was about to fall out of her world, she just knew it. Whatever he was about to say terrified her.

'Isla, we've worked together a long time.' He was struggling to choose the right words. 'I want you to know that I've enjoyed every minute. You are an outstanding teacher and an amazing person. Nothing will ever change that.' His face was white.

Her gut twisted into a knot. She nodded. 'I love my job. It's my life.'

'That's why this is so bloody difficult.' He released her hand, rested his elbows on the desk. He looked utterly distraught.

'Isla, they're going to close the school.'

'No way! I read some rubbish in *The Morning Post* last week but Corella High will never close. It'd be a huge mistake. The community would riot.'

'It will close, believe me. The Regional Head phoned me Saturday. I was on the green of the eighth hole. Two under par. After the call I couldn't finish the game.'

'Then we'll fight! The government will *have* to listen. Remember Vietnam? Remember the moratorium marches? People power can win every time.'

'This isn't the seventies, Isla.' He opened the top drawer, took out a dun-coloured envelope. Without fanfare he slid it across the desk.

'As principal of this school, it is my unfortunate duty to offer you a voluntary early retirement package. Everything is set out in this letter. At the end of this term, the school will close forever. The land has been sold to a property developer.'

In a whirlwind of disbelief, Isla took the envelope. It was unsealed and had no stamp. The deer-and-brolga coat of arms of the State of Queensland was printed on the front, along with her name and the school's address. Her eyes brimmed with tears. She looked around the room. Everything was distorted. The envelope, her hand, the bookshelves, Brian's hang-dog expression. She blinked and condensed sorrow rolled down her cheeks.

All of a sudden she was boiling and freezing at the same time. Shivering, she stood up to leave. The room began to spin. Strong arms wrapped around her, the only body contact in all those years. Nothing sexual, nothing suggestive. Just the firm embrace of one person comforting another. His chest was a barrel; his skin was soft. For a moment she relaxed, purring almost. Then the sharp edge of the envelope dug into her wrist and she crashed back to reality.

In four weeks' time the school would no longer exist. The umbilical cord would be cut and she'd be cast into unemployment for the first time ever. *Voluntary early retirement.* What a misnomer! She was only fifty-seven. Fifty-seven was too young to retire. She'd always imagined working until pension age. That was another eight years. What would she do now without a job?

Brian released her and perched on the edge of the desk. He was so close she could smell his aftershave. Spicy with a hint of cinnamon. Her heart was ripping apart. The best of days and the worst of days.

'I'm sorry, Isla. If it were up to me …'

'Wait. Didn't you say this was *voluntary*?'

'That's the term they use. I don't know a person yet who's knocked it back. Have you seen the dollars? Have you thought about the alternatives?'

With trembling fingers she opened the envelope and took out the letter. The price of buying her out was truly staggering. Five weeks' notice, two weeks' pay for every year of service, cash for her leave entitlements, an additional twelve weeks' pay if she signed by the end of the week.

'Thought you'd be pleasantly surprised. Imagine what you could do with that money!'

'I … I don't know what to say.' Another flush was brewing. She fanned herself with the redundancy letter and miraculously the heatwave disappeared.

'Think about it. Talk to your accountant. This could be the start of a new life.'

'What if I don't accept?'

'Oh, they'll place you in another school. You might have to drop a pay-point or two, or you might end up at the back of Bourke.'

'What about you, Brian? What will you do?'

He chuckled. 'I'd be mad if I didn't take it and run. Mary and I always wanted to do a grand tour of Europe. None of us is getting any younger. It's the chance of a lifetime!'

From a man who'd dedicated much of his career to excellence in pedagogy, the flippant response was unexpected. Perhaps there was truth in the adage that *every man has his price*. Whatever incentive they'd offered Brian, it was enough to make him gleefully dump his vocation and crack open the French champagne.

Outside, the first bell jangled. In five minutes, classes would begin.

Brusquely Isla tapped the envelope on the desk. 'I'd better be going.'

'I'm calling a staff meeting at three. Until then, please keep this to yourself. There'll be food and a few drinks and also a counsellor. It's a good chance to talk it all through.'

'Okay, see you then.' She opened the door and was half-way along the corridor when she remembered the reason she'd gone to see him. The break-in had paled into insignificance. In a few short weeks, the school and everything it stood for would be bulldozed. She tried to imagine the gaping hole it would leave in the suburb and in their lives. Like a bad tooth extracted and the gap filled with a sparkling new implant that didn't fit.

This school was part of Isla's DNA. What she'd been offered—small fortune that it was—was a pathetic bribe. The reward for all those years of devoted service was little more than a kick in the guts. No appreciation, no recognition, no future.

Every man has his price.
Did she too have her price?

3

Gone to the dogs

Twenty-one months ago: early summer

Wednesday was Lola's day.

Of all Claude's clients, Lola Molloy was the most interesting and also the most lucrative. He'd been seeing her for nearly a decade, the arrangement starting shortly after he gave up being a public servant and struck out on his own. Not for one moment had he regretted the decision to resign. His microbusiness earnt enough to cover expenses such as smokes, beer and pizza, and to top up his account at the betting agency. There was also a small cache of cash, hidden under the floorboards in his bedroom. Soon he'd be able to get the age pension and then he'd be set for life.

Summer had begun in a furious heatwave and the traffic was chaos. Too hot to walk or cycle to work, or (heaven forbid) make the kiddies catch the bus to school, everyone was driving their cold-rooms on wheels around the city. The road to Lola's rural property on the outskirts of town was bumper to bumper all the way. By the time the ute turned into the driveway, it was half past nine. Shirl's mag wheels bumped along the rough dirt track that ran between the weatherboard cottage and the kennels. She nosed in beneath the canopy of a giant Moreton Bay fig tree that would have been older than the house itself.

Waiting for him in the shade was Lola, accompanied by two of her retired greyhounds, Bessie and Freeman. Both were favourites that she couldn't bear to part with.

'Claude Fabergé, where on earth have you been?' she said in mock anger. With hands on hips she waddled to the driver's side. Her navy sundress with yellow flowers ballooned around her, making her seem twice as big as she was. While she waited for him to get out, she fanned herself with a large floppy hat. The dogs' tongues were lolling out and their tails were slapping her skirt like riding crops.

Claude cut the engine and opened the door. Moist snouts pushed into his hands. 'You want a pat, do you?' he said, ruffling their long eager faces.

'Me too,' said Lola, holding out her arms for a hug.

Going to Lola's was the same as going home. Warm and familiar and comfortable. Sadly for him, home—both the place and the feeling—vanished when he was six. Perhaps that was why he treasured Wednesdays in the outer suburb of Greenfield amongst paddocks, trees and animals. And big-hearted Lola who bred and trained racing greyhounds for a crust.

'Come in and have a bite.'

Claude's stomach rumbled at the thought of a nice cup of milky tea with sticky buns from Coles. Having risen at dawn to mow the lawn before the heat set in, he'd forgotten to have breakfast. The physical activity of looking after his own place and his clients' kept him trim and strong. Never had he felt more alive and in control. Every day he thanked the worst boss in history for forcing him to ditch the desk job.

'Did you see the article in *The Morning Post*?' said Lola.

'Didn't have time this morning.'

Lola set the kettle on the stove and filled a metal bowl with fresh water for the dogs. They lapped noisily then flopped on the kitchen floor for a nap. Between them they took up most of the spare space. Lola had to step around legs and tails to bring the plate of food to the table.

'Here, read this.' She opened the broadsheet at page six, folded it in quarters, and pushed it across the table to Claude.

The headline read *Gone to the dogs*.

Claude groaned. For ages animal rights activists had been pressuring the government, and anyone else who would listen, to shut down the greyhound racing industry. The latest round began with an expose on a current affairs program about an unscrupulous breeder who'd kept dogs in cages not much larger than the ones for battery hens. For the animal activists, the media frenzy that followed was like the announcement of free beer at the pub. They flocked to the bar with stories that grew bigger and more righteous by the minute.

With trepidation he skimmed the article. It was about 'blooding' greyhounds using rabbits. Surprisingly the reporter had gone to the trouble of interviewing not only the passionate objectors but also some owners, trainers, and vets. While most of the critters had been shot before being tied to the lure, one trainer had been secretly filmed using live animals. The article ended with the trainer receiving a hefty fine and facing deregistration. But the most amazing part of the exposé was that all dog racing enthusiasts weren't painted as animal abusers who only cared about profits. In the last paragraph was a quote from *a female trainer of Greenfield* who said *if you don't love animals, you're in the wrong business.*

Claude couldn't have agreed more. His eyes flicked to the by-line at the top. *Seth VerBeek.* There was also a picture of two happy greyhounds resting in the shade of a tree.

'What do you think?' Lola smiled.

'It's you, isn't it? And these two lovelies.' He stroked the sleeping dogs with his foot.

'Best press we've had in years. Truth to tell, when he phoned and asked for an interview, I was a bit wary. Reporters can be real mongrels. But he's different. He's been around the block a few times, if you know what I mean. And his voice …' A dreamy look crossed her ruddy face, as if she were in lust with the fellow. 'Anyways, in the end I couldn't say no,' she concluded.

For several minutes they sat in silence, mulling their own thoughts. For Claude it was a welcome relief that not everyone was against a sport that he followed with a passion. Those dogs of Lola's were treated better than any other animals he'd seen, including several stables of racing thoroughbreds that he'd been involved with.

Lola tucked into the Coles brand roly-poly cake while Claude re-read the newspaper article.

He drained his cup of tea. 'Right. What's on the list of jobs for today?' The Wednesday afternoon race meet at Albion Park meant there was always plenty to do.

'Give me a hand cleaning the kennels. Lightning Flash is sick, poor girl. Called the vet yesterday and he gave her a jab.'

'Sure thing. Lead the way. Any of your dogs running this arvo?'

Lola put on her hat. 'Two were. I've had them scratched in case it's contagious.'

Together they walked to the business end of the property, which was enclosed in a high chain-wire fence. By the gate was the old Moreton Bay fig tree. Beyond, a dozen greyhounds of various colours came running to greet them. Lola lifted the latch and they sidled through, careful not to let anyone out. The enclosure itself was an acre of lawn fenced into runs with an exercise circuit at the rear. To the left was a large iron shed that housed the night kennels.

At the shed, Lola measured disinfectant into a bucket and half-filled it with water. Claude unhooked the hose and ran it along the concrete floor inside. The night kennels were large and airy, each furnished with a hammock bed, a water bowl and a chewy toy.

At the far end, separated from the other cages, was *sick bay* as Lola called it, a larger pen with an examination table and a washbasin. Lightning Flash was asleep on her side on one of three doggy beds reserved for invalids. She was aptly named, for her entire body was the colour of charcoal except for a jagged streak of white down her chest. For a black dog, her face looked awfully pale. The floor was a mess of diarrhoea and bile. Yesterday's injection hadn't worked.

Claude called out to Lola. As soon as she laid eyes on the dog, her face blanched. From a pocket in her voluminous dress, she produced a phone. Her fingers tickled the screen, then she held it up to her ear.

'Wayne?' A pause. 'Nope, no better. Can you come? Sure, see you then.'

'What should we do?' said Claude.

Lola frowned and chewed the corner of her lip. 'Let's move her so we can clean up. The vet will be here shortly.'

Between them they lifted the dog, still on the bed, into her usual kennel. Claude hosed out the muck and Lola sluiced the floor with phenol. The stench of the disinfectant flashed him back to the orphanage where he'd grown up. More specifically, the boys' toilets. As the reward for good behaviour, his job every morning was to slop out the stalls with a mop and bucket. The smell of phenol still made him gag.

When they were done, they moved Lightning Flash back into the isolation ward and then finished cleaning the other kennels. The sun was directly overhead. The joints of the metal building were cracking and creaking in the heat. Lola brought in a large pedestal fan to keep the sick dog cool.

Outside, they splashed their own sweaty faces with water from the tap and waited in the shade for the vet. Lola began clicking her fingernails, an annoying habit that surfaced whenever she was worried.

The cigarette packet in Claude's top left pocket was burning a hole in his shirt. What he wouldn't give for a smoke! Lola didn't approve of cigarettes, especially around the animals. Minutes ticked into half an hour and still the vet hadn't arrived.

Usually on a Wednesday, Claude would leave with inside knowledge about racing form. At least one of Lola's dogs would be coming to its peak and she was kind enough to let him know. Under the circumstances he was loath to ask, but she seemed to read his mind.

'Hot Tamales has been training well.' She gave him a sly wink. 'Tomorrow night.'

'Hope Lightning gets better soon. She's a real nice dog.'

'Don't worry. Wayne will do whatever it takes.'

Desperate for a smoke, he picked a stalk of grass and sucked on the end.

'Look love, why don't you tootle off? I can manage fine on my own.'

'You sure?'

She gave him a peck on the cheek. As he turned to go, she followed it up with a slap on the arse. 'See you next week. Let's have a special treat to make up for today.'

With a grin, he reversed the ute onto the rocky drive. Before he was out the gate, a cigarette was between his lips and he was humming along to a seventies disco number on Classic Hits radio.

First stop was the betting shop at Greenfield Village, where he placed a hundred bucks to win on Hot Tamales in the Thursday night races at Albion Park. The odds were a bit short, so he also took her in a quinella, along with that tried and true sprinter, Red Rover. Closer to home he bought a tub of deep-fried chicken from KFC and a six-pack of cold lager.

Yep, despite today's small upset, Wednesdays at Lola's were the best.

4

Hangman

Thursday 6 August

After taking Cate home, Seth returned to his cubicle at Newspaper House. Alone to ponder his next move, he weighed the scarlet key in his hand. He examined the markings on the shaft, flipped it over, rotated it. Like red-hot embers, the office lights reflected off the anodised surface.

On the computer he reopened Cate's message, examined the scanned image of the address on the notepaper. The result had been scientifically generated and was feasible. Despite this, the key was undoubtedly wrong for 53 Maryland Avenue, Corinda. How could he gain access to the house? It seemed important that he did. Should he call a locksmith? Or should he jemmy open a window?

He laid the key on the desk. The tiny red saw was rounded at one end and serrated at the other. Was he missing something important? What if the key had nothing to do with the post-war cottage in Corinda?

Perhaps it was meant as a symbol. When he was a cadet journalist, the mayor of Blue Gum had given him a gold key for helping stop the construction of a dam that would have flooded the town. Later, on his twenty-first birthday—more years ago than he cared to count—his mother had given him a silver key to mark his coming of age.

What did a red key signify?

He typed *red key* into the internet search engine but Google couldn't find anything remotely likely. Other variants—ruby, crimson, scarlet, vermillion—also returned nothing of interest.

He flicked the key with his finger. It spun across the desk, collided with his water glass. *TING!*

Maybe that was it. A key was a bit of metal. Cut to specification, its shape was fixed forever. While a lock could be reset, a key was inalterable. There was no such thing as *the wrong key.* The problem was the address! *Scrawl Wizard,* that piece-of-crap app that Cate swore by, had made a mistake.

To the best of his knowledge each house key was unique. Of the million residences in this city alone, it would fit only one. The *elderly gentleman* who'd delivered it must have known the right address. Sadly he'd provided no contact details and no clue to his identity.

The scrunched-up piece of notepaper lay on Seth's desk like an unsolved riddle. Perhaps he should show it to Peter O'Day, the retired chemist who lived in his apartment block. That man could make sense of any sort of handwriting, from a post-card written by a doddery aunt to the straight-line signature of an overworked physician. As a pharmacy student in the days before computers, Peter would have done entire courses on how to work out unintelligible writing.

Seth scratched his head. Times like this he depended on Cate. When in a bind about what to do, she always came up with bizarre but brilliant ideas. Besides having brains, her female intuition often won out over his rational pig-headed approach. Luckily the extent of Cate's injuries from the morning's mishap amounted to nothing more than a sore head, bruises, and a deflated ego. She assured him she'd be back at work tomorrow.

With a magnifying glass he examined the scrap of notepaper. What jumped out was the name of the suburb. *Corinda.*

One by one he stepped through the poorly-formed letters. The first two were undeniably C and O. The last was an A. The middle was a series of loops.

He scratched his head. There must be another way.

Then it came to him. As a kid, he loved to play *hangman*. In the guessing game, four-letter words were the hardest. Not the foul ones he used later as a teenager, but simple words. *Have, most, love, want.* Seldom did he lose.

On a fresh sheet of paper, he marked seven dashes and wrote in the known letters.

<u>C</u> <u>O</u> _ _ _ _ <u>A</u>

Although it was cheating, he opened the post office website to get a list of suburbs. Corinda was wrong. What was alongside it? In less than a second it was solved: CORELLA.

Spurred on by success, he set to work on the street name. On Google Maps he located the suburb. Using the low-tech *hangman* methodology, he again marked out the letters that were legible.

<u>M A</u> _ _ _ _ _ <u>D</u>

Commencing at the northern boundary of the suburb, he worked his way south.

Eureka! He dragged and dropped the little Google man onto Mayfield Avenue and walked around the virtual neighbourhood. From the lush gardens and neatly-painted exteriors, he deduced that the locality was prosperous and predominantly owner-occupied.

Number 53 was a Queenslander situated at the end of the avenue. It was adjacent to an expanse of parkland that was bounded by a mangrove-lined creek. Goal nets for hockey or soccer were stored face-to-face beneath the paperbarks along the eastern side.

Clicking the directional arrows, he zoomed up and down the street. On the road was the odd-shaped shadow of the Google car as it captured a vignette of suburban life.

Click. A grey cat, startled by the car, raced across the road.

Click. The cat ran into the driveway of number 53.

Click. The cat was half-way up the stairs. In the doorway was a stout woman in a blue dress. Was she the owner?

With any luck he'd find out before the afternoon was over. Seth grabbed the red key from his desk and headed for the Jeep. He punched the address into the satnav, turned up the radio and sang along to a classic rock hit from the seventies. All in all he was feeling rather pleased with himself for having outsmarted Cate and her less-than-impressive software.

By the time he reached Corella the sun was angling in from the north-west. It was nearly two and his stomach was growling. Due to the earlier altercation between his colleague and a septic tank, he'd overlooked lunch.

A new block of townhouses had sprung up where the high school used to be. Opposite was an old-fashioned corner store. Advertisements for soft drinks and ice-blocks covered the windows. According to the chalkboard outside, the shop served the *Best Bloody Burgers in BrisVegas*. Salivating at the thought of a good old-fashioned hamburger, he pulled over and went inside.

The fellow behind the counter was a refugee from the sixties with long white hair tied in a ponytail, faded jeans, and a string of love-beads around his wrist.

'What'll it be, mate?' His Aussie accent was as broad as the Nullarbor Plain.

'Hamburger with the lot, thanks.'

'Sure, mate.'

Seth paid in cash and the old bloke went out the back to cook.

On the counter were large glass jars of lollies. Jelly snakes, red raspberries, chocolate freckles, liquorice allsorts. On the shelves were grocery items he hadn't seen in years. The décor was the colour of a lime milkshake. Seth stood there drinking it all in and feeling slightly off-beat. He was stepping back in time. For a moment he was no longer a man on the wrong side of middle-aged, but a kid with a threepenny bit in his pocket and all the choices in the world.

When he was a boy, the corner store in Paddington had looked exactly the same. In the days before gargantuan shopping malls, the corner store sold everything a family would need. Milk arrowroot biscuits for the babies, tailor-made cigarettes for the dads, headache powders for the mothers, and purple aniseed squares just for him.

The Paddington corner store ran a tab that Pa paid at the end of the month. On the way home from school, young Seth would call in for a 'free' ice-block or a chocolate frog, never realising that every penny went straight onto his father's tab. After a particularly social period in which he supplied after-school treats to the entire class, the dream run came to an end when Pa confronted him over the bill. A man of few words, Pa deferred to the strap. Seth promised not to buy another thing. After that, his popularity rating at school fell off a cliff.

Outside the Best Bloody Burger store, Seth sat on a garden bench beneath a striped awning and sank his teeth into the tastiest feast he'd had in decades. He had to lean forward with his legs apart so that the beetroot juice wouldn't drip onto his pants.

Nearby was a red payphone booth, an endangered species in the era of mobile technologies. Did anyone in the world still use them?

Across the road, a flock of white cockatoos screeched from the towering ironbarks. While the high school itself had been erased from the landscape, the trees that once graced its boundary line still remained. For a moment he wondered what had happened to the disadvantaged students who'd been displaced. Once more, politics had shunted them aside in favour of bright young things with obscenely large salaries and even larger mortgages. In the struggle of life, wealth always beat poverty.

Parked down the road was a ute with a curious number plate: SH1RL. Cigarette smoke drifted from the cabin. There was no logo on the door and no tools in the tray. The driver kept glancing nervously in the rear vision mirror. Seth imagined it as the get-away car for a robbery or a homicide. Wouldn't a scoop like that earn him brownie points with the Chief!

He bundled up the lunch wrappers and wiped his hands. With a belch of contentment, he eased himself into the Jeep. Now to concentrate on the task of finding the right lock for the red key.

The house he'd seen on Google maps was easy to find. From the outside, the Queenslander was as neat and well-maintained as the others in the street. The lawn was neatly mown; the daisy bushes along the front fence were in glorious full bloom. The casement windows along the northern side were open, suggesting someone was home.

He parked the Jeep. Trying not to act like a plain-clothes cop, he took his time climbing the front stairs. The brass knocker was the shape of a cat.

He rapped twice and waited.

From inside came no sound. The shape of the keyhole warned that this too was the wrong lock. To reach the rear entrance, Seth took a side path, bordered by long-tongued agapanthus and hippeastrums. The smooth leaves slipped reassuringly through his fingers.

The coir mat on the back porch was coated in a film of fur. He recalled the grey cat on Google maps and wondered where it was. The wooden door was painted blue with panels of ripple-glass. A sheer white curtain provided a modicum of privacy. Again he knocked and again there was no response. The keyhole looked promising. With a galloping heart, he took the scarlet key from his pocket and slotted it in.

Hallelujah!

The old boy still had it. Seth: one. *Scrawl Wizard:* nil. Turning the key, he heard the satisfying clink of the lock releasing. A sudden breeze rattled bamboo chimes that hung beneath the awning.

Klink, klik, klok ... klik, klok.

Muted, malicious. The sound of the Indochine jungle. His body was frozen, yet the sweat poured out of his skin. Anything could be a trigger. Flashbacks to the ugly days were intense and came without warning. The whop-whop-whop of an electric fan, the stench of rotting fish, the sound of heavy rain on the roof. He closed his eyes and whispered the words of affirmation that usually worked like magic. He paused, listened to the rhythm of his breath. The wave of panic broke and washed over him.

When he opened his eyes again, he was standing at the door of a nice middle-class house in a nice middle-class neighbourhood. Far, far away from the battlefield.

He pushed on the door and stepped into a retro-style kitchen. The air was thick and dank. In the subtropics mould grew fast. A hairline crack in the chamfer boards or rust in the roofing iron would let moisture in. A sooty bloom would creep across the ceiling and down the walls. Within a day, the carpet, curtains and upholstery would pong like a pack of wet dogs.

In his gut he knew this was a bad idea. This was more than innocent mould. The odour was imprinted on his olfactory sensors and it was unforgettable.

He forced himself on.

What he should have done was dial 000. Or he should have called Detective Sergeant Dave Frame, his boyhood friend and neighbour from the Paddington days. That way he'd have police backup as well as a terrific story. But he was a bloodhound on a scent and there was no way he'd stop until his nose was buried in shit. Of course he'd take precautions. Of course he'd not disturb any evidence or leave careless fingerprints lying about.

He slipped off his shoes and gently closed the ripple-glass door behind him.

In bright blue socks he padded through the kitchen. The green laminate benches were spotless; not a pan or a cup was out of place. On the table was a vase of dead roses. The ancient refrigerator was covered in gaudy magnets, notes and business cards. As the motor kicked in, the fridge shuddered. The bottles inside played *Jingle Bells*.

He jumped in fright; his arm bumped the table. The vase teetered. Somehow he caught it before it toppled. A close call. He rubbed his sweaty palms together. Realising there'd be fingerprints on the vase, he wiped the glass clean with his hanky.

His reflexes might be good but his nerves were shot. Already he'd survived too many horrors for one lifetime. Some people turned to grog, some turned to God. He'd tried both and neither had worked. His philosophy was simple: *what doesn't kill you makes you stronger*. Easy to say, hard to do.

Half of him voted in favour of getting out and letting the old house rest in peace. The other half urged him on. *Seth VerBeek will know what to do.* The confidence of an elderly gentleman had sent him on this mission to unlock a secret. He had a reputation to live up to; he must press on.

He entered a central hallway of polished wood, rooms off to either side. Mostly they were dark and airless with heavy drapes drawn against the sunlight. On the right was a smaller room with black-and-white tiles on the floor. Here the smell was stronger. He knew what to expect and it wouldn't be pretty. His nose, unlike his lips, never lied.

He peered around the door jamb. The white tub stood proud and solid on clawed feet. Swallowing, he took one last step into the bathroom.

On the floor was a doona, as white and puffy as a cloud. Peeping out was a foot. Pink varnished nails, cracked heel. He grasped a corner of the doona and lifted it. Beneath was a naked woman. Clearly she was dead.

Although beyond her prime, she certainly was not old. Her hair was dyed neon pink. Her skin was one all-over tattoo that covered every part of her except for her face, hands, and feet. There were colourful cherubs and garlands, birds and beasts, flowers and fruit. The images flowed together to form patterns within patterns, swirls within swirls.

In awful fascination, he squatted and took several photos with his phone. Some of the tattoos looked as fresh as yesterday, while the rest would have been no more than a few months old.

The body was lying on its side and partly wedged between the shower screen and the hand basin. Judging by the state of decomposition, she would have been there a couple of days.

There was no blood, no obvious sign of a struggle.

One thing bugged him. Why the doona?

Shaking his head, he stood up. *Seth VerBeek will know what to do.* Except now he didn't have a clue. He ought to get out. What if he'd been seen? What if the cops caught him with pictures of a naked corpse?

Five more minutes, barked his inner newshound. *Get the story first.*

As best he could, he replaced the doona exactly as he'd found it and padded deeper into the house. Everything seemed to be in order. No evidence of a break-in or robbery.

In the lounge room were two plush armchairs and a brown sofa with bright cushions. On the coffee table was an open magazine. *Art and Australia.* The bookshelves held weighty tomes about Michelangelo and Constable and the Heidelberg School. The wall was a gallery of paintings. A beach scene, still life with plums, a creek in the bush, portrait of a grey cat. Seth took a few photos and moved on.

At the southern end of the house was the main bedroom. Block-out curtains made it as dark as night. Using the flashlight app, he swept a beam around the room. The double bed was a tangle of sheets and several pillows lay on the floor.

On the duchess, piled with feminine bric-a-brac, was a bowl of dried lavender. Some had spilled and he'd trodden on it. The scent of lavender reminded him of his Gran—mother of ten including his mother—who used to douse herself in the stuff. She was a wonderful cook in an old-fashioned way. Her sherry trifles and rum cakes were legend but she always acted a bit vague. Later he found that she gargled lavender cologne to mask the smell of gin, which she drank by the bottleful.

One side of the bedroom was set up with a glass desk and swivel chair. Black leather, chrome, glass. In the old timber house the ultra-modern furniture looked vulgar and out of character. On the desk was a wireless mouse, sitting snug on a patterned mousepad. There was a space where a laptop might have been.

His five minutes was up; he had to go.

Returning to the kitchen, he pulled on his sneakers, shut the door and ran down the stairs. Cicadas in the neighbour's mango tree whirred like circular saws. The house next door was as quiet as a morgue. Up and down the street, not a soul could be seen.

In the Jeep he made a U-turn and planted his foot on the accelerator.

What a story! He'd have his work cut out to get to the bottom of it and not much time. Three pieces of a jigsaw puzzle were all he had: an elderly informant, a scarlet key, and a gaudy female corpse.

5

Mandala

Twenty months ago: summer

In a flurry of activity, Isla Bright navigated the end of school celebrations. The academic presentations, the official farewells, the wake put on by 'retiring' staff to mark the death of their careers. For these she had donned a protective coating as durable as steel. In the tumultuous sea of emotions, she had been their anchor. Calm and sensible. The purveyor of reason and hope.

Even through Christmas dinner, which she'd held at home with the usual assortment of adult orphans and nomads—most of whom were fellow teachers—she'd remained positive. Everyone wanted to talk about the good old days when the school was young. Sweet white wine and ice cold beer fuelled the stories. Laughter rippled around the table.

Remember the time ...

One of the benefits of the teaching profession was the six-week break through the hottest months. Summer rolled out ahead, an endless welcoming carpet of recreation. Travel plans were swapped, itineraries critiqued, links to useful websites shared. Starting on Boxing Day there'd be a mass exodus from the city for everyone except Isla.

Paula was going bird watching in New Zealand; Abigale was trekking in the Border Ranges; Tony was driving to Melbourne for his cousin's wedding.

Maxine, the hippie music teacher, was off to Byron Bay to commune with other alternate life-stylers and to beat the tribal drums. She'd probably get high on hash cookies and grow skinnier on a diet of organic lentils and kale.

Maddie, the only non-teacher in the group, was going to Kathmandu in search of bliss and positive energy. She'd bought an open ticket so the date of return was uncertain. As she was between jobs and her current husband was away, time was not an issue. Isla didn't know exactly what Maddie did for a living, apart from a glib one-liner. *I'm a lifestyle consultant, dahling.* Whatever that entailed, it was better paid than teaching. She always had plenty of cash to splash around.

The last of the Christmas regulars, Principal Brian Dean, was conspicuous by his absence. The day after the redundancy money came through, he and his wife took off for Paris. A postcard of the Moulin Rouge arrived two weeks later.

Having a ball. Wish you were here (not). Don't expect me back any time soon.

And so, full of merriment and good cheer, the afternoon faded into night. Not once was the upcoming work year mentioned. It was too alien to contemplate. In their minds, it seemed, nothing had changed. Come January, they'd be preparing lesson plans and gearing up for the influx of new students who'd arrive the day after Australia Day.

Except next year would be different.

At last the *silly season* was over and the tinsel and baubles were packed away. With nothing else to do and no-one around to visit, Isla began to ponder her prospects. At age fifty-seven they didn't look promising. Who would employ a dyed-in-the-wool art teacher with no other skills to speak of?

She paced the hot airless lounge room. Could she make a living from her passion? Perhaps she could paint on weekdays and run a market stall on the weekends. Her pictures weren't commercial; they were expressions of the heart. The idea of compromising creativity for the sake of a few dollars didn't sit well.

Perhaps she could get a job at Bunnings *selling* paint instead. She had a good eye for colour. No, that would never work. Her painting technique didn't extend to sandpaper or putty, and she'd never sold a thing in her life.

The future seemed deep and dark. If she planned nothing, the days and weeks and months would run together into a lazy meandering river of inactivity. Slowly and without realising it, she would drift with the flow only to find herself, twenty years from now, entangled in the jetsam of old age.

The redundancy money she'd received in December lay untouched in the bank. Apart from splurging on prawns and turkey at Christmas, she'd spent practically nothing. She worried that her nest egg would disappear. An interest rate near zero meant no income, but she needed an income to live. Financially she was on the brink of a downhill slide.

A plan was what she needed.

She wandered into the sleep-out where the temperature was a few degrees cooler. Amongst the indoor jungle of philodendrons, African violets, and parlour palms she always felt calm. On the coffee table she laid out sheets of A3 paper and some colour felt-tip pens. A plan must be in writing or it's nothing but hot air. She chose a sky-blue pen, twisted the lid, sucked on the end, put it back down on the table. Sitting in a cane chair amongst the greenery, she tried to imagine the rest of her life. Barring a horrible accident, she'd probably reach her eighties. Although her mother had died young, both her aunt and her grandmother had lived to eighty-seven.

From now until eighty-seven was thirty years. Thirty years was a long time to watch soapies on TV. She stared at the blank white page and it glared back at her.

Purring, Venus leapt onto the table. With a swish of her feather-duster tail, she swept pens and paper to the floor. Isla picked up the beloved Persian cross and hugged her. Long grey fur stuck to Isla's sweaty skin. The air was as thick as molasses. Later there'd be a storm.

'What should I do, darling puss?'

The cat meowed and touched her pink nose to Isla's. A raspy tongue licked her chin, triggering an attack of menopausal itches. She put Venus down and went to the kitchen to make a nice strong pot of tea. While it was brewing, she cut a slice of leftover Christmas cake, the fruity one with Grand Marnier and ginger made to her mother's recipe. She followed it up with a rum ball, a wedge of shortbread, a fresh apricot.

Feeling full and a bit queasy, she carried the steaming mug to the sleep-out.

Brainstorm, she said out loud. *What do I like? What do I want to be?*

The answer was obvious: an art teacher. It was not what she intended, but she wrote it down anyway. That was what brainstorming was about: generating ideas, crazy or otherwise without judgement or editing. She shut her eyes, put the pen to the paper and allowed her mind to guide the path.

Seduced by David, she wrote. An image of Michelangelo's famous nude flashed into her mind. She giggled. Where did that come from? She'd never been to Europe.

Florence and Venice, she wrote.

With the first seeds sown, a garden of ideas began to grow. Her pen was moving faster than her mind. Possibilities and desires trailed all over the page. After a ten-minute burst of energy, she turned the page face down and went to the kitchen for another slice of cake. Her blue dress was far too tight but her soul craved sustenance. In any case, she reasoned, it was summer holidays and she was on a break from diets.

Later when she reviewed the sheet, it was clear that the right side of her brain—the creative side—was in control. Random words were joined together with doodles and arabesques. Some were written strong and bold, while others were daddy-long-legs squiggles across the page. Calligraphy with design. Of all those words, three caught her attention.

Conquer. Dare. Create.

Conquer your fears. Dare to be yourself. Create new meaning.

The trio of ideas promised a wonderful new beginning after an odious end.

With India ink, a nib pen, and handmade paper, she turned the words into a mandala. The circular shape was dynamic and never-ending. The three words were inspiring. Life was meant to be lived and enjoyed.

It was the most meaningful plan she'd ever made. Satisfied, she pinned the mandala to the cork board in the kitchen.

*

The worst day of all was January twenty-seven, the first day of the new school year. On purpose Isla didn't set the alarm. Nevertheless at five-thirty sharp the biorhythms of her body jolted her awake.

In every suburb and in every town, parents would be cutting lunches and getting their kids ready for school. Toddlers barely out of nappies would be starting prep. At high school, excited year sevens would arrive in crisp new uniforms two sizes too big. On the first day the older students would turn up neat and clean, while the rest of the year their clothes would be lucky to find their way into the weekly wash.

Already teachers would have submitted lesson plans for the semester, spent the final week of the holidays preparing lecture notes and assessments, and wasted time cajoling the gatekeeper of the resources room for precious equipment. Every school had its own dragon.

Isla had done none of that. She was no longer Head of Art. Her status was *early retiree*. Like it or not, she'd have to get used to it. Perhaps she should join the lawn bowls club or play the pokies at the RSL or take up knitting or crosswords.

How utterly boring and depressing!

As an *early retiree*, she'd dared to let her hair return to its natural colour. Instead of rich chestnut, the dye of choice, her hair was now the colour of driftwood. As a result, she'd become completely invisible. In crowds, people pushed around her as if she weren't there. At the shops, she was last to be served. If she'd have stripped naked or dropped down dead on the floor, no-one would have noticed.

While new-year's resolutions sent others to the gym or to Weight Watchers, Isla had spent the last week of January cleaning out the cupboards. Oh, the memories she'd found! Things she'd forgotten, stored out of harm's way, up high or right at the back. Things that belonged to her mother, treasures inherited from aunties or given to her by friends.

Her house was drowning in *stuff*. In the spirit of starting afresh, she decided to clear out the old. To keep on track, her intention was to remove everything from its storage place and put back only what she wanted to keep. She'd even gone to the trouble of labelling three cardboard boxes. *Dump. Sell. Donate.*

The contents of the hall cupboard sprawled along the entire corridor. There were souvenirs from New Zealand, embroidered sheet sets, Barbie dolls, photo albums, a blue tutu, old university assignments, tracing paper, crystal wine goblets, stoneware mugs, purple roneoed flyers for an art show in 1976.

Everything was part of her life history. Everything had a story.

In a calico bag she found her all-time favourite shoes: cork platforms, caramel and tan. Eagerly she tried them on but her toes wouldn't go beyond the cross-band. Either the shoes had shrunk or her feet had swollen. One of the leather ankle straps crumbled in her hand.

Whatever would she do with them?

Overwhelmed, she sat on the hard polished floorboards and wept. After hours of procrastination, she dusted the shelves and put everything back where it belonged.

By eight-fifteen on January twenty-seven, Isla had cooked and eaten two slices of French toast with bacon and tomato, read *The Morning Post* from cover to cover, washed the dishes, played cat-tag with Venus outside, watered the plants, and taken a long cool shower. Her household chores were done and the morning had barely begun. The neighbourhood echoed with the squeal of excited youngsters leaving for school.

Her heart took a leap. Oh my, she'd be late for work.

Except there *was* no work.

Biting her lip, she paced the hall. On the sideboard lay her work bag. Brown leather, a gift from Maddie for helping when she left husband number one. That bag had been packed and unpacked every school day for ten years. The lining smelt of the art room; the handles were shiny from wear. Instead of being fat with papers and books and anticipation, it was as sad and hollow as a drought-starved calf. Each time Isla passed the sideboard, it seemed to call her. *Get ready, hurry up.* She couldn't make it stop.

The kitchen clock became a ticking time bomb. Nine o'clock limped by. Isla was irritable enough to climb the walls.

What had become of Corella High? Were the buildings still there? For the first time since the gates were padlocked, she felt compelled to go and find out.

She grabbed the car keys and shooed Venus outside. All summer holidays she'd avoided that well-worn route. The Camry practically steered itself along Park Esplanade, across Reedy Creek bridge, left at the lights, right into School Road.

Near the turnoff to the staff carpark she was stopped by a man in a high-viz vest. Hazard lights flashing, a heavy tip truck was reversing out of the grounds. The skip was full of demolition materials: bricks, slabs of concrete, reinforcing steel, metal frames. The rig took up the entire width of the road. The front wheels tip-toed over the kerb and righted, the driver gave a salute and the truck roared away.

The lollipop sign flipped to *SLOW*.

That was when Isla noticed the security fencing. Two-metres high, anchored with concrete blocks, finished at the top with barbed wire and punctuated with orders to *Keep Out*. The barrier ran the length of the footpath, imprisoning the school buildings and walkways, proclaiming that this was a demolition site and no longer a place of learning.

With a sunken heart, Isla parked the car and crossed the road to where the main entrance used to be. She laced her fingers into the chain wire and surveyed the scene.

What was left of her workplace was enough to make her weep. Clumps of weeds sprouted from the rose gardens, fallen branches littered the stairs, the windows of B Block had all been smashed, spray-paint tags defaced the walls. In the barren quadrangle beyond, an enormous yellow bulldozer basked in the morning sun.

The quadrangle was once the heart of the school, where the kids congregated before class. Like mobs of teenage wallabies they would laze on the benches or graze on sweets and packets of chips. They'd flirt or play handball or swap homework answers or send messages on those infernal brain-sucking electronic devices.

Over the decades, how many of the city's residents would have been part of that morning ritual? How many enduring connections would have been made? How many careers would have been launched over a shared carton of chocolate milk? The school's alumni included prominent people of every race, creed and profession. Some ran the city as elected officials or public servants. Some owned businesses or worked in trades, others were dentists, lawyers or accountants. No doubt, there was also a jailbird or two.

An era had ended. As early as this afternoon, the entire place could be reduced to a steaming pile of rubble.

Isla tried to imagine Corella without the familiar red-brick buildings. How would it have looked two centuries ago, before white settlers razed the eucalyptus forests and carved contours into the hillside? Although her British ancestors had been here for but a short episode in the history of this ancient land, each generation seemed hell-bent on destroying the artefacts of the past. In her lifetime gracious old buildings had been demolished to make way for bigger, better, brighter structures. In fifty years' time, those buildings would be torn down in turn and the cycle would be repeated. It was all so temporary and superficial, an exercise in scratching the surface. The soul of this country ran deep, far too deep for Europeans to appreciate. She loved Australia but in her heart she knew she didn't belong.

Isla closed her eyes and rested her head against the chain wire.

Behind her, footsteps crunched on the gravel.

'Isla Bright?' said a female voice.

Isla jumped, turned to face the interloper.

The last person she expected to see was Antoinette Collier, past student and sole parent to Amber, the wild-child of the year before. Following a rift in their friendship, they'd reconnected at a teacher-parent interview in November after Amber wagged school.

Not surprised Amber's playing up, Antoinette had said at the time. Her skirt had ridden up her thighs. She wiggled it down an inch or two and readjusted her bra. *Like mother, like daughter,* she added with a shrug.

A good teacher knows what her students get up to, Isla said with meaning.

Their eyes locked in mutual understanding. Then they both laughed.

In recent times Antoinette had undergone a transformation. Gone was the devil-may-care attitude of her youth. Eighteen years separated the ages of mother and daughter. Both were resourceful and forthright and showed absolutely no fear of anything.

'My dear, you gave me a start,' Isla said.

Antoinette wore a strapless polka-dot top, teamed with brief cut-off jeans. The denim was shorter than the calico pockets, which hung below the leg-holes like pudding bags. She'd dyed her hair purple and varnished her nails vermillion. Although her blood was pure Anglo Saxon, an upward tick of eyeliner made her look part-Asian.

Most astounding were the 'sleeves'. Antoinette, an artist herself, had been amassing tattoos as fervently as a philatelist collected stamps. Although Isla had never been interested in tattoos, she had to admit that the colours and designs were gorgeous.

On a previous occasion Antoinette had announced that she was working with *the most awesome tattooist on the planet*. Isla had smiled primly and congratulated her on the new job. At the same time, she'd wondered why an attractive young woman would want to ruin her appearance with all that ink.

Antoinette threw her colourful arms around her in a warm hug. 'I've been thinking about you.'

'Really?'

'Yeah, I wondered where you were teaching. Now that … you know.' Her gaze took in the sorry state of the school.

Isla swallowed a lump in her throat. 'How come you're not at work?'

'I start late and finish late. Thought I'd pay my last respects to the old place. Lots of good memories. Best time of my life.' Antoinette sighed. 'And you?'

'I'm an *early retiree*. That's the term they use. It means I'm all washed up.'

Antoinette looked shocked. 'You're not teaching anymore?'

Isla shook her head. 'Didn't Amber tell you?

'Amber and I have an understanding. We share only what needs to be shared. In our family, trust is everything.'

In Isla's opinion, Amber wasn't worthy of anyone's trust. That girl was headed down a slippery path. But as a retiree from the teaching profession, she was no longer authorised to give advice to parents. Quickly she changed the subject. 'How's the job? Keeping busy?'

'We're run off our feet and I'm loving it.' Antoinette snapped off a stalk of paspalum and squished it between red claws. 'If you don't mind me saying, you don't look too happy. My aunt retired last year and you can't wipe the grin off her face.'

'I loved my job, but now it's over.' Tears welled. The tell-tale rash was crawling up her neck; her head was filling with heat. She pressed her nails into her palms and let the breath roll over her tongue.

Antoinette hugged her again, this time in sympathy. 'Come and see me at work. I'll buy you a coffee and introduce you to my partner. He's the coolest dude. Reads my every mood and helps me sort through my issues.' She dived into a voluminous shoulder bag and produced a business card. The details were printed in gold on black, which seemed a bit of overkill for a tattoo parlour. In small print was the tagline *ink art and psychic healing*.

The logo was a seated cat. Perhaps it was a sign.

Isla gasped. 'I know the place!' The old-world shop near the Goongulli station had once caught her eye. Although the outside was tastefully unadorned, she'd glimpsed fantastic designs of dragons, unicorns, angels, and devils displayed on the walls inside. Of course she'd never ventured in. Tattoos were for old sailors and whores. This current fascination, she was sure, was a passing fad.

'Gotta go.' Antoinette turned to leave. 'Good to see you, Isla.'

'Take care of yourself and your daughter.'

'Promise you'll come and see me?' Antoinette shouted from the car. The yellow Hyundai Getz was stencilled with filigree swirls.

'I'll call you.' Isla smiled at the mental image of herself, dressed in pedal pushers and a neat striped shirt from Millers, entering a forbidden den of ink.

She wouldn't *dare*, would she?

Now that she was not a teacher, she was no longer expected to be a pillar of virtue. Retirement had set her free. There'd be no more criticism from parents or other teachers for being a mere mortal. No longer would she be the butt of juvenile jokes. She thought of the mandala pinned on the corkboard in her kitchen and the words that made it up.

Conquer, dare, create.

At that moment, Isla Bright made a decision. She'd do it. She'd go to that tattoo parlour and see what all the fuss was about. Now that she was retired, she could do whatever she damn-well pleased.

To *dare* was part of her plan. What did she have to lose anyway?

6

Scratching the surface

Thursday 6 August

By the time Seth reached the far end of Mayfield Avenue, he was shaking so hard he could barely keep the Jeep on the road. The enormity of what he'd seen and done hit him with the force of a tropical storm. Pulling over to the curb, he mopped sweat from his brow and patted his pocket for the habitual pack of cigarettes. Instead, his fingers hit the edge of a small tin that rattled. Of course! He'd left his emergency smokes on the desk in the office. He was supposed to have quit, at least that was what he'd told his doctor. Sometimes it was hard to stay nicotine-free. He flipped open the tin and tossed two Eclipse mints into his mouth. He checked his watch. It was going on four: too early to go home but not too early for a drink.

There was a lot to do; he'd be working well into the night. He took out his phone and asked Siri, the female electronic know-it-all, for directions to the nearest pub. She told him how to get to the King's Arms.

The mental image of honey-smooth whisky calmed him enough to drive to the next suburb without hitting anything. From the outside, the hotel looked a tad run-down and in need of a lick of paint. The chunky brick structure with curved external walls would have been built in the nineteen-twenties. Green-and-black floor tiles and geometric stained-glass windows made a welcoming entrance. Inside, five bar-flies—all well over the age of seventy—had attached themselves to the wood-panelled counter. Three were pontificating loudly about last year's rugby league final as it was replaying on the flat-screen TV. Another was relating a long and convoluted

36

story to the barman. The fifth sat alone, elbows on the bar top, sadly contemplating the foam at the bottom of his glass.

Seth ordered a Scotch with a beer chaser, took the glasses to a table in the corner away from the rabble. The whisky barely touched the sides of his throat, but its warm comfort flowed deliciously through his body.

He took a swallow of beer, placed his phone on the table and opened the *HouseSales* app. Itching for answers, he typed in the Mayfield Avenue address. Within seconds he had the name of the registered owner. Isla Jean Bright. Back in 1978 she'd purchased the property for a mere thirty-six thousand dollars. He whistled softly. The place would now be worth twenty times that. As a young man, why hadn't he listened to his own advice and invested in real estate instead of hot women and fast cars?

Was Isla Jean Bright the deceased?

He copied and pasted the name into the Google search bar. Not much came up apart from advertisements for an American brand of jeans. He scrolled through several pages of irrelevant rubbish until he found a reference to her on the Teachers Union website. He clicked on the link.

The document was a petition addressed to the State education minister protesting the proposed closure of four Queensland high schools. One was Corella. Eagerly, he skimmed through the diatribe. Isla Bright was listed as one of the long-serving union members who would be made redundant. A related article was about the government forcing mature-age teachers out of the system by stealth and without regard to their future job prospects. According to the union, the redundancy packages offered were an insult to experienced high-quality professionals. Immediate industrial action would be taken unless the affected teachers were reinstated or given a better settlement. The article was dated twentieth November, nearly two years ago. Sadly there were no photos of any staff members. A picture of Isla Bright would have sealed the deal. On the surface, however, it was improbable that a tattooed lady with fluoro pink hair fitted the profile of a respected middle-age teacher.

Seth guzzled beer while he opened the photo reel on his phone. Until now he had no idea of the quality of the pictures he'd snapped at the Mayfield Avenue house. With trepidation, he flicked through the shots. The first few were of a shit-encrusted Cate at the bottom of a pit. So much had happened since this morning, it could have been a week ago. He wondered how she was feeling and sent her the ugliest along with a text and a smiley-face to cheer her up. If she didn't show up for work tomorrow, he'd give her a call. Maybe he'd send her some flowers. No, then she'd think he was doing her a line. And he wasn't. Really.

He turned his attention to the photos of the corpse on the floor. Four were clear enough for newspaper reproduction. Sadly the face was either concealed by the doona or badly underexposed. On a brighter note, the shots of the tattoos were clean and sharp, in particular the one across her back. A sweep of colour in the form of angel wings. Why hadn't he noticed it before?

Astonished, he enlarged the pic. The wings were magnificent, detailed, alluring. In the shock of finding her, scrambled emotions must have blinded him to it. That tattoo was an omen. And it was fresh. On its surface was a liquid sheen, similar to gravel rash he'd endured as a kid whenever he fell off his pushbike.

Hailing the bartender, Seth ordered another Scotch. The sight of those wings sent shivers down his spine. Graceful and curved, they were exquisitely drafted down to the last feather. What set them apart from the pale wings of graveyard angels were the rainbow colours. These wings were vibrant and bursting with energy.

In this life you never knew what was around the corner. Since turning sixty, he'd become acutely aware that the easy years were numbered. Some of his mates had already departed this world. Grog and weed and depression had taken their toll.

In one mouthful he downed the Scotch and set the empty glass on the table. He couldn't afford to get pie-eyed and maudlin; he needed to keep his mind sharp. As it was, he'd have to abstain for at least another hour before he could drive without being over the legal limit.

If the dead woman wasn't Isla Bright, then who was she? Seth thought about matching the tattoos to pictures on the web. A woman with a full body suit would surely be out there somewhere. In his experience tattoos were for showing off, the same as graffiti. Without maximum exposure, what was the point of all that pain?

On his phone he trawled through hundreds of photos on Instagram and Pinterest, but to no avail. Then he stumbled on a tattoo website that was closed to casual browsers. Should he? He touched the button to join and was confronted by a questionnaire. They wanted to know everything about him: his age, sexual orientation, favourite food, where he went to school, what he wanted in a relationship. The non-refundable fee was five hundred dollars; it came with a written guarantee he'd find a soulmate. Yeah right. How many wood-ducks had fallen for that old trick?

He was tempted to cut his losses and turn his attention to an exposé of dating site rip-offs instead. Already he had plenty of dirt on that topic, gained mostly through personal experience.

In a last attempt, he searched *Isla Bright* on Google images. Up came gorgeous snaps of rolling fields and soaring white cliffs. *Visit the Isle of Wight*, said the promo.

His suspicions were confirmed: the owner of 53 Mayfield Avenue was not the woman with the angel tattoo. Isla Bright, retired schoolteacher, would have been wary of social media and technology in general. She never would have joined the millions of privately public young people compelled to share every intimate detail with thousands of virtual friends.

He understood completely. For him, social media was for self-promotion and making others envious. Even as a journalist, who was expected to be connected twenty-four seven, he often 'forgot' to check his Twitter account. In the four months since Cate had nagged him into becoming an official Twit, he'd contributed eleven times, four of which were the one word. *Testing.*

He returned to the central question: who was Angel Tattoo?

Was she a tenant? A relative? A guest? An intruder?

Perhaps she was a squatter who'd broken in and made herself at home while Isla Bright was away. After years of teaching, Isla had been forced into retirement. Maybe she'd gone overseas on an extended holiday. The scenario had possibilities.

The Scotch honed his skills of deduction. Seth VerBeek might yet live up to his reputation of being the one who'd *know what to do.*

'This isn't rocket science,' his editor would have said. 'It's pure common sense.'

Of course! Why hadn't he thought of it sooner? He should *phone a friend.* The friend he chose was Davo, his boyhood mate from Paddington.

These days he was better known as Detective Sergeant Dave Frame of the Criminal Investigations Branch. Knowing a senior detective sometimes came in handy.

'Can I see you, mate?' Seth said into the phone. 'I got a tip-off about a crime.'

Dave Frame repeated the Corella address and said he'd get his team onto it. He also agreed to meet Seth at the King's Arms in half an hour to get the full details.

Now Seth faced the usual dilemma when dealing with his police officer mate. How much should he admit? A fine line existed in both their worlds about the information that could be shared without breaching the ethics of their respective professions. On occasions such as this, that line was so fine it was practically invisible.

While he was waiting, Seth did a search of the online yellow pages directory for tattoo shops. For Angel Tattoo to have acquired that much ink in a short time, her tattooist had to be somewhere close by.

Up came the list. There were around fifty within easy driving distance. Those were businesses that paid to advertise on the directory site. There were probably dozens more: backyard operations and those on the wrong side of the law. To find them all and check them out would take a couple of weeks.

Exactly half an hour later, Detective Sergeant Dave Frame strode into the bar. He was a tall man: six foot seven. His spine curved into a permanent S-bend in a vain attempt to appear shorter. Behind his back, junior officers called him *String Bean*. Of course he knew it, but he never lost his temper. Today he was in plain clothes: blue jeans and a shirt with a tablecloth check. *Undercover* was the term he preferred.

The pair slapped each other's backs and exchanged greetings. Within minutes they'd established that it'd been far too long between beers and they should get together more often.

With that, Dave loped to the bar and returned shortly afterwards with two frothy schooners, a packet of roasted cashews, and a cup of steaming chips smothered in black sauce. He scraped back the chair and sat down. 'What do you *know*, mate?'

That clever opener belonged to Seth. He'd used it to great effect ever since he graduated from uni. For some curious reason, people felt compelled to provide an answer. Over the years, the responses he got to that innocuous question were legend.

Caught wrong-footed, Seth shrugged and opened his hands. 'Oh, you know … this and that.' The words tumbled out as a bit of a slur.

Dave lifted the schooner. 'How many of these have you had?'

'Look mate, I'm no more pissed than you are.'

Dave raised an eyebrow but said nothing.

Without further fuss, Seth launched into an edited story of the elderly informant who'd given him the address in Corella. He omitted the morning mix-up which might implicate Cate, and the gift of the scarlet key which would incriminate him on several levels ranging from trespassing to interfering with a corpse.

'When I went to the house, I knocked but nobody answered.' Seth mopped cold sweat from his forehead. 'I knew there was something wrong. The smell …'

'You don't have to spell it out,' said Dave. 'I know the smell of death too well. The boys texted me a few minutes ago. They found a body inside.'

Seth lifted his beer glass. His hand was trembling so much he could barely bring it to his lips. 'Must be getting weak in my old age.'

'Is there anything else?' said Dave, finishing his beer. 'I'd love to stay and chat, but it's been a big day and it's not over yet.'

'No, that's it.' Seth drained his glass. 'Keep me posted?'

'Sure, mate. In the meantime, keep yourself out of trouble.'

On the way out, Dave had to duck his head to avoid a collision with the door lintel. Seth watched him all the way to the car.

He knew. Somehow he knew what Seth had done.

There was a bigger question. *Would he tell?*

7

Jet Ink

Eighteen months ago: late summer

Not in her wildest imaginings did Isla think she'd ever set foot in a tattoo parlour. Yet there she was, on the pedestrian bridge of Goongulli Station, about to make good her promise to Antoinette. Apparently she was about to meet *the most awesome tattooist on the planet.*

After the chance encounter at the high school on the first day of term, Isla had been tossing it around in her mind. Once, the two women had been close. Very close indeed. Their relationship was no different from mother and daughter.

When Antoinette morphed from a wayward girl into pig-headed teen, things began to fall apart. After an argument she moved out and took up residence in a squat in the Valley. There she hooked up with a series of dubious youths who treated her like dirt. At the age of eighteen the inevitable happened. By the time Amber was born, the dead-beat who was the father had long gone. Destitute, Antoinette contacted a long-lost aunt in Dubbo and went to live there with the baby.

According to the sanitised version of the story, she'd struggled on the sole parents' pension and supplemented her income by selling charcoal sketches at the markets. That was before Jet the Magnificent came on the scene. The truth was probably more sordid. Sometimes it was better not to know. Details of the relationship with Jet were scant to say the least. Isla assumed they were lovers.

At the station, Isla descended the white-railed staircase to the footpath of Innovation Drive. The weather was blistering hot, one of those airless days at the tail-end of summer when the asphalt melted and stuck like black chewing gum to the soles of your shoes. Sweltering, she stood on the kerb of the busy thoroughfare that ran parallel to the interstate railway line and waited for the traffic lights to change. On the main connector between the airport and the CBD, trucks and vans flowed in a constant stream both ways. In the wake of passing vehicles came blasts of dust and stinking diesel fumes.

On the strip of shops opposite were the rooms rented by her naturopath. Victoria Bennett was a wise woman who listened to problems and prescribed herbal potions to cleanse the blood and cure female ailments. Since the onset of menopause, Isla had been a regular client. Over the last ten years, she'd devoured more pills and elixirs containing black cohosh, evening primrose, red clover, ginseng, and kava than she cared to count. It was debatable whether any of the remedies actually helped to reduce hot flushes and mood swings, or the sensation that a battalion of spiders in feather-soled boots was marching all over her body. It was equally debatable whether the recent warnings by doctors about side effects of *untested botanical ingredients* were scientifically-based or scaremongering campaigns funded by the pharmaceuticals industry.

Despite this, Isla always looked forward to the consultations. The naturopath's level-headed approach and unhurried ear were better than bottles of pills. For a moment she was tempted to detour to Victoria Bennett's instead of barrelling into a den of iniquity. She was probably crazy coming here. What did she hope to achieve?

In answer to her own question, she whispered aloud. *But a promise is a promise.* Embarrassed, she glanced around to see if anyone had caught her talking to herself. The nearest person was a lone teenager leaning against a wall. Although he was several metres away, the one-way conversation was so loud that she could hear every word. Despite the absence of a physical listener, wires in his ears and a slab of shiny plastic made his behaviour socially acceptable. Technology had made the world a curious place.

After crossing Innovation Drive she turned right and continued walking along the row of small businesses until she reached a quaint timber building with a horse trough and hitching post outside. It could have been a saloon in a John Wayne western.

The sign on the window was exactly the same as the logo on the business card Antoinette had given her. A gold seated cat with its tail curled around its paws. *Ink art and psychic healing.* It had to be the right place.

Taking a shallow breath, she pushed against the timber-framed glass door. It pivoted inwards as easily as the flap of a litter bin. Suddenly she was catapulted from the glare of a summer's day to a dim and alien world.

The entry foyer was as cool as a limestone cave. A carved teak desk and chairs with red-and-gold cushions gave the waiting area the feel of a Balinese retreat. Soothing sounds—waterfalls and birdsong—mingled with the tinkle of wind-chimes.

On the walls was a myriad of tattoo designs, framed in black. The variety was astonishing: tribal, fantasy, geometric, freeform, caricature. The drawings were well executed; the colours were luminous. Here was an entire field of creative expression that she'd never considered legitimate art, yet each one was undeniably gorgeous.

At the centre of the gallery was the stand-out: a grey part-Persian identical to Venus. The markings and expression on the cat's face were so appealing that she caught herself wanting to have it placed on her skin. Mesmerised, her fingers touched the glass.

'Isla, you're here! I didn't think you'd come.' Antoinette's unmistakeable twang floated from the inner sanctum.

Caught with her hand in the proverbial cookie jar, Isla spun around. 'Of course I'm here. I made you a promise.'

Dressed in a chrome-studded leather bodice and black tulle skirt, Antoinette swept into the room. Today her hair was electric blue with yellow ends. By some trick of the lighting, the tattoos on her arms seemed to glow.

They hugged briefly, Isla careful to avoid the sharp metal studs.

'Phew, it's hot. You must be parched.' Antoinette poured a drink from a jug on the counter and handed it to Isla.

Its perfume was a mixture of ginger, rosewater and cinnamon. She took a sip; the flavour was hard to define. Herbal and neither sweet nor bitter, not only did it clear the dust in her throat but also the brain-fog of menopause. A shot of distilled energy.

'Jet will be here in a minute. Can I show you around?'

'Sure. Why not? I haven't been in a tattoo parlour before.'

'It's a *studio*,' corrected Antoinette. 'And we refer to it as *ink art*.'

'Did Jet do these?' Isla indicated the pictures on the wall.

'Yes, he's the artist but some are based on my designs.'

'He's very good at what he does.' This was the closest Isla could come to complimenting a subculture she struggled to understand.

Antoinette led the way from the entry foyer to the inner studio. Surprisingly spacious and airy, the room was furnished simply in timber and leather. Padded lie-flat benches, recliner chairs, a stool on wheels, shelves displaying a kaleidoscope of powdered pigments in glass jars, sets of tattoo needles, soldering equipment, assorted paraphernalia for creating pictures on skin.

Photographs of finished works filled the walls. These tattoos were completely different from the ones in the foyer. The oriental-style back-pieces covered every square inch of skin from the neck to the upper arm to the thigh. Golden carp, dragons, phoenixes, or tigers were the main feature. Images were positioned to conform to the curves of the body. So tantalising were the designs that it was not immediately apparent that the models were stark naked.

'Living canvases,' Isla breathed.

Antoinette caught her gaze. 'Jet's a *horishi*. One of the few in Australia.'

'What's that?'

'He was taught by a traditional master in Japan. Tattooing is an ancient craft.'

'That sort of detailed work would take ages.'

'Around eighty hours for the back piece alone. But it's not the time, it's the pain. Not even childbirth comes close. Believe me, this is a life-changing decision. Once you've started, there's no turning back.'

Isla was about to say that they were similar to ancient woodcut prints that she'd seen in the art gallery but she was interrupted by a tinkling bell.

Antoinette dashed out and returned arm-in-arm with a middle-aged man in denim jeans, black t-shirt, two full sleeves of tattoos, and an impressive beard. 'Here's the master himself.'

'Pleased to meet you at last, Isla. I've heard lots about you.' Jet offered a handshake.

'All good, I hope,' said Isla. As his palm touched hers, she felt a buzz of electricity. A sudden flush of heat raced up her neck and crawled across her scalp. Her face was burning red. Quickly she turned away.

'Isla was admiring your work.' Antoinette came to the rescue. 'But I don't think she's ready to sample our wares,' she quipped.

'Leave us, Nettie,' Jet said.

Without further comment, Antoinette exited the studio. A moment later, the bell jingled again and the front door latch clicked shut. Isla was alone with the tattoo wizard. At least ten years her junior, he could have been handsome beneath all the facial hair.

Her heart was fluttering. What had come over her? She was as silly as a schoolgirl on a first date. Last time she'd felt this way was when Brian Dean gave her a farewell kiss on the final day of her teaching career.

'Let's talk.' He indicated that she should sit in a recliner chair.

Without hesitation she sank into the soft upholstery. He leant forward, placed his hands on her forearms. There it was again: the electric buzz, stronger than before.

'Relax,' he whispered. 'Relaaaax.' His voice was as smooth as warm caramel.

Despite her proximity to this outrageous-looking stranger, a sensation of calmness washed over her.

'Nettie brought you here for a reason,' he said.

Isla stiffened. 'I certainly don't want any tattoos!'

'That's not what I meant,' he said evenly.

Mollified, Isla lay back down. Her blouse had pulled up at the back, exposing a wedge of flesh above the waistband of her pedal pushers. The smoothness of the leather against her skin was like seduction.

Jet's hands smoothed along her arms, across her shoulders, and up her neck to her forehead. There he held them, warm and pulsing.

She closed her eyes. In her mind, the colour she saw was blue. Electric blue. She was floating on clouds. The continuous self-depreciating commentary in her brain went on hold. In the state of bliss, nothing mattered. She slipped into a deep slumber.

Sometime much later, she woke.

Jet was on the stool beside her.

'How long did I sleep?'

'A few minutes.'

'It seemed like ages.'

'Your aura is blue, same as mine.'

Her mouth opened slightly. 'I have an aura?'

'Everyone does. *Conquer, dare, create* are evocative words,' he said.

Now she was speechless. Had she been sleep-talking or could he read her mind?

'Don't be alarmed; my gift is rare. If you'll allow me, I can help you.'

In awe she nodded. The power of his charm was beyond comprehension. 'Can you really help me? I'm a woman who is utterly lost.' Her voice sounded foreign to her own ears.

'You won't know unless you give me a try.'

He helped her up and escorted her to the door. 'Lesson one: *conquer your fears.*'

She stood on tiptoe and kissed his cheek. 'Thank you, *horishi*. I shall see you soon.'

8

Pants on fire

Sixteen months ago: autumn

Tuesday was Maddie's day.

Claude had never known anyone like her. Maddie was the living definition of high-maintenance. Some would have called her a gold-digger. Certainly she had a penchant for attracting famous and obscenely wealthy men. Amongst the trail of broken hearts—those that he knew about—was a gynaecologist, a rugby coach, a property developer, a TV host, and the male lead of an X-rated film called *Hot Rox*. Of the last, he suspected Maddie had been a fellow cast member.

When she wasn't in town—which seemed to be every second week— she was pampering herself at some fancy beach resort in Fiji or Bali or Phuket. He never knew if she paid for the 'me time' herself or if she had a sugar daddy on the side as well.

So, how did high-flying Madeline Hilton-Byrne become one of his clients? The reason was hard to pinpoint, but it probably boiled down to his being completely different from all the other men in her life. First of all, he knew how to fix things. Everyday things such as door latches, toilet cisterns, smoke alarms, leaky taps. Despite her show of extravagance, Maddie hated waste. And second of all, he treated her as an equal and not as a trophy. The more he came to know her, the more he came to realise that her origins were as humble as his.

Currently she was living with her second husband in a mansion in Hamilton with a billion-dollar view over the river. Once she'd told Claude there were enough bedrooms and bathrooms to accommodate an entire cricket team without anyone having to share. All those rooms for two people seemed a sacrilege.

At ten-fifteen on Tuesday morning, Claude turned left off Kingsford Smith Drive and wound up the narrow terraces of the hillside suburb. Concealed behind high stone walls and neat clipped hedges were magnificent stately homes. Only the vast rooflines and an occasional stone turret were visible from the road. The sweet fragrance of port-wine magnolias and roses offset the musty odour of old money.

At Maddie's place, he stopped at the security gate and pressed the intercom button. On a Tuesday, she was guaranteed to be home alone. The wrought-iron gates rumbled apart and he drove Shirl along a circular driveway fringed by garden beds overflowing with petunias. Under the porte-cochere he parked beside the black Bentley.

He didn't bother to lock the ute, a poor cousin to its neighbour. Stepping back, he took in the grandeur of the white-rendered residence. Although he'd been there many times, he remained in awe of its sheer size. Designed in the plantation style of the Deep South, the façade featured four soaring columns spanning two entire storeys. Picture windows with green shutters were symmetrically placed on either side of the main entrance.

Maddie glided out. Her batik sarong was tied in a complicated knot at the neck. The fabric billowed out, giving the impression of an exotic butterfly. Her shoulder-length hair was coiled into a bun, held in place with a pair of chopsticks. Frowning, she consulted a gold Rolex, one of many in her collection. All genuine, she claimed.

'What kept you?' Her voice crackled like ice.

'Traffic.' He shrugged and forced a lopsided grin.

She sniffed. 'This city's getting too big for its boots.'

'Hey Maddie, good to see you too.' He opened his arms and gave her the traditional French greeting, one kiss on the right cheek and one on the left.

Straight away she began to thaw. 'Sorry to be such a grouch, *dahling*. Marital issues. Do come in. Is it too early for a drink?'

He didn't need a second invitation. Licking his lips he trailed behind her, through the white-marble foyer decked with Romanesque statues and gilt-framed paintings of dour men, down a bowling-alley hallway. At the rear they entered a spacious glass room with an indoor garden that she called the *orangery*.

Maddie's home was dripping with affluence. Some days he had to pinch himself that a privileged few thought nothing of such luxury. As a boy, he'd lived twelve years in a rambling old residence that he supposed might once have been grand. In his day, it was bare of creature comforts and worn down to the bones of its arse. So too were the boys who shared his dorm. Stripped of dignity, as well as clothes, they kowtowed to Father Doherty when he came to supervise them at shower time. *Devil Doherty*, they used to call him behind his back. What he made them do was worse than Hell itself.

Maddie opened the cocktail cabinet and rummaged about inside.

Sinking into one of the cane chairs, Claude loosened his muscles and gazed at the azure pool. Although officially autumn, intense sunlight beamed through the glass. Steam rose from the leaves of the philodendrons. He reached for the remote and turned on the ceiling fan. Artificial breeze rustled the red lipstick palms growing in massive stone troughs.

Maddie brought two crystal flutes, an ice bucket, and a bottle of champagne. She popped the cork, filled both flutes and handed one to Claude.

'To a new beginning.' They clinked glasses and drank.

Claude frowned. 'Are you going to tell me or do I have to guess?'

'I've made a momentous decision, *dahling*. After much thought and soul-searching, I've decided to leave Darren.'

'You *what*!'

'Yes, I know it's only been two years. But a woman like me knows when she's wasting her time. Honestly, he and I have nothing *at all* in common.'

'Have you told him yet?'

She shot him a sly look. 'Not officially. That's where you come in, *dahling*.'

Claude groaned and shifted in his chair. He chugged down a quarter of the champagne without taking heed of the bubbles. Then he was choking and spluttering and trying to breathe all at the same time.

Maddie took his glass and slapped him on the back. 'Want some water?'

He shook his head, belched and finally caught his breath.

'I need your help to move my things,' Maddie continued unfazed.

His heart sank; this was bound to get ugly. As a practising lawyer, Darren knew his rights. Not only that, but his pockets were as deep as the ocean.

'He's going to Melbourne on a case. I'll be gone when he returns.'

'When?' Claude croaked.

'Tomorrow. Please help me, *dahling*. I'll make it worth your while.'

He buried his head in his hands. 'Does he know about me? About *us*?'

'Of course not!'

'Then why are you leaving all this?' He expanded his arms to take in the magnificent room. 'If you ask my opinion, you're nuts.'

'I didn't ask for your opinion. I asked for your help. So the answer is?' She paused while he scratched his head and searched for excuses.

At length he said lamely, 'But I've got other clients.'

'Just this once?' The expression in her brown eyes was as pitiful as a puppy. She poured more champagne and handed back his flute. 'You're the only man I can trust.'

In the bat of an eyelid, he was hers. Manipulative, conniving, irresistible. That's exactly what she was and he loved it.

She planted a sensual kiss on his lips. He drew her onto his lap.

Her hands roamed his body, massaged the sensitive spots, dipped beneath his belt and sought him out. Her tongue ran over his lips and pushed into his mouth. She tasted as sweet and fruity as the champagne. His mind was whirling, partly from the alcohol, partly from this sudden turn of events, partly from raw animal desire.

'Come upstairs,' she breathed into his ear. 'I'll give you an incentive payment in advance.'

His body was eager but his conscience niggled. What would he tell Lola about tomorrow? He hardly ever missed a Wednesday.

She led him up a sweeping staircase to the first floor. Out of self-preservation, he baulked at the matrimonial bedroom so she took him to one of the guest rooms, which was as large and impressive. On a round silk-covered bed they indulged in a passion that began when Maddie was last between husbands.

Afterwards, she rolled onto her back, purring with pleasure. 'Mmmmmmm. Claude Fabergé, you're worth your weight in diamonds.'

From downstairs came the sound of footsteps on the tiles.

'Someone's here,' Claude whispered.

'Shit, it must be Darren.' Maddie leapt off the bed, pulled on her knickers and straightened her sarong. 'How do I look?' Her cheeks were pink with the tell-tale afterglow, a neon sign that screamed SEX.

'Orgasmic.' He gave her a kiss and retrieved his jeans from the floor.

'Quick, there's a staircase at the other end of the hallway.' She bustled about, smoothing the bedspread, checking the room for evidence. 'Go out through the *orangery* and pretend to be working in the garden.'

As an afterthought she whispered, 'I'll call you about tomorrow.'

In less than a minute, he was standing outside by the pool. On the slate pavers was a scoop for fishing out leaves. Thankful for whatever prop came to hand, he seized it and began trawling the bottom for litter. He'd never had much to do with pools; he was acutely aware that his technique looked less than professional.

Ten minutes to make it seem fair dinkum, then get the fuck out.

He'd finished the first run when a baritone voice boomed out. 'That'll be all.' The Irish-Australian accent was the same as Devil Doherty's.

Claude nearly peed his pants. He dropped the pool scoop and prepared to flee.

A rotund man in an expensive dark suit strode toward the enclosure. His face was tanned and wrinkled; his eyes beetled beneath heavy brows. His hair was receding at the temples.

So this was Darren.

Claude froze. For a moment he was a rabbit caught in the headlights.

The two men stood motionless, each sizing the other up. Then Darren slipped his hand into the pocket of his jacket.

A dozen scenarios streamed through Claude's mind. All featured a gun. His life hung in the balance. Saliva turned to dust. He said a mental prayer along the lines of *please God, don't let him kill me* and steeled himself for the worst.

'Is one hundred enough?' Darren opened his wallet and took out a banknote.

Claude couldn't believe his ears. Not only had he screwed the man's wife and plotted her escape from their marriage, but he was getting paid for his services. Not one to pass up an easy buck, he answered without hesitation.

'Been here since seven-thirty, mate. Make it two.'

Without raising an eyebrow, Darren gave him the money.

With as much bravado as he could rouse, Claude stashed the notes in his fob pocket. He swaggered out of the enclosure and around the side of the house. Minutes later he was in his beloved ute, roaring down Kingsford Smith Drive. He slapped the steering wheel, laughed out loud. What luck!

It wasn't quite midday, there was money in his pocket and he was free to do whatever he pleased. At the Newstead turnoff, he swerved into the right lane and took the Inner City Bypass. Near the Royal Hospital he exited through the maze of flyovers onto Bowen Bridge Road. He continued driving along Gympie Road, the main arterial route north. His destination was yet to crystallise, but he hadn't been to the Sunshine Coast in years. Today, on the cusp of autumn, was perfect for the beach. The sparkling north-facing shores of Noosa would be a glorious sight.

For company he turned the radio to his favourite station: a mix of classic rock, sport, a bit of news and talk-back. The host was embroiled in a heated discussion about the greyhound racing industry. His two guests were on opposite sides of the track. A woman with a polished Melbournian accent was berating the treatment of racing dogs while a man with a North Queensland drawl kept interjecting. It promised to be a monumental battle of words.

As the ute zoomed along the six-lane Bruce Highway, that massive scar of bitumen that sliced through pine forests and coastal scrub, Claude lit a smoke and turned up the volume.

The woman wouldn't be swayed. 'The poor creatures are kept in cages. I've been to these places. Anyone with a heart would want to stop this sort of abuse.'

Finally the host squeezed in a question. 'Can you describe what you've seen?'

'I'll do my utmost but it won't be pretty.'

'Okay listeners, a warning: graphic descriptions to follow. We'll be back right after the break.'

A guitar riff preceded advertisements for Oz Insurance, Whisper tampons, and Innapickle relishes. Claude flicked between the stations but found no better offering.

Two minutes later the talk-show host was back. For the benefit of newcomers he gave a brief recap. 'Today our guests are Jane Foster representing Animal Freedom and Peter Hall of the Racing Industry Association and we're discussing greyhound racing. Jane Foster, what are your objections to the methods used by trainers?'

'First and foremost, Animal Freedom objects to the practice of blooding greyhounds. We have filmed instances where small animals are attached to the lure while they are still alive. The speed is set to give the dog a good chase. At the end of the session, the dog is allowed to catch the lure and the animal is mauled to death. It is absolutely revolting! Over weeks of surveillance, we observed rabbits, possums, and cats used for this abhorrent practice.'

'What absolute rot!' spat Peter Hall. 'Get your facts straight before you make accusations. Rabbit pelts are sometimes used, but never live animals.'

The woman ignored him as if he were an annoying puff of wind. 'Then there's the treatment of the greyhounds themselves. Some disreputable trainers deprive them of food and water and keep them in cramped accommodation. They are often inbred because they are selected for speed alone. If a dog doesn't reach expectations, it is exterminated. And when I say *exterminated*, that's exactly what I mean. Not euthanized painlessly by lethal injection, but bludgeoned until dead. The bodies are disposed of in bushland. During our investigations, we found a greyhound graveyard with the skeletal remains of sixty-three dogs. All the skulls showed severe trauma, consistent with being beaten with a blunt instrument such as a hammer or a baseball bat. The dogs were dumped soon after death or else they were killed—'

Claude snapped off the radio, his good mood gone to the pack. Greyhound racing was his passion and had been for twenty years. He loved the grace of the animals running at full speed. And he had utmost respect for their trainers, of whom Lola was one.

What a beat-up! Those animal rights activists got on his goat. All emotion and little evidence. In his experience of the real world of dog racing, the sorts of things Jane Foster described hardly ever happened. For a start, it would be professional suicide for the trainers. Why would they want to make a racing dog aggressive? Complete lunacy! It would be nothing but a distraction on the track.

At the next exit he veered left off the highway and turned east towards the coast. Forget rubbing shoulders with toffee-nosed tourists and yuppies at Noosa. He wanted to be with *real* people. Punters like him.

Twenty minutes later he crossed the bridge from the mainland to the island, headed straight for Woorim on the surf side and the Blue Pacific Hotel. There, amongst retirees and the thong brigade, he drowned his frustrations in beer while reruns of *Sex in the City* played silently on the screen.

Tomorrow was Wednesday. He'd promised to help Maddie move out.

But Wednesday was Lola's. Apart from when he'd had his appendix removed years ago, he'd never missed a day with Lola. After the radio talk show, there'd be more bad publicity for sure. Lola would be looking for a sympathetic ear.

What if there was a public outcry and they shut down the dog races? What would she do to earn a living?

Feeling annoyed and guilty about the predicament he was in, he ordered another beer. A sparrow flew in and pecked crumbs off the floor. In an adjacent room, poker machines jangled and flashed. A couple of old codgers set up a triangle on the pool table. One was on crutches and the other had part of his nose missing. Old age could be harsh, but the alternative was harsher.

Somehow Claude would get through this day.

Tomorrow, he'd worry about tomorrow.

9

Photographs

Friday 7 August

For Seth everything was going according to plan. Dutifully, he'd informed the cops about the corpse without spilling the beans on his involvement and he'd emailed his initial report to the editor at *The Morning Post*. Rather than risk a drink-driving charge, he'd taken an Uber car from the King's Arms back to Mayfield Avenue to get some external shots of the house. His return coincided with the removal of the body, so he took a few action snaps as well.

Safe in his pocket was the scarlet key.

His run of good fortune continued the next morning when he arrived only fifteen minutes late for work. At the nearby showgrounds, the Ekka was in full swing. Fine weather was forecast for the weekend and the public holiday to come. The short working week was an excuse for thousands of the city's public servants to cash in their flex-time and head for the coast. After the gridlock of the day before, it was a dream to drive to Newspaper House without any traffic holdups.

In the office he set the habitual take-away coffee cup on his desk and connected the laptop. On the other side of the grey cubicle divider, Cate was tapping away at her keyboard. Apart from sticking plaster on her forehead, she seemed to be in good shape.

Folding his arms on top of the divider, he said, 'Hey Cate, how's the sore head?'

'I'll live.' She looked up from the computer screen and narrowed her eyes. 'So, boss? Was it you?' Her sense of anticipation was almost palpable.

'What?' he said mystified.

'Didn't you hear the morning news? A body was found in a house at Corella. The police are tight-lipped. Anything to do with a certain tip-off?'

Seth scuttled around the divider. 'Shhhhh! Keep your voice down.'

'It *was* you,' she whispered with a hint of awe. 'Can you fill me in? Maybe over a coffee? My treat.'

'I never refuse a woman who offers coffee.'

A block away from the office was a run-down shop that sold lunches, soft drinks, and cigarettes. The sandwiches were usually soggy and the service was atrocious. The saving grace was the espresso machine. It wasn't the finest coffee in town, but it wasn't the worst either. Upstairs at the rear was a rustic verandah that overlooked a checkerboard of tin rooves and postage-stamp back yards, the perfect setting for clandestine meetings between lovers and spies and reporters.

While Cate placed the order, Seth claimed a rickety table as far from the other customers as he could get. After glancing over his shoulder and being satisfied that no-one else could hear, he said, 'Promise you won't breathe a word.'

'Whatever it is, we're in it together,' said Cate glibly.

'I mean it Cate. There's a lot at stake. Criminal charges for trespassing, possibly break and enter, withholding information, interfering with a corpse—'

'What *have* you been doing?'

'I'll get to that in a minute. There's a story here and we're going to be first to get it. On your grandmother's grave, promise you'll keep it quiet.'

'Both my grandmothers are alive.'

'You know what I mean.' He sat back and waited for her to respond.

At last realisation dawned that he was deadly serious. 'Cross my heart and hope to die.' She made the appropriate actions. 'I mean it, boss. I won't let you down.'

He shifted the chair closer and lowered his voice. 'After your little accident, I went back to the office and deciphered the address. 53 Mayfield Avenue, Corella.'

Visibly she paled. 'How did you work it out?'

'Hangman.' The response slipped out without thinking. What a dumb thing to say. Here he was, a world-ranking journalist who'd scooped stories on par with Watergate, employing a simple child's game for research.

Quickly he added, 'It's a great new app. All the rage in the States.'

'Hangman?' She narrowed her eyes. 'Oh yeah, I heard about it on Twitter.'

'To cut a long story short, I went into the house.' He opened the camera roll on his phone and slid it across the table. 'This is what I found.'

As she flicked through the photos, her jaw fell open. 'Oh my God!'

When the coffees arrived, Cate quickly covered the screen.

Seth paused until the waiter was out of earshot. 'I called the C.I.B. straight away. The cops were there within the hour. The house will be cordoned off for a few days.' He flashed the red key. 'Then we can get back in.'

'Do you know the identity of the deceased?' She seemed anxious, as if she were keeping something important to herself.

'No. I checked out the owner. I'm certain it's not her.'

Looking relieved, Cate sipped her latte and studied the shots of the corpse. At length she said, 'Poor thing, she's had cancer.'

'How on earth do you know that?'

'See here?' She expanded the image. 'Do you notice anything unusual?'

Seth rubbed his chin. He'd seen plenty of naked women in his day but none as decorative as this. On her back were the angel wings, on the thighs and arms was a feast of botanicals, and across the chest were arabesques and blue lotus flowers.

'Here's a hint,' she said. 'What's missing?'

He examined the photo again. Of course! The nipples.

'Cate, you're a genius!'

'Double mastectomy. Might give us a clue.'

'You want to drive past the house?' he suggested.

'Another time. I've got a deadline and it's not going away.'

In silence they walked back to the office.

Later when Seth reflected on the conversation, he could pinpoint exactly when Cate had gone a bit strange. It was the address. What else did she know?

He tucked this thought into a fold of his brain. At this stage of an investigation, any information—no matter how obscure—might be important. His training was to get answers in whichever way he could. He was well-practiced in asking straight questions and piecing all the clues together to reach a logical conclusion. That was the way he operated. The process had served him well as a foreign correspondent covering wars in the Middle East, and in Bosnia before that. It worked perfectly on the logic of men.

All he had to do now was figure out how to influence one intelligent but evasive young woman.

10

The case of the missing cat

Sixteen months ago: autumn

Daylight was growing shorter and soon the cold weather would set in. Then the roaring westerlies would seep through the cracks in the weatherboards, dropping the temperature into single digits. At night the casements would rattle and wail. For Isla, alone apart from a furry companion, the eerie hours would drag on.

Ever since her early retirement, the weeks had blurred together. Only the mechanics of human existence—eating, shopping, cleaning, sleeping—marked the passage of time. Morning drifted into midday, which flowed into the afternoon and evening. Life was an empty vessel.

Although she'd tried to create structure out of nothing, she'd found it tough. Really tough. Her ambitious plan—the mandala of *conquer, dare, create*—made months earlier had stalled. From her checklist of things to do, she'd ticked only a few. Her finger ran down the sheet. Visit the galleries of Italy (tick); volunteer at Meals on Wheels (tick); improve computer skills (question mark); clean out the cupboards (crossed out). What remained far outweighed the accomplishments. If she were to rate her efforts, she'd struggle to get a C-minus.

Slow start and lots of room for improvement.

The first element of her mandala was the crux of the problem. *Conquer your fears.* Fear shut her down. Fear of failure, fear of ridicule, fear of change. She knew this was irrational, for she had no-one to answer to but herself. That didn't stop her from being frozen into inaction.

'Why are you so scared?' she said aloud.

57

As if in sympathy, Venus rubbed against her legs. Her feline motor rumbled. Isla picked her up and scratched the downy fur beneath her chin. Venus tipped up her pink nose, closed her eyes and kneaded her claws into Isla's thigh.

'Naughty!' She unhooked the talons from her skirt and dropped the cat to the floor. Frustrated and restless, she donned yard shoes and tramped downstairs.

Liquidambar leaves, crisp and orange, skittered around the concrete. The smell of dry earth from the unsealed section beneath the house filtered through the bannisters. She walked through the downstairs laundry and undid the storeroom padlock. As the door opened, she pulled the dangling cord for the light.

On the shelf was the plastic fishing box that held her art equipment. Once canary-yellow, the coating of dust and gecko crap was so thick that the lid was brown. Gingerly she carried the box to the lawn and hosed it off. After drying it with a rag, she unclipped the latch. Inside were her oil paints and brushes, old enough to be classified as vintage.

One by one, she took out the tubes. Surprisingly, most were in good condition. Emerald green had sprung a leak and four others were fused together. The boars' hair brushes were stiff and true. The Conte crayons— black, white, terracotta, grey—were as straight as soldiers lined up in a clear plastic case. Four palette knives and two small bottles containing linseed oil and turpentine were present and accounted for.

Perversely, she felt a pang of disappointment. If they'd been ruined she'd have an excuse to delay, a reason not to start today … or any day. Once she'd loved painting, but rekindling the passion at her age was probably a bad idea. Her hands were no longer steady, her eyesight was getting weak. What did she expect anyway?

As it turned out, art had provided her a living but not in the way she'd first imagined. As a student in the 1970s, she'd fantasised about fame and fortune. In her daydreams, her work would be exhibited in galleries across the world. Well-meaning lecturers had lavished her with praise. Her paintings were *vibrant, luminous, evocative*, they'd said. She was *a female Brett Whiteley*, they'd said. For her assignments she received top marks and her confidence soared.

The year after graduation came the reckoning, swift and merciless. After ten months of solid creative effort she produced thirty paintings and organised her debut exhibition. Not a cent of income had she received in the entire period. The Plantation Gallery in Paddington was booked and prepaid with a loan from her old man. As a newcomer to the city's art scene, publicity was hard to get. She couldn't afford advertising so she sent press releases to

The Morning Post and all the free neighbourhood papers. No-one picked up the story. A few shops along Given Terrace agreed to display her screen-printed posters but it wasn't enough. Two days before the event, Maddie helped her letterbox-drop the suburb. Up and down the hills they trudged. Two hundred and seventy worker's cottages in Paddington received a purple roneographed flyer.

At ten o'clock on the day of the exhibition, the gallery doors opened for business. To save money she'd baked biscuits and made finger food for the guests and Maddie had agreed to be her sales manager. In the space of six hours, ten people came in, two of whom were her parents. At four p.m. the gallery doors shut. One painting had been sold. The ninety dollars it brought was barely enough to cover costs.

Defeated, Isla took a job at Bandicoot Press packing and despatching text books. Her wages covered food and rent and not much else. At the end of the year she was accepted into teachers' college. She'd taught art ever since, proving yet again the self-fulfilling prophesy. *Those who can, do. Those who can't, teach.*

Except she could. She knew she had talent. Resurrecting her art career was at the very top of her bucket list. It fitted perfectly with her plan.

All that stood in the way was one woman: herself.

In the back yard she sat on the lawn, absently twirling a boars-hair brush. With the regular income from her superannuation, she no longer needed to work. She was free to do whatever she chose.

The trip to Italy had been the catalyst. Never had she felt more inspired, but she hadn't done anything about it. Three months ago she'd returned, bursting with intentions, yet she was still stuck in a tangle of procrastination.

Okay, Isla Bright, she said. *Damn-well do it this time.*

She jammed a straw hat on her head and lugged the easel, paintbox and canvas board into the park. The vast expanse of grassland, twenty hectares in size, was mostly deserted on weekdays. In the late afternoon it would come alive with schoolgirls, training for the hockey fixtures that were held every weekend. The first busload would arrive at three-thirty. By then she intended to be packed up and gone.

Directly across the park from her home was the creek, the lifeblood and the curse of the neighbourhood. Most of the time it was alive with birds. But if the king tide coincided with a stretch of solid rain, the creek would breach its banks and flood into the houses.

Overlooking the swirling milk-coffee water, she set up the easel. Native shrubs—grevillea, golden wattle, lemon myrtle—screened her chosen spot from the playing fields. The fragrance of honey offset the salt breath of the mangroves and the rotten-egg stench of the mud.

At that moment she felt good. She was in control. *Making progress*. If this proved to be a dismal waste of time, at least she'd made a start.

She stretched her arms, cracked her knuckles, opened the art box. Closing her eyes, she visualised the surroundings. The fraying trunks of the paperbarks. Crabs scuttling on the mudflats. Redtop grass, riffling in the breeze. Yellow panniers of pollen on bees' hairy knees.

Keeping her eyes shut, she touched crayon to paper. Guided by imagination and non-visual cues, she sketched out the vibrations of the landscape. The sensory exercise was what she'd taught students but hadn't practised herself in years. Meanwhile mickey birds squabbled, swallows twittered, willie wagtails gyrated. All the urban creatures went about their business as if this plump middle-aged woman in a blue dress and purple cardigan were a normal part of their territory.

In an hour, she completed six sketches. She laid her work in a semicircle on the grass. The lines were strong and confident; the scale was good. *Solid effort*, she said aloud. Hearing the affirmation boosted her confidence.

The paint tubes—ultramarine, vermillion, cadmium yellow, magenta—were stiff and unyielding. Eventually she coaxed them out. Globules of oil paint formed glistening pearls on the palette.

Her first study was of the creek framed within an arch of foliage. The mid-morning light was perfect; the chocolatey water was dappled with golden spots of sun. She blocked in the background with a thin wash then added dollops of colour. The brush seemed to find its own rhythm as she caught a transient moment of time.

Transient: not lasting, enduring, or permanent. The perfect description of her life since her career was rudely interrupted. The wings of freedom had come at a price. Even the trip of a lifetime to Europe had been difficult. So many choices, so little time. Usually she deferred decisions to a circle of wise friends. Without them she was rudderless.

Change was inevitable. Change came and went with the wind. Often she'd helped others—students, parents, teachers—to cope. The endings, transitions and beginnings mirrored the stages of grief. That's what the text books said. Her current stage was transition: the twilight zone of neither here nor there. The only way out was through the passage of time.

Isla continued to paint until heavy clouds gathered in the west. Distant thunder rumbled. The creek bank rang with the *coo-eeeee* of a storm bird and the screech of low-flying lorikeets.

All at once, the birds fell silent. The only sounds were the rattle of the mangrove leaves and the whisper of wind through the grass.

There was something else: a deep thrumming, almost too low to hear.

Isla put down her brush and cocked her head.

Through the foliage, she saw a flash of blue near the bridge where the road made a U-bend. A tradie's ute. Kingfisher blue, chrome bars, mag wheels. A mobile Christmas tree. The ute stopped near the bridge and the driver cut the engine.

Goosebumps prickled the back of her neck. There she was, completely alone. Only a screen of native shrubs stood between them.

What if ...?

Pull yourself together, she told herself.

Isla loaded the paintbrush with cadmium yellow and stippled it over green. She stepped back to examine the result. It was awful! Worse than a beginner. Her muse had packed up and gone, scared off by the intruder.

Resentment shot heat to her head. She tried to fix the mess but her eyes kept wandering to the bridge and the man who appeared and disappeared between the nodding vegetation.

From the tray of the vehicle, he took a hessian sack and swung it onto his shoulder. Bent under its weight, he staggered onto the bridge. Half-way across, he stopped and threw the sack over the side.

Empty handed, he returned to the ute and sped away.

Isla shook her head. Illegal dumpers were mostly lazy creatures. Rubbish was usually left on the verge. Nobody bothered carting things onto the bridge or tossing them into the creek.

Often what was left by the roadside was re-useable, which benefited not only poor students and families down on their luck but also the council workers whose job was to remove it. One thing was clear: the man who threw the sack off the bridge was not your average illegal dumper.

Isla wiped the paintbrush with a rag and ventured out of the hide. The ute was long gone. Curiosity gnawed her. What was inside that hessian sack?

Meanwhile, layers of shifting cloud in the west congealed and swelled into a nasty bruise. Purple was tinged with green. The atmosphere crackled with electricity. Lightning pulsed. Soon the storm would break.

Hastily she packed up the art materials and anchored them beneath the easel. Shivering, she pulled the cardigan tight around her chest. With each step her skirt snatched at her ankles. She edged along the line of bushes toward the bridge. Cicadas buzzed. The clouds closed in, shutting off the sun.

As she reached the concrete ramp to the bridge, day turned to night. Common sense warned her to turn back but curiosity urged her on. Wind flailed the paperbarks. Confetti of leaves and bark swirled through the air.

In the middle of the bridge, Isla stopped and leaned over the rail. The outgoing tide lapped the edge of a mud island. Stranded in the shallows was the hessian sack. In the middle was a pregnant bulge; the neck was strung with rope.

Did she dare go down?

To reach the island she'd have to wade through hip-deep water. It would be cold and she'd most certainly catch her death. Excuses drowned the idea before it was fully formed.

Flash! The creek, the bridge, the trees became stark images in black-and-white. Thunder rocked the bridge. Fat drops of rain smashed onto the timber.

Five metres below, the sack wallowed in the oozing mud. What could be inside? Stolen goods? Body parts? Garden clippings?

With one last look, she turned and fled the storm.

With the art materials bundled under her arms, she half-walked half-ran toward home. Crosswinds propelled her forward and sideways; she was as helpless as a yacht in a cyclone. The canvas was a flapping sail; the easel was a treacherous boom that threatened to capsize her.

Simultaneous lightning and thunder struck as she raced up the back stairs. In semi-darkness, she unlocked the door. A gust wrenched the knob from her hand and slammed the door against the VJs. Inside, she snapped on the light and laid the sodden art materials on the table.

'Ve-nus,' she called. 'Here puss, puss.'

The cat was nowhere to be seen. Not surprising. When it came to storms that animal had a sixth sense. At least an hour before the Bureau of Meteorology picked up activity on the radar, she'd vaporise into a secret place. No amount of calling would bring her out. When the last drops of rain pinged onto the aluminium awning, she'd stroll in dry and calm, acting as if nothing had happened.

'Veeee-nus,' Isla sang.' Where are you, scaredy cat?'

Irrational fears began to rise. What if she'd gone out through the cat-flap and was lost in the storm? What if she ran away forever? Panicking, Isla searched all the usual hidey-holes. Under the bed, behind the sofa, beneath the coffee table, in the hall cupboard where the door was permanently ajar.

Not a whisker, not a trace.

She placed her hands on her hips, told herself not to worry. Easy to say. If anything happened, it would be her fault.

Damn curiosity! She should never have gone onto the bridge. What had she seen? A muddy old sack. What a stupid waste of time!

Tears filled her eyes.

Irritably, she brushed them away. Of course Venus would turn up when the storm had passed. A cup of tea was what she needed; a good strong cuppa would set her mind at ease.

Flash! CRACK!

The timber house shuddered in the aftershock. At the same time the lights went out. Isla raced to the park-side windows. Firefly sparks flew in all directions. The next explosion of lightning revealed that one of the old paperbarks had been split down the middle. Half the tree had fallen onto the power lines, bringing them down onto the road.

Retreating to the kitchen, she filled the kettle and lit the cooktop burner. In the glow of the gas flame, she tracked down the emergency candles at the back of the utility drawer. Ahead was the prospect of a long lonely night. No cat, no internet, no TV. Isolation in a city of two million. Hailstones attacked the window glass. The wind moaned like a lost soul.

Where is my darling Venus?

In the pantry was a jar of choc-peanut biscuits, home-baked yesterday. She wolfed three straight down and kept another two out for later. The comfort food provided little comfort. Chewing her nails, she sat at the table and waited for the tea to brew. The hammering of hail on the roof reminded her of a blacksmith's shop. The candles cast creepy shadows on the walls. Her stomach contracted into a tight wad of fear. Ever since childhood she'd been scared in storms. Alone she felt especially vulnerable.

As quickly as it began, the storm blew itself out. When the rain eased to a patter, Isla opened the casements. The freezing air was fragrant with the scent of lush grass and wet linen. Street grime was rushing down the drains, gushing into the creek, flowing into the river and the bay. The sun was already peeping out. Tomorrow the wash-and-dry cycle would start anew.

She opened the kitchen door, hoping that Venus would be there. She wasn't. Perhaps food would bring her out. Isla filled the empty bowl with kitty-bits. Downstairs, she sang, 'Vee-nus! Here, puss!'

A greenish tinge to the evening light made her feel slightly woozy.

In the back yard, drifts of hail were half a metre thick. Naked branches were dark skeletons on the lawn. Along the side path, slippery ice-slush was littered with shredded leaves. Out front, the daisy bushes were knocked flat and the trellis of sweet peas had gone over. A huge tree limb had smashed the fence, narrowly missing the house. Tangled powerlines—black spaghetti—were strewn across the road.

Returning to the kitchen, Isla picked up *The Morning Post,* rolled in plastic wrap, from the bench. Newspapers: good old-fashioned entertainment. No electricity required. She poured another cup of tea, spread out the paper and forced herself to read.

On page three was the headline *Cat-napped!* The opening paragraph made the hairs on the back of her neck stand at attention.

> *Lock up your pets, residents are warned as more cats disappear. 'Fifteen cats went missing last week alone,' said an RSPCA spokesman.*
>
> *Four days ago Marilyn Carpenter, 41, of Corella lost her blue-point Burmese. 'We've put up posters everywhere. My daughter is heartbroken.'*
>
> *Janet Torrens, 75, also of Corella is another victim. Ten-year old Felix, a white Persian, disappeared Thursday morning. 'One minute he was playing in the yard, the next he was gone.'*

Isla's mouth fell open. How awful! And in her suburb too!
What has happened to Venus?
With mounting dread, she began a thorough search of the house. This time no nook or cranny would escape her attention. She opened every cupboard, lifted every curtain, groped beneath every piece of furniture. There were dust balls and cotton balls and fur balls. But no cat. Outside, she scoured the back yard, the garage, the garden shed. In failing light, she battled through the storm debris to reach the scrubland by the creek.

There was no sign of Venus.

What should she do? She knew that the police didn't act on missing person reports for forty-eight hours. If she called them about a missing moggy, they'd probably laugh her off the phone.

In the lounge room, she sat on the brown couch with the candle on the side table and the phone in her hand. Who would understand? Who would help? Over the course of a lifetime she'd known thousands of people, yet few were true friends. She flipped through her address book, starting at the letter A.

Antoinette Collier? No, she'd be at work.

She bypassed Brian Dean (still overseas) and several other workmates who'd politely traded phone numbers at year's end.

Under M were three names.

Marjorie Wippet? No, not in this lifetime.

Maxine Daniels? In all the years they'd worked together, not once had the hippie music teacher inquired after Venus. Recently she'd adopted a rescue greyhound, which confirmed the suspicion that she hated cats.

Madeline Hilton-Byrne? Firstly, Maddie wouldn't be at work. It was doubtful that she'd done a day's work in her life. Second, she had a soft spot for animals.

Isla punched in the number. By the time the phone answered, her heart was thumping and her lungs refused to breathe.

'Can you ... come over? It's a matter ... of life ... and death.' She could scarcely get the words out. As a teacher, she'd had to deal with plenty of panic attacks. Every time there were exams, one of the students would have to be taken out and treated. Until now she'd viewed a panic attack as a sign of weakness or a ploy to get attention.

But now it was her. These things were real. The struggle to speak coherently, and the inability to do so, created more panic.

'Who *is* this?' Maddie sounded doubtful, as if she might hang up.

'Isla ... Isla Bright. Listen ... can you help me?'

'*Dahling, y*ou sound absolutely dreadful! What's wrong?'

'It's ... it's Venus.' At the sound of the name, she began to sob.

'Ooooh *dahling*! I'm *soooo* sorry. She was such a *dear* little thing,' Maddie cooed.

'She's not ...' Isla fished a tissue from her sleeve and gave her nose a good blow, which made her feel a bit better. 'She's gone. I mean, she's *missing*. There's an article in the paper.'

'About catnapping? I saw it. How awful! Have you called the animal shelter?'

'Oh my lord! Why didn't I think of that? I'll call you back.' Of course that was the answer. Venus was microchipped; she'd be easy to identify.

Half an hour later, Maddie arrived bearing gifts: a cheerful bunch of gerberas, a cake box, a bottle of white wine. As usual she was immaculately dressed: the latest in designer jeans and a luxurious silk blouse. Although she'd trowelled on a variety of expensive cosmetics, the bags beneath her eyes showed through, taking an edge off perfection.

'My poor *dahling*.' She aimed air-kisses at Isla's cheeks.

'Thanks a million for coming.' In the window glass, Isla caught her own reflection. Dowdy was the only way to describe the paint-splattered blue dress and purple cardigan that she'd recently liberated from years of banishment in a camphor chest. Her eyes were puffy from weeping. 'Sorry, I'm such a mess.'

Maddie smiled. 'It's only me, honey. Not the Queen of Sheba.'

Isla slumped into a vinyl kitchen chair. Maddie would know what to do. Maddie had worked her way out of dozens of scrapes. Already she was ransacking the cupboards for wine glasses and plates. It was not quite wine-o'clock, but today it didn't matter. For once Isla wouldn't be indulging alone, not that she was much of a drinker. These days, one chardonnay with dinner saw her snoring on the sofa by eight.

Maddie poured out two generous glasses. 'Now, tell me exactly what happened.' She took a deep swallow and leant her elbows on the table.

Isla gave a sketchy recount of the afternoon's events. 'I did as you suggested and phoned the animal shelter. No luck, I'm afraid.'

The newspaper was open at the catnapping article. Maddie moved the candle closer and read it aloud. At the end, she snapped her fingers and rummaged in her Valentino bag for her phone. After scrolling through a list of numbers, she touched the screen. Her sculpted nails tapped a rhythm on the tabletop while she waited for an answer.

'Hello. May I speak to Cate Bradshaw?' Maddie used her upper-class British accent usually reserved for cocktail parties and wealthy men. With this accent she could make outrageous demands and get whatever she wanted. The accent was as fake as her boobs, yet it worked every time.

Isla couldn't help but smile.

'Hello, Ms Bradshaw? This is Madeline Hilton-Byrne. Congratulations on today's catnapping article.' A pause. 'Yes. Beautifully researched and written.' Another pause. 'Sadly, there's been another disappearance … my friend's cat … in Corella.' After a longer pause, Maddie gave a description of Venus, naming the breed a *Latvian Grey* and providing Isla's contact details. By the end of the conversation her eyes were sparking.

'What did she say?'

'Cate's all over it. Her phone's been running hot. More cats missing—all pedigree—and a couple of leads on suspects. She thinks it's a trafficking racket linked to an online pet shop. She wants to interview you tomorrow at three.'

'Okay, that sounds promising. But what on earth is a *Latvian Grey*?'

'Venus is a unique and special feline. She has to *sound* impressive.'

Isla rolled her eyes and skulled the wine. 'I hope that reporter is right. About the pet shop, I mean. At least my precious darling will be alive.'

'Google *cats for sale*. You'll find her in no time.'

Feeling somewhat reassured, Isla cut herself a slice of chocolate cake. The icing was slathered on thick and glossy; the centre was oozing with whipped cream and fresh strawberries. She could feel the calories going straight to her hips but she couldn't care less. She ran her finger along the flat blade of the knife to collect the oh-so-irresistible combination of cream and chocolate.

Maddie was busy checking text messages; the shadow of a frown crossed her brow. 'Sorry *dahling*, must dash. If you're not busy next Tuesday, come to my place for lunch.' The invitation was phrased as a statement: decline it at your peril.

Isla opened her diary, which was completely blank. 'I'll check my busy schedule.' She paused to see if her friend picked up the little joke. Maddie didn't seem to notice.

'I'm free.' She wrote down the solitary appointment.

Maddie gave an enigmatic smile.

Isla frowned. 'Anyone else going?'

In an expression that typified vagueness, Maddie waved her hands. 'Oh … you know … maybe.'

'Hmmm. You know I don't like surprises.'

'You'll like this one, I promise. Just what the doctor ordered. I'll text you the address.'

Before Isla could ask why she'd need the address when she'd been to the Hamilton mansion dozens of times, Maddie gave her a final hug and rushed out.

Her voice floated back through the open door. 'Hope you find Venus, *dahling*.' Her stilettos clip-clopped down the stairs. Why a woman in her late fifties chose to wear those ankle-breakers was beyond her comprehension.

Isla refilled her wine glass, retrieved the laptop by her bed and commenced a *Google* search for cats. The task was more than daunting than she expected. Around three hundred were listed on *Sell 'n Trade* alone. Humble moggies were going for a song. Some advertisers were asking the cost of de-sexing and vaccinations; some said they wanted the family pet to go to a good home for free. On the other hand, rare pedigrees were fetching thousands of dollars.

If there were such a breed as a Latvian Grey, Venus would be worth a lot of cash. Sadly, as an ageing bitser, she had no monetary value at all.

With moist cheeks, Isla laid her head on the table. For a short while her spirits had been boosted; now she was back to square one.

What other explanation could there be for the disappearance of her darling pet?

11

Lost and found

Sixteen months ago: the day after the storm

At the appointed time of three o'clock sharp, the rap of the brass doorknocker resounded through the Queenslander. In the kitchen, Isla had just finished icing a batch of patty cakes. To open the front door, she had to drag away the brown couch that had never quite fitted and lever out three rusty bolts. Friends and neighbours always came around the back. In the suburb of Corella, it was an unwritten rule that the front entrance was for debt collectors, Bible bashers, and travelling salesmen. Or in this case, a reporter from *The Morning Post*, there for an interview about a missing pet.

With a tug, the hinges moved and the door creaked open. On the landing was a young woman with long dark hair, perfect eyebrows, and cherry red lipstick. Wearing a slim black dress, tights, ankle boots and red tote bag, she could have easily passed as a catwalk model.

'Hello,' she said with a smile. 'I'm Cate Bradshaw from *The Morning Post*. Are you Ms Bright?'

'Please, call me Isla.' She returned the smile as they shook hands. 'Do come in. Mind your step. Sorry the place is bit of a mess. I haven't had the heart to do the housework since losing Venus.'

Isla fussed nervously about the living room, gathering up papers and plumping cushions. Not used to being the centre of media attention, her heart was fluttering like a bird in a dust-bath. 'Actually, do you mind if we do the interview in the kitchen?'

The fragrance of vanilla wafted down the hall.

'Sure.' said Cate. 'Mmmm. Something smells good.'

The kitchen was where Isla felt most comfortable, never more than on a warm autumn afternoon when the sun filtered through the mango tree and dappled the lino with gold. The table was set with white linen, floral crockery, and a tiered cake-stand with the fresh-baked patty cakes.

'How do you take your tea?'

'Black with one. You shouldn't have gone to all this trouble.' Cate helped herself to a dainty cake. She took a notepad and pen from her tote bag, and set up her phone in the middle of the table. 'Do you mind if I record? It keeps me honest and guarantees an accurate report.'

'Fair enough.' Isla brought the tea and sat down opposite.

'Are you ready?'

Isla nodded, unsure of what to expect. In a past life it was she who interrogated young people, generally when they'd done something bad. And here was this *girl*, not much older than her students, about to grill her about a possible crime in which she was the victim. She hid behind the floral teacup and readied herself for a barrage of questions.

'Just tell me what happened,' said Cate simply.

Isla's eyes began to prickle. *Don't blubber, woman.* She bit down hard on her lip, which triggered an inconvenient rush of heat to the brain.

Cate touched her arm. 'Take your time. I know this is hard.'

'I miss her,' Isla said in a tiny voice. She fanned herself with a serviette. 'You must think I'm a crazy old cat-lady.'

'Not at all. I have a cat myself. Thomas. He's part-Persian and part-Ragdoll and he's gorgeous. I don't know what I'd do without him.'

Isla softened. 'Venus was my family. I don't have children of my own, but I've spent a lifetime teaching other people's. I'm recently retired, you see. They gave me an *early retirement* package because they closed the school.'

'Corella High?'

'Why yes. How did you know?'

'I have my sources.' Cate tapped her nose with a finger. 'Seriously, I wrote a piece on the proposed closure way back when the community was up in arms. Can't say I agree with the government's decision. But, as a reporter, I'm obliged to present facts and not opinions. It was a wonderful school. Some of my friends went there.'

Despite her spectacular appearance, this young woman seemed to have a heart.

Isla laid a photo on the table. 'There she is: my darling Venus.'

'Why, she's absolutely beautiful!' The comment sounded genuine. 'So that's a *Latvian Grey*. I searched the Internet and couldn't find anything. Is it a new breed?'

Isla shook her head. 'It's not a breed at all. My friend—the one who phoned you—is prone to exaggeration.'

They both laughed.

'Well she's adorable anyway.'

Isla explained the circumstances of the disappearance in as much detail as she could remember. As an afterthought she mentioned the man, the ute, and the sack that was hurled off the bridge.

Cate's mouth opened slightly. 'Did you get a good look at him?'

'No, I was too far away. Later I went down to investigate, but the water was deep and a storm was coming in.'

'Have you been back since?'

'To tell you the truth, I'd almost forgotten about it.'

'Can you take me there?'

Isla blinked in disbelief. 'I suppose. It'd be a miracle if it's still there. That creek might look mild now but after rain it's a raging torrent.'

'You'll never know if you never go.' Cate jumped to her feet. 'But first I need to change.'

Isla showed her to the bathroom.

Two minutes later an entirely different Cate appeared. She was dressed for action: red button-down shirt, tight blue jeans, red Cons. With hands on her hips and flowing black hair, she was Wonder Woman personified.

Together they paddled across the playing fields and dodged debris remaining from the storm. Earlier, workmen had removed the damaged paperbark and restrung the powerlines. Isla showed Cate the spot on the riverbank where she'd set up her easel the morning before. She pointed out the bridge, partially obstructed by mangroves, and the road that ended in a U. They paced the distance between the open-air studio and the northern end of the bridge. One hundred and thirty-eight metres.

Isla walked to the middle of the bridge and rested her elbows on the rails. As usual the water was the colour of milk coffee. She scanned both banks, littered with flotsam from the deluge, and decided this was a complete waste of time.

A few steps away, Cate clung to the top rail, a rapt expression on her face. 'Was the sack made of hessian?'

'Yes, at the time I thought it was an old sugarbag.'

'Look over there!' Cate pointed to a mangrove about fifty metres downstream. 'See the branch hanging into the water?'

Isla could see the tree but couldn't make out anything else. Last time she'd renewed her driver's licence, they'd tested her eyesight and she'd managed to fake it so she wouldn't have to wear glasses. She rubbed her eyes and squinted at the dark branches that dipped into the water. From this distance it was hard to tell if the lumpy shape in the creek was the sack, a fallen log, or a shadow.

'I reckon that's it. Come on.' After snapping several photos, Wonder Woman set off at a cracking pace.

To reach the place where the sack was marooned, they had to slide down a mud embankment and dodge a large concrete pipe with an iron grille over its mouth. On the shore, slippery ooze sucked at the soles of their shoes.

Isla found the going tough. In one spot she sank up to her knees in muck. In another she had to tip-toe between the peg-roots of the mangroves. She was walking across a bed of nails: one wrong step and the spikes would skewer her foot. Thank God she'd worn her oldest joggers. She wouldn't bother to wash them later; they'd be going straight in the wheelie bin.

Agile as a cat, Cate took each obstacle with ease. Several metres ahead, she waded into the murky water, unhooked the sack from the branch and began to haul it ashore. 'God this is heavy. Give me a hand.'

Isla grasped the lower edge of the hessian and lifted with all her might. The stench seeping through the cloth turned her stomach but she battled on, aware that this might become headline news. Between them they carried the lumpy load up the creek bank out of the reach of the tide. From her jeans pocket, Cate took a Swiss army knife and began to saw through the cord around the sack's neck. The little crabs were congregating, their claws snapping in anticipation of a feed.

'Stand back,' said Cate gasping. 'Whatever's in here is coming out.' She hoisted the sack from the bottom. What fell onto the mud was worse than a nightmare.

Hair, lumps of grey flesh, jaw bones with pointy teeth, flaps that might once have been ears, vertebrae, ribs, moth-eaten hides.

Spurred by the thrill of discovery, Wonder Woman was madly taking photos. Isla, on the other hand, crept into the bushes and threw up her lunch.

'Thankfully these aren't human,' said Cate. 'I'll call the cops anyway. You know what I think?'

From a safe distance Isla mumbled, 'What?'

'I think this is linked to the missing cats. In fact, I'd put money on it.'

'Can we go now?' said Isla, feeling fragile.

Leaving the sack and the gruesome contents on the creek bank, they sat on the bollards by the road and waited for the police. In the fresh air, away from the dreadful smell, Isla soon recovered. What she wouldn't give for a glass of water! She was about to suggest going back to the house when she heard a soft mewling.

The sound reverberated as if in a cave. She remembered the Ear of Dionysius on her whirlwind tour of Italy. Once a Roman prison, the acoustics amplified every whisper. In ancient times, guards were positioned to eavesdrop on prisoners' conversations. The penalty for treason was death.

'Did you hear that?' Isla whispered.

'Oh my God!' Cate ran towards the creek bank, heading for the concrete pipe.

'Ve-nus,' Isla sang as she scrambled to her feet. 'Veee-nus!'

The cat meowed weakly.

Everything happened so fast it was hard to say what came next. Cate crawled up the bank carrying a bedraggled bundle of fur. The police car—a fanfare of flashing lights—screamed around the bend. The creek was marked out with crime-scene tape. The sack and its revolting contents were gathered up and taken away as evidence.

And Isla, reunited with her precious pet, almost fainted with joy.

12

A farewell

Thursday 13 August

One entire week after the discovery of Angel Tattoo's body, Seth finally received the call he'd been waiting for.

'Autopsy's been done. Body's been released to the family.' The rest of the one-way conversation was about football games on the weekend and the woeful state of the economy. If nothing else, Detective Sergeant Dave Frame was an affable man who could talk the leg off the proverbial iron pot about any topic on the planet.

Seth was half-way through writing a piece about a typhoon recovery effort in the Pacific. The Australian navy had gone in with food, water, and machinery to help the villagers rebuild their homes. Good news sometimes followed bad, and for a journo who'd seen plenty of bad news in his time, this was a welcome respite.

While Dave ran his commentary, Seth was quietly pecking out letters on the keyboard, surreptitiously trying to get the piece finished before the deadline. To show he was listening, he punctuated the monologue with encouraging grunts. Hopefully his detective friend would talk his way back to the point and offer up some useful information about the autopsy.

At last Dave seemed to notice the absence of intelligent input. 'You still there, mate?'

'Yeah, but you still haven't told me anything.'

'What about?'

'Who she was and how she died.'

'Classified information. I can say an illicit drug was found in her system.'

In frustration Seth sniffed. 'Then can you tell me if there's a suspect?'

'Maybe.'

'Maybe there's a suspect, or maybe you can tell me?' Irritation was creeping into his voice. Soon he'd turn into a whinging old bastard, the sort they showed on current affairs programs complaining about barking dogs or rattling air conditioners.

Dave Frame seemed to get the hint. 'All I can say is this: keep going. There's more to this than meets the eye.' With that puzzling comment, he hung up.

Seth tossed the phone onto the desk. He needed to concentrate on the typhoon report, but he wanted to get cracking on his investigation of a *maybe* crime that *might* have been committed in a sleepy inner suburb.

As soon as he'd submitted the three-hundred-word article, he grabbed the Jeep keys and took off for Mayfield Avenue. The day was cold and bleak; the sky was the colour of wet concrete. He turned on the heater. It made the car stuffy, so he turned it off again. Probably it was a little premature to gain access to the house itself. He hadn't yet done any door-knocking of the other houses in the street. With any luck, he'd scoop the story before the TV news-sharks caught a whiff of blood. One of the benefits of keeping old neighbourhood friendships alive was an occasional pearl of insider information.

In times past, neighbourhoods were at the heart of a community. When he was a boy, couples would scrape together a deposit for a modest timber box on stilts. For the next thirty years, they'd live there and work to pay off the mortgage. Neighbours would chat over fences while their offspring played on the streets or in each other's backyards. A headcount would be taken at teatime. More often than not there'd be extra kids at the table. No-one would have asked parental permission to stay out after dark and it wouldn't matter. Everyone was fed and no-one went missing for long. In a neighbourhood, people cared and everyone belonged.

How times had changed! Although Seth had lived five years in his Clayfield apartment, the only residents he'd actually spoken to were Peter O'Day the chemist in number one about a double-parked car, and Stefan vanBroek in number four about a mix-up with the mail. Removal vans regularly parked in the driveway as various tenants came and went. Other apartments were empty or the residents worked the same crazy hours he did. The burgeoning suburbs of sleek new apartment blocks had become dens for lone wolves just like him.

Solitary apartment living suited his hectic lifestyle. It was nice to get home at ten p.m., strip down to his underpants and watch the football with a glass of Scotch on ice. It was nice to have the place to himself and not be interrupted by irritating neighbours or housemates. But that didn't stop the niggle deep inside that mourned the extinction of that cosy neighbourhood spirit.

At Mayfield Avenue, Seth stopped outside number 47, three doors up from the property owned by Isla Jean Bright. A weatherboard cube with glass louvres at the front, it had obviously been raised and bricked-in underneath to make room for a growing family. The windows along the northern side were open, a promising sign. At the federation-green front door, he pressed the buzzer. Behind his back, his fingers were crossed in the hope he'd uncover useful information.

'Who's there?' called a wavering old-woman voice.

'Seth VerBeek of *The Morning Post*. Can I talk to you about an important matter?'

'Wait on.'

From the depths of the house came the clink of china, the sound of a chair scraping back, plodding footsteps on a timber floor, the squeak of a wheel. She was certainly taking her time. He wondered whether she were playing him along or alternately making an escape down the back stairs.

When she finally appeared, he blinked in surprise. Her spine was bent double as she inched the wheelie walker toward him.

The woman would have been about ninety, the same age and build as his mother. Guilt pinched his conscience. He made a mental note to visit her at the nursing home, even if he'd be as much a stranger to her as he was to this old lady.

'What do you want, young man?' The question was mumbled as if she'd forgotten to put in her teeth. 'I haven't got all day you know.'

'Sorry to bother you, ma'am. I'm looking for information about the owner of the house at the end of the street. Can I ask you a few questions?'

'Miss Bright? Dreadful business. You'd better come in.' She swivelled the walker and clomped across the verandah to a recliner chair draped in an orange-and-blue checked blanket. After dropping heavily into the warm nest, she motioned to him with an arthritic hand. 'Come, take a seat. What did you say your name was?'

'Seth.'

'Take a seat, Mister Seth.'

'And yours?' He took out a spiral-bound notepad and pencil. Shorthand was his preferred way of recording interviews.

'Mrs Green,' she said. 'I've lived in this house since 1948, ever since it was built. The whole street was new then. Nice families, good people. This suburb isn't what it used to be, mark my words. The young ones coming and going, I can't keep up with them all.'

Seth nodded in sympathy. He understood her sentiments. The world he knew and loved had also disappeared. Although thirty years her junior, he too was a relic of the past.

'Do you know Isla Bright well?' he said.

The old lady frowned and examined the liver spots on the back of her hands. 'Not really. I see more of her cat. Cheeky little mite comes in begging for food. Before my knees gave out, I'd put down a saucer of milk. She has the silliest name. What is it now?' She sucked her gums. 'One of the planets.'

The conversation was in serious danger of being side-tracked by a cat. 'And her owner?' he prompted.

'Oh, that one is never home. She used to be a school teacher at Corella High. When it closed down, she lost her job. Not that you'd know it. She's always off here and there. Once she went to *France* for a holiday. Or was it Russia? Sometimes I get things mixed up. Anyways, Mrs Taylor on the corner is always looking after the cat.'

Her eyes lit up. 'Venus! Yes, that's the name. I knew it would come back.' She pressed a button on a remote control. The chair made a whirring noise and a footrest sprang up from somewhere beneath the blanket. 'Come to think of it, I haven't seen her around in a while.'

'Isla Bright, Mrs Taylor, or the cat?'

Mrs Green tutted and absently shook her head. 'No, I haven't seen much of her at all. She loves a good feed, that one. Can't get enough when there's bacon.'

Seth reframed the question but the response was equally vague. This was as futile as talking to his mother before dementia completely stole her mind. The more he tried to understand, the more confused *he* became.

Mrs Green looked as if she was set for a good long chat. He needed to cut and run before frustration made him snap. He attempted one last question. 'Which house is Mrs Taylor's?'

'White picket fence.' She pointed a crooked finger in the direction of the creek.

Seth thanked her and stood up to leave.

'Thanks for coming to visit, dear. See you next time.'

Thankfully Audrey Taylor was at home, both in body and in mind. A sprightly seventy-something, she told Seth that she'd seen neither Isla Bright nor the cat Venus in a fortnight. Until the police came knocking a few days before, she'd assumed they'd gone on holiday. Other than the cops and neighbourhood gossips, she had no idea of what happened. Not as hospitable as her elderly neighbour, she kept him standing at the door.

'Does Isla Bright have any family?' asked Seth.

'Not exactly ...' Audrey hesitated.

As a journalist, he was well versed in the art of silence. Sometimes it felt awkward and he still had to make a conscious effort not to fill in the gaps with talk. Silence was a powerful tool that could be far more effective than a truckload of questions.

He maintained eye contact. Pressure built.

As if on cue, Audrey turned her attention to the empty house opposite. She seemed to be having an internal debate about whether or not to tell. It would have been easier to use words like a cattle prod to get her moving but the process of questioning would break the spell. Holding the position of interested silence, he waited.

Audrey cleared her throat and spoke as if she were talking to herself. 'It happened long ago so it probably doesn't matter anymore.'

Seth nodded and remained silent.

'Isla once took in a teenager who'd lost both parents in a dreadful car crash. Her name was Antoinette. By all accounts, she was bit of a handful and was often in trouble. Nothing major. Truancy, shoplifting, that sort of thing. Isla always tried her best and stuck up for her. Managed to get her out of most scrapes with nothing more than a warning. One day, the ungrateful minx just up and left. But not before helping herself to all the cash in the house.

'Poor Isla was in a terrible state, so I asked her in for a cup of tea. We hadn't spoken much until then, apart from exchanging a few pleasantries. After that we became friends. Many years passed. Then out of the blue Antoinette turned up again, this time with a daughter in tow. No husband, of course. Typical.'

'How old is the child?'

'About sixteen now, I suppose. Nasty piece of work. Worse than her mother at the same age. Sometimes they'll blow in and stay a day or two.' Audrey lowered her voice. 'Man trouble, if you know what I mean. And is it any wonder! The way that woman presents herself! I've never seen anyone like her, not in *this* neighbourhood, any rate.'

Seth raised an eyebrow.

Audrey gave a snort of disgust and folded her arms. 'All those bloody tattoos! I wouldn't have given her the time of day.'

A breakthrough! So, he'd been right when he deduced that Angel Tattoo's body was not that of a retired high-school teacher. With his mind racing, he pressed on. 'Do you know where she lives now?'

Audrey shook her head. 'Can't say I do. She's a bit of a mystery, that one.' She was fidgeting with a bunch of keys. 'Sorry to cut you off, Seth, but I must be going. Dentist appointment.'

Seth gave her a business card and asked her to call if she remembered anything more.

He did a walking tour of the houses along Mayfield Avenue but as elderly Mrs Green had forewarned no-one else was home. Outside number 53, a barricade of blue-and-white police tape ran along the fence. If he intended to use the scarlet key again, he'd have to bide his time. In the interim there were plenty more leads to investigate, starting with the tattoo parlours on the north side of town.

By now Antoinette would be in her late thirties and her appearance would be striking to say the least. Surely someone could identify her from a photo. He was turning the ignition to start the Jeep when his phone pinged with a message.

It was Cate. *Your friend's brought another envelope. Can I open it?*

He was about to respond *which friend* but the answer was obvious. Instead, he pressed the call button. 'Hi Cate, it's me. Of course you can.'

Through the phone came the rustle of paper, followed by a curse. 'Why can't this dipstick do text messages like everyone else? His handwriting's getting worse!'

'Scan it to me. Better still, run it through your handwriting app and we'll compare notes.'

A scan of the scribbled message pinged onto the screen. Straight away, he set out the recognisable letters and blanks in a game of *hangman*. Within seconds he'd deciphered it and compared his result to *Scrawl Wizard's.*

294 Graham Rd, Bridgeman Downs. 2pm today.

Man versus app: this time the outcome was identical. Either Cate had found a more reliable version or she'd taught the sucker to read.

Two o'clock today! To make it on time he'd have to move fast.

Cate phoned him back. 'Well?'

'Perfect match! Want to come?'

'As long as there are no septic tanks.' She laughed and his day lit up.

'Wait outside the office. I'll pick you up in fifteen.'

*

Bridgeman Downs was on the northern outskirts of the city. Graham Road ran due west from the highway, through red-soil country that was once farmland and market gardens. Green and leafy, the district was in the process of being transformed from acreages with gargantuan executive residences into small-lot developments and townhouses.

Their destination was signposted and easy to locate. The approach was tranquil and green. On the neatly-mown lawns were hundreds of concrete pavers, set out in rows two metres apart. On the left side of the road was a derelict tennis court; on the right was an entrance gate.

'Who'd have thought?' Cate breathed as they drove in.

Seth glanced at his clothes: blue jeans and red button-down shirt. Cate wore a yellow-and-white polka dot dress. Both were totally inappropriate for the event they were about to gate-crash. They exchanged grins and shrugged. He followed the arrows to the carpark. The place was milling with people of all ages. Most wore black.

'Let's split up,' he suggested.

She nodded and strolled toward an animated group of young people.

Near the chapel was a shapely blonde in a black lace dress and high heels. The outfit was finished with a corsage of roses, and a thick gold chain. From her proprietorial stance she seemed to be in charge. Seth hovered as she greeted each set of new arrivals.

'*Dahling*, how nice of you to come!' She embraced him warmly.

Adopting the demeanour of a long-lost friend, he kissed her cheeks. 'I'm so sorry for your loss.' His baritone voice was as smooth as melting chocolate.

'Thank you, *dahling*. Poor thing, we'd been friends forever. We were like sisters. Lord, how I'll miss her!' She brushed away tears.

'Sorry, I don't remember your name.'

'Maddie. So many people … I don't know half of them.'

'Yeah, me too,' he said with a smile. 'I'm Seth.'

She flashed teeth so white and perfect they had to be caps. 'Relative or friend?'

'Friend.'

From the corner of her eye, Maddie was looking him up and down. If it weren't for the circumstances, he would have sworn she was doing him a line.

'Your friendship, was it *recent*?' she said.

'I can't recall where we first met. We kept bumping into each other here and there. She was such a lovely person I wanted to pay my respects.' How easy it was for Seth to lie.

Maddie nodded. For a moment she seemed satisfied with his explanation, then her eyes widened and she turned so they were face to face. 'I'd advise you not to listen to any of the gossip that's going round.'

Seth was a ball of curiosity. He was trying to think of a way to gently dig deeper when the funeral celebrant called everyone inside.

'Must go. Catch you later, *dahling*,' Maddie made a move towards the chapel door. At the last minute, she pressed a business card into his hand. 'Don't leave without saying goodbye.'

He gave her a little wave then trailed behind the crowd.

A metre or so in front of him was Cate, talking to her newfound friends. Their clothing was as bright as hers and most had sleeves of tattoos. Seth shook his head. Even in a canary yellow frock, Cate had found a way to fit in at a funeral. She'd probably spun them a yarn about yellow being the deceased's favourite colour.

Come to think of it, he still didn't know the dead person's identity.

Outside the chapel a notice board gave the order of service for the day. He skimmed down the list to two o'clock.

It was a name he knew well.

13

An introduction

Fifteen months ago: early winter

Two hours before Tuesday's luncheon with Maddie, Isla received a text message with an address in New Farm. Thinking the venue must be a trendy café, she took extra care getting dressed. As she could never compete in the fashion stakes, she decided classic was the best way to go. Tailored black pants, silk blouse, cobalt jacket: clothes she'd worn when she was proud to be called Head of Art. After slicking on lipstick and pinning up her hair, she rated herself in the mirror.

A-minus. *Keep up the good work.*

As it turned out, the appointed meeting place was not an eatery but a block of new high-rise apartments. Feeling slightly intimidated, she pressed the intercom at the front gate. Her mind flooded with questions. There had to be an ulterior motive.

Lately Maddie had been acting a bit odd. More than once she'd put Isla under the microscope, quizzing her about relationships and finances and plans for the future. Some days she felt more like a science experiment than a best friend. Frankly, it was getting on her nerves.

The intercom buzzed and the lock released. Isla opened the gate. In the glass-walled elevator she glimpsed the river through the trees. On the tenth level the doors slid open and she stepped out directly into a modern apartment.

'*Dahling*, so glad you're here.' Maddie, all dimples and glamour, led her through an immense living room while prattling on about people Isla didn't know.

81

Leather and chrome furniture exuded the expensive perfume of an interior design showroom. Outside on the tiled balcony, they settled into moulded resin chairs. For the moment they were alone, which raised further questions.

Maddie launched into a detailed account of the former loves of her life. Isla held her tongue.

'You're always moping about.' Maddie chided. She was fiddling with her phone, the latest model of course. The case was red ostrich leather. 'You need to get out more. Get yourself laid.'

According to Maddie, the solution for everything was to get laid. Her latest obsession was a dating app that linked her to potential suitors who drifted onto the radar. Isla wondered why a married woman would want to dabble in deception but thought better of asking.

'I'm fine as I am!' Isla snapped.

The notion of mature women chasing men for sex was downright pathetic. In her opinion the whole online dating thing was bizarre. One night stands were for teenagers, not responsible middle-aged adults.

The balcony overlooked a broad sweep of the river. The word *balcony* didn't do it justice. It was more a botanical garden suspended high above the ground. The chairs were arranged in clusters. In between were spiky succulents, the latest fad in potted plants. The apartment was as stylish as a six-star resort. If that wasn't impressive enough, there were two kitchens: one indoors and the other on the balcony. The indoor kitchen had European appliances and benchtops of black granite with flecks of mica. The outdoor kitchen had a commercial-grade cooker and stainless steel benches with a plumbed-in sink and bar fridge.

An icy wind blustered in from the south, buffeting the river gums and whipping the muddy water into white-caps. Behind the glass barricade it was warm and snug.

Maddie took a cigarette from a silver case and slipped it between her lips. She flicked a lighter, drew back and released the smoke with a sigh. 'Don't be a goose, *dahling*. Every woman needs a man. By the way, did you know I've left Darren?

Isla shook her head. 'When?'

Maddie waved the cigarette airily. 'Last week. I'm better off without him. He was cramping my style. So, what do you think of my new digs?'

She opened her arms to take in the river, the steel-girder bridge linking the north side to the south, the sawtooth silhouette of the cityscape, the bright winter sky.

'Most picturesque,' Isla said. At the same time she wondered how Maddie could afford such an apartment without Darren's seven-figure salary.

The sun was at the meridian and Isla's stomach was growling. Maddie brought out two platters of food that could only be described as *edible art*. Ordered from the caterers, the display was perfection. Shot glasses of green liquid, slivers of pink meat curled into roses, five different cheeses, colourful sushi rolls.

'Here, try one of these.' Maddie offered the sushi.

Apart from chicken chow mien from the local Chinese take-away, Isla had never tried Asian cuisine. She eyed the rolls, trying to identify the fillings. A cat-lover she might be, but be damned if she'd eat raw tuna. She settled for the safety of mushrooms.

While Maddie prattled on about the virtues of vice, Isla wondered how two old schoolmates like them could remain friends. Their lives were as different as chalk and caviar. Perhaps that was the reason the friendship had endured. Their divergent personalities complemented each other.

'Now, about my other guest. His name is Claude.' Maddie took a sip of wine. 'And he's my ... um ... handyman.'

There was something in the way she said *handyman* that raised Isla's eyebrows. 'You mean he's going to work while we're having lunch?'

Maddie stroked her chin. 'He's not that sort of handyman, though he can fix anything. He also mows lawns, digs gardens and paints fences. And for very reasonable rates, I must say. But that's not why I've invited him.'

Isla said nothing. Sometimes it was better to let Maddie babble on.

'Actually he's more a handyman of the heart, a person you can talk to. Really talk to. He's helped me through some of my darkest hours. It's so liberating to have a *platonic* relationship with a man.' She placed undue emphasis on the word platonic.

'Is he gay then?' Isla asked. She'd never known her friend to have a platonic relationship with any male, apart from those in her own family.

Maddie ignored the question. 'We agreed at the outset, the last thing I need now is another sexual relationship. He's such a sweetie.'

The intercom buzzed.

'That's him! *Dahling*, you'll absolutely adore him. He's *fabulous!*' With that, Maddie dashed into the apartment to release the security gate.

Isla stuffed another mushroom roll into her mouth and washed it down with sauvignon blanc (another of Maddie's exotic selections). *Always from a bottle dahling, never from a cask.* The wind's icy fingers reached around the glass barricade and nipped at her skin. She buttoned her jacket and prepared for an encounter with the *fabulous* Claude.

Their chatter was coming down the hall. Standing up, Isla turned toward them. Hand in hand, they came through the kitchen with the sparkling benchtops and the virgin appliances. The glass door opened and two human forms stepped into the spotlight. They could have been a pair of ageing rock stars about to make a comeback.

In blue jeans, white shirt, sports jacket and scarf, Claude cut a fine figure. Judging by the salt-and-pepper stubble, he was in his late fifties. Slim and tanned, he looked as fit as a marathon runner.

Maddie made the introductions.

He grasped Isla's hand and brushed it with his lips. 'Enchanté,' he said in a terrible French accent. 'Your poor hand is freezing.' He warmed it between two calloused paws.

Off-guard Isla said, 'Pleased to meet you.' She stood there awkwardly, her hand in a sandwich press, not knowing what to do. She hadn't felt this gauche since her first high-school dance when she was thirteen. Johnny McMullan had sat too close and she'd felt the warmth of his thigh against hers. Now, as then, she didn't have the confidence to speak up or move away.

'Loosen up. We're all friends here.' Claude smiled in a larrikin way. Thankfully he gave her hand a final squeeze and set it free.

That was the moment her inner thermostat decided to go haywire. The embarrassing flush shot up her neck. In a split-second she went from just right to bodice-ripping hot. Sweat trickled down her spine. For one crazy moment she contemplated leaping into the river to cool off. If she were lucky, a bull shark would take her and that would be the end of the problem forever.

Maddie came to the rescue. 'Anyone want a drink?' Without waiting for an answer, she squatted at the bar fridge. Bottles clinked as she sorted through the stock. 'Lordy, what will I do with all this wine? Claude *dahling*, do me a favour and take some home? There's no way I can ship it all to Dubai.'

'Dubai?' said Isla. 'Since when are you going to Dubai?'

'Didn't I mention it, *dahling*? Next week.'

Maddie was full of surprises, but never like this.

Triumphant, Maddie held up a bottle of France's most expensive champagne. 'He must've been saving this for a special occasion. Today definitely qualifies.'

She brought the bottle to the table, together with an ice bucket and three champagne flutes. The cork shot off with a *POP*; liquid gold geysered out. She poured. Bubbles fizzed over the rims of the glasses. About twenty dollars' worth shimmied down the side and onto the tiles.

'A toast. To friends old and new.' Maddie lifted her glass.

The champagne was pure sunshine laced with old oak.

'Why Dubai?' Isla persisted.

'That's where Andrew lives.'

Isla shook her head. 'Andrew?'

'We go way back. His wife left him—poor pet—and he's devastated. I offered to help by packing up his apartment and renting it out. Then he asked me to go to Dubai and keep him company.'

Isla was utterly speechless. She gulped the bubbly and tried to smother the urge to say that this was the most hare-brained idea ever.

'Here's a little going-away present.' Claude pressed a small box into Maddie's hand. 'To remind you to come back.'

She flipped the lid and removed a piece of tissue paper. '*Dahling*, how gorgeous!' The gift was a tiny boomerang on a keyring. Cheap tourist kitsch. She threw her arms around his neck and kissed him full on the lips. You'd have thought it was a diamond ring with all the fuss she made.

'Speaking of going away ...' Maddie handed him a grey plastic card. 'Security access. In case something happens ... you know ... to Andrew or me. You are officially appointed as the property manager.'

At last Isla found her voice. 'Is this a permanent move then?'

'*Dahling*, in my world nothing's permanent. I prefer to say *indefinite*.'

Claude put the security card on the table. 'As we agreed, I'll clear the letterbox, water the plants and generally keep an eye on the place until you get a tenant.'

Maddie turned to Isla. 'I've told the other residents that Claude is my cousin. They've seen him before; he moved my things in. All the old stickybeaks spy through the shutters.' She flashed him a suggestive look. 'You *come* every Tuesday, don't you *dahling*?'

He chortled and patted her thigh.

Platonic relationship indeed!

As if making Claude responsible for the apartment weren't enough, Maddie seemed hell-bent on sharing him further. Over the course of the luncheon she brokered an arrangement: Isla needed a handyman and Claude needed extra cash. In the vacated Tuesday timeslot, Isla would become the temporary substitute.

Maddie raised her glass. 'To the future! A brilliant outcome all round, don't you agree?'

Isla wasn't so sure. Did she want an interloper who could fix dripping taps? She hadn't trusted a man in decades. But Maddie was hard to refuse and she seemed to think the world of this jack-of-all-trades cum lover.

She glanced at Claude across the table. He was cleaning his nails with the corner of the security card. To be fair, he didn't seem particularly enamoured with the arrangement either.

*

A week later, Maddie boarded an A380 flight bound for Dubai. According to the promotional blurb, the A380 was *the fastest and most advanced passenger aircraft in the world.* She'd booked business class of course. For the next fifteen hours she'd sip fine wine and slumber in cocooned lie-flat comfort. In Dubai she'd wake refreshed and ready to begin the next instalment of her high-octane life.

What a contrast to Isla's *el cheapo* flight home from London via Singapore! Twenty-eight hours of plastic food and discomfort, sandwiched between two portly gentlemen who alternated between belching and farting while she pretended to sleep.

From the glass viewing platform of the International Terminal, Isla waited until the massive metal bird pushed back from the boarding bridge. She paced the vast expanse of glistening tiles between rows of check-in counters, packed with people and kids and bags. After taking the elevator to the ground floor, she paid for her parking ticket and took another elevator to the second floor of the carpark. As she drove through the boom gates, the A380 raged down the runway. Slowly it lifted and momentarily flew parallel to the road. Climbing, it turned in an arc over the city. White with red on its tail, it looked like a dinky toy. Smaller and smaller it shrank, until a wispy cloud in the west swallowed it whole.

Feeling abandoned by her only friend, Isla brushed away tears.

Stop that whimpering, she told herself as the Camry sped along Sandgate Road. She should be glad Maddie was off to an exciting new life.

Wallowing in self-pity was not allowed. At home was the best friend a person could have: her darling Venus.

Her mind replayed the poor creature's recent brush with death. When Isla had gone down to the creek to paint, Venus must have followed. So engrossed was she in her work, that she didn't notice two green eyes watching. When the storm blew in, Venus would have taken fright and found a place to hide.

Then there was the mystery of the stinking bag of bones. It was only through sheer determination on the part of Cate Bradshaw that the dear pet was found. Isla's heart was bursting with gratitude. Without that young reporter, the story would have had a very different ending indeed.

14

Desperately seeking Angel

Friday 14 August

The day after the funeral, one name was on Seth's mind. Maddie.

She and the dead woman had been best friends. Of course Maddie would know all her secrets. Then he remembered that he'd left before the end of the service. She'd invited him to stick around. No, she'd *expected* him to stay. And he'd probably blown his chances by making a hasty exit. It would be a miracle if she spoke to him again.

On his desk was the business card she'd given him. Apart from her name and professional status—*lifestyle consultant*—there was a mobile number and an address at Hamilton.

It was going on nine on a Friday morning. Was it too early to call?

He reached for the phone and punched in the number. While he listened for the ring tone, he popped an Eclipse mint in his mouth. Finally he'd kicked the filthy habit. Not one cigarette had he smoked all year. The emergency packs with their graphic pictures of ugly cancers were lined up at the rear of his desk. There were five. Each contained one cigarette: a sort of break-glass for nicotine addicts.

In the next cubicle Cate was busy searching for new leads. Some time ago, she'd written a report about catnapping. She was trawling through her old notes and the newspaper archives for something that might shed new light on the case.

As Seth was about to hang up, the phone answered. 'This is Maddie.'

'Hi. It's Seth VerBeek. We met yesterday.'

'I hoped to see you after the service.' In her voice was a trace of indignation.

'I'm really sorry. Got an urgent call from work,' he fibbed. 'Can I see you today?'

'I happen to know what you do for a living, Mister VerBeek. I've been reading your articles in *The Morning Post* ... and loving them.'

'I would have told you yesterday, but it didn't seem right under the circumstances.'

'Did you really know Isla? I want the truth now.'

'Our paths had crossed.' It wasn't a straight-out lie. 'There are questions about the circumstances of her death that I'd like to clear up.'

'Out of respect for her, I'll meet you. Where?'

'So you know *La Belle Vie* on Racecourse Road?' The café was close to the address on her business card.

'Can you come to New Farm instead? Around five this evening would suit. I've just returned from Dubai and my Merc's in for a service.'

'Would you like me to pick you up?'

'Hmmm. Can I trust you Mister VerBeek?' Her tone was teasing.

'Of course. My word as a gentleman.'

She laughed and gave him the New Farm address where she was staying.

At the appointed time, he parked outside a modern apartment block in Oxlade Drive and pressed the buzzer. Ten storeys up, the lights were on. Canned laughter from an American sit-com cascaded over the balcony.

Her voice crackled through the intercom. 'I'll be right down.'

He stood at the security gate beside a trio of polished granite spheres that stepped down in diameter from a metre to the size of a medicine ball. It wasn't clear if they had any purpose, other than to impress the friends of the residents.

Minutes later Maddie appeared, dressed provocatively in a skin-tight black cocktail dress and silver stilettos.

'Good evening, Mister VerBeek.' She offered her hand. 'There's a nice bar called *Blade* in James Street where we can talk.'

'I know it well.' He opened the Jeep's passenger door and she climbed in. A hit of expensive perfume filled the cabin. To him it felt like a first date.

While he drove, they talked about the weather, food, travel, life.

'Until recently I was living in Dubai,' she said. 'Things didn't work out. So now I'm back and single again. What about you?'

'My job has cured me of living out of a suitcase and staying in places where nobody wants to go.'

'That's not what I meant.' She regarded him with deep simmering eyes. 'Are you … *available*?' It was hard to keep his mind on the road.

'You certainly don't pull any punches,' he said. They'd reached their destination. He reverse-parked into a vacant spot in a street of coffee shops, restaurants, cinemas, and bars.

At Blade, she ordered a Manhattan and he a Scotch on ice. They sat on steel benches, overlooking the sidewalk and a constant flow of traffic fuelled by the Friday night dilemma of whether to make an early escape or stay and drown the week's woes with your workmates.

The bar was filling with bright young things in smart business suits or designer dresses. Everyone was laughing and talking over each other. A singer, accompanied by an acoustic guitar, began a set. The music was good, if you wanted to chill out and give up on small talk. The exuberant Millennials ramped up their volume in competition. The noise bounced off the floor and echoed off the walls. Steel, glass, and tiles did nothing to muffle the din.

'You want to go somewhere quieter?' Maddie shouted into Seth's ear.

'Sure. I forgot it was Friday.'

They skolled their drinks and beat a retreat.

'Where to?' he said outside.

A light breeze had sprung up. Maddie shivered and hugged her body. 'Come back to my place,' she said quickly.

At the apartment, she led him into the living room, furnished with black leather sofas and a long-pile rug. Two table lamps cast a golden glow on the polished wood floorboards.

'How can I tempt you?' She opened the cocktail cabinet. The array of spirit and liqueur bottles would have put the bar at Blade to shame.

'Scotch on the rocks, thanks.'

'Chivas or Johnnie Walker Blue?'

Now that was a woman who understood whisky. He chose the Blue.

She bent over to reach the ice-maker, which gave him a bird's-eye view of the delightful chasm between her breasts.

He eased into a leather sofa, inhaled a scent reminiscent of a brand new Porsche and thought how lucky he was to be an investigative journalist.

'Push the lever on the side. It reclines,' she said.

As the footrest lifted, she handed him the Scotch along with a dish of shelled pistachios. She made herself a blue cocktail in a V-shaped glass, then sat on the sofa opposite and sipped her drink through a straw. All the while her dusky eyes caressed his body. He was acutely aware of where this was leading. A self-confessed devotee of the opposite sex, he could read women as easily as newsprint. This one was no shrinking violet and the stakes were mighty high.

'Now *dahling*, you wanted to ask some questions. Fire away.' She kicked off her shoes and tucked up her legs on the sofa. Nestled between cushions, she looked as sexy and self-assured as a Hollywood starlet.

'First, do you have a photo of Isla?'

Maddie reached for her phone on the side table, scrolled through the images. She smiled. 'I'll send you this one.' The phone whooshed as the email sped into the cloud.

Ping! Seth opened his inbox. The photo was of a stunning Maddie sitting alongside a plain middle-aged woman with grey hair. Her shapeless blouse and pedal pushers would have been at home in an op-shop. If this was Isla Bright, she was not the woman he'd found dead in her house.

His nose wrinkled from the imagined stench of red herrings. For some unknown reason, an *elderly gentleman* was drip-feeding him information that was either grossly untrue or intentionally misleading. Why?

'Tell me about Isla,' Seth said.

Unshed tears glistened in Maddie's eyes. 'We'd known each other ever since I can remember, yet we lived very different lives.' Her forefinger circled the rim of the cocktail glass and it resonated like a bell.

She continued. 'You see, Isla was very conservative. She liked to be organised, to know what was scheduled from day to day. That's why she gave up being an artist and turned to teaching. My, how the years have flown! To think I once helped promote her debut exhibition in a gallery at Paddington.'

'The Plantation?'

She sat upright. 'How'd you know?'

'I grew up in Paddington. We used to walk past the gallery to catch the bus.'

'That's funny, so did I.'

They scrutinised each other's faces, attempting to peel back the patina of time.

'Hayward Street,' he said.

'Mort Street.'

'You were just around the corner. Do you remember the fire?'

She shook her head. 'Mum used to talk about the night the tram depot went up. I remember the blackened ruins well enough.'

Sipping the Scotch, Seth contemplated the fallout of that dreadful night. It spelt the beginning of the end for his father who was a tram driver. Not long afterwards, he departed this world leaving Lorna VerBeek to raise two young sons on her own.

Maddie must have sensed the change in mood, for she sidled in beside him and laid her head on his shoulder. 'It was bad for you, wasn't it?' she said gently.

He turned to face her. She lifted her chin, softened her eyes. Before he could stop himself, he'd pressed his lips to hers. The flavour of blue curacao was on her tongue. She wrapped her arms around him and drew him close. The scent of her body was an aphrodisiac. In a heartbeat he would have had her there on the couch but either his conscience or his work ethic pulled him away.

'Hey what's the matter? Worried about your *wife*?'

'Business first, then pleasure. And, for the record, I'm not married.'

She feigned annoyance but took the hint. Retreating to her original position on the opposite sofa, she folded her hands demurely in her lap and crossed her ankles. Above the left ankle was a small tattoo of a butterfly.

'How many questions before we get through the *business* part?' she said.

'Never you mind.' He drained the glass and cleared his throat. 'Now, back to Isla. What sort of person was she?'

'Dedicated, hard-working, kind. She was an art teacher at Corella High until it shut down. Apart from other teachers, she didn't have many friends. After she stopped working she sort of dropped her bundle. I'd call her a couple of times a week and make sure she was okay.'

'After you went to Dubai?'

'Yes, we'd talk for hours on Skype.'

'Did she ever do anything out of character?'

'Nothing I can think of. In my opinion, her life was nothing short of boring. Most of the time she was totally predictable, apart from a spur-of-the-minute trip to Europe last year. And that only happened because I talked her into it.'

Seth nodded at the tattooed butterfly. 'Did you talk her into anything else?'

'Of course not! As I said before, she was very conservative. She wouldn't have gone to a tattoo studio in a fit.' Maddie answered with absolute conviction. Either she was telling the truth, which meant that Angel Tattoo was definitely another person, or she was the best liar in the world.

'What about men? Was she seeing anyone?'

'She never admitted to having a *boyfriend*.' Maddie gazed thoughtfully at a spot on the floor. 'I wonder ...'

He waited, confident that silence would shed new light.

As if answering her own question, Maddie shook her head. 'Nah, forget it.'

Seth pushed on. 'Apart from you, is there anyone else she might have confided in?'

Maddie shrugged and raised her palms. 'Isla was a lovely person and she was my best friend. She lived a decent life and deserved a decent death.' She rose from the sofa and opened the fridge. 'If you don't mind, I'd like to make a toast.'

In a flash, she'd cracked a bottle of champagne and poured out two glasses. 'To Isla, wherever she may be.' Liquefied grief rolled down her cheeks.

Seth stood up and raised his glass. 'To Isla.'

Clearly, question time—and with it the business part of the evening—was over. To give her some emotional recovery space, he opened the sliding door and went onto the balcony. The nightscape of the city lights and reflections off the river reminded him of sideshow alley.

He sipped the bubbly and tried to arrange the jigsaw pieces of information. His initial hunch—that the owner of the house was not the victim—had been verified. But if Angel Tattoo was not Isla Bright, then who was she? Was it mere coincidence that she and the owner of the house had died at the same time? Both times the informant had been an elusive *elderly gentleman*. What puzzled him more was that Maddie, the so-called best friend, didn't seem to know much about Isla at all.

What was he missing?

His glass was empty. Not normally a lover of champagne, he had to admit this one was the nectar of the gods. Not too many bubbles, easy on the palate, crisp aftertaste. He could have easily polished off the entire bottle.

In bare feet, Maddie padded towards him. Without asking, she refilled his glass. 'Is it time for *pleasure* yet?' She smiled coyly and proceeded to unbutton his shirt.

He took her in his arms, drew her in close and kissed her deeply. She melted into him and shivered as his hands caressed her skin. He unzipped her dress and the straps fell back, revealing a black lace bra. Above one breast was a tattoo of a love heart. The outline was crisp, the colours were bright. He bent his head and brushed it with his lips. It was so new that he could practically taste the ink.

She led him to the sofa, pulled him down onto her, smothered his neck in kisses. His shirt was off. She was tugging at his belt, moving her body against him. He unhooked the bra, slipped it off and dropped it to the floor. His tongue circled her nipples and she moaned with pleasure. She folded herself around him, moist and warm and glorious.

Nothing in the world existed but the thrust and rhythm of their bodies.

The pain, the ecstasy, the release.

Afterwards, as she dozed in his arms, he counted her tattoos. There were five. All beautifully executed, all with a spirit of their own. Whoever had done them was a master of the craft. However Maddie was a blank canvas in comparison to Angel Tattoo. He wondered what had drawn them down that path and whether there was any connection. Soon alcohol and fatigue combined. His eyelids closed and he drifted into a deep and satisfied sleep.

In his dream, he heard the beat of a tribal drum.

Boom ... boom ... boom.

The rhythm was as regular as footsteps. Faint at first, then gradually it grew stronger.

In the dream he was crouching in a makeshift hide in a forest. It was late at night and the wind was icy. The throb of the war drum was ominous. They were coming to get him. Who they were and what they'd do was not known. He was sweating with fear.

Sleep came and went. *It's only a dream*, he told himself as he snuggled into Maddie's body for warmth. His mind teetered on a knife-edge between wakefulness and the scrambled logic of dreams. The beat of the drum resumed.

Except now the sound was real.

Boom ... boom ... boom.

It wasn't a drum at all, but the fall of boots.

Someone was in the apartment.

All of a sudden he was flung onto the cold hard floor. One of those nightmarish boots sank into his ribcage. He yelped and curled into the foetal position; his arms cradling his head for some measure of protection.

'You bastard! What the fuck are you doing, fucking my wife! I'll kill you!'

Seth scrambled under the coffee table while Maddie yelled at the intruder to stop.

The man seemed to lose interest in Seth and turned his attention to Maddie instead. There was a loud slap followed by a high-pitched scream.

No-one hit a woman and got away with it, not on his watch. White-hot fury boiled in Seth's belly as he crawled onto the long-pile rug. The pain in his ribs was excruciating. He was gasping for breath. Pure adrenaline drove him on.

The intruder had his hands around Maddie's throat. Pinned down on the sofa, her arms and legs flailed about. She was making an awful gagging sound, as if she were fighting for her last breath.

Seth leapt to his feet and delivered a goal-scoring kick to the man's balls. He howled and buckled to his knees, which gave Maddie a chance to escape.

He was twice the size of Seth and built like Arnie Schwarzenegger. Every spare minute must have been spent at the gym. His dark features contorted in a combination of agony and rage. Seth cast about for a likely weapon, grabbed the only thing he could reach: the bronze statue of a giraffe. It was club-shaped with a long neck and a solid metal base.

In a race between life and death, he raised the statue ready to strike. Pain shot through his ribcage. The room was spinning. Determination to either kill or be killed spurred him on.

From the corner of his eye he saw Maddie, naked, talking into the phone. The last thing he remembered was a red-hot poker thrust into his side.

When Seth woke, he was in Heaven.

A beautiful face hovered over him; her head was surrounded by a halo of gold. With a touch as light as wings, she stroked his forehead. Her voice tinkled like a harp. Whatever language she spoke, he couldn't understand a word. But the sound of that voice was so lovely that he closed his eyes and drifted on a glorious cloud of bliss.

All his life he'd been an unbeliever, yet somehow he'd been allowed into Paradise. He sent a thought of thanks to his mother for making him go to Sunday school and praying for his soul.

'Seth!' hissed a female voice. This wasn't the voice of an angel.

He was being shaken. Vigorously. His head was knocking against the floor.

'Seth, wake up!'

He opened his eyes and saw Maddie. Was she dead too? Where the angel had been a minute before, Maddie crouched over him and rattled his bones. The ache in his left side snatched his breath. Lying church bastards! There wasn't supposed to be any pain in Heaven.

'Seth! Can you hear me?'

15

The arrangement

Fourteen months ago: early winter

The first Tuesday of the 'arrangement', Claude arrived at Isla's house at exactly ten o'clock, dressed in a work shirt, navy shorts, and yard boots. He'd splashed his face with citrus aftershave, possibly to prove to her that he was more than a common labourer.

Despite her protestations, he insisted on removing his boots before entering the house. In thick socks he padded behind her as she led him into the kitchen.

Earlier that morning Isla had a made a chocolate cake and a batch of buttery biscuits which she'd arranged at the centre of the table along with her best floral china and a vase of fresh-cut daisies. Without waiting for an invitation, he sat on her favourite chair with his back against the wall.

'Thank you for coming,' she said stiffly. 'Maddie can be very persuasive. It wouldn't have surprised me if you had second thoughts.'

With a smile he waved the suggestion away. 'As of last week, my Tuesdays are free. I'm all yours.'

She spooned tea-leaves into the pot and began prattling about the weather, the state of the economy, the art galleries of Florence, and cats. All the while he kept nodding with feigned interest, as if he were a student out to impress the teacher for the purpose of improving his grades.

The kettle whistled. She filled the pot, set it on the table and slumped into a chair. In a small voice she said, 'Sorry, Maddie's such fun and I'm an old bore.'

'Not at all,' he said. 'Your voice is lovely. I was enjoying your stories.'

95

'I'm a big girl. You don't need to humour me.' She turned the pot three times clockwise, as her mother used to do *for good luck*. The thought crossed her mind that she'd already outlived her mother by a decade, all the more reason to conclude that she'd passed her use-by date. 'By the way, I used to teach high school. My voice is a foghorn.'

'Not to my ears.' He helped himself to a biscuit. It was the shape of earmuffs stuck together with white icing.

She added a dash of milk to both cups and then poured the tea through a strainer.

He ate the biscuit and picked the crumbs off the plate. 'These are great. Did you make them?'

'Yes, I love cooking.' She patted her middle. 'But I shouldn't eat them myself.'

It was a test of sorts. If he bought into a debate over her weight, she'd put an end to this ridiculous arrangement before it got off the ground. Not that she'd call herself obese, but since she'd retired her waistline had blossomed.

Ignoring the bear trap, he reached for a second. 'What are they called?'

She loosened a little. 'Melting Moments.'

'Mmmmm, they're Heaven in a mouthful.' Crumbs trickled onto the floor.

Venus slunk in and began mopping the lino with her tongue. Isla picked her up and ruffled the fur beneath her chin. 'We have a visitor, my sweet.' The cat yowled and struggled to get down.

Looking alarmed, Claude shrank away.

'Oh God, are you allergic?'

'Not exactly. I'm not very good with cats.'

Isla shooed Venus outside. Nothing was going to plan. Why did Maddie insist on this *handyman* person when she was quite capable of managing on her own? On top of that, the hideous hormonal rash was shooting up her neck again, making it look as if she were blushing.

'Sorry,' she said again. 'I'm not very good with men.' She fiddled with the paper serviette, folding and unfolding it on the table.

Sunrays refracted through the ripple-glass door, scattering shards of brilliant colour across the floor. The wall clock ticked slowly. She could have sworn the second hand was moving backwards.

'I'm not like most men,' he said.

Isla looked him square in the eye. 'Maddie didn't explain *exactly* what you do. Are you some kind of counsellor? Am I supposed to tell you my secrets or talk about my dreams?'

'We can do whatever you want. It's entirely up to you. Tuesdays I'm yours for the asking.' He flashed a lopsided grin that others might have found charming. To Isla, it came across as sleazy.

She bit her lip, aware of how different she was from her school friend. For Maddie that grin would have been the signal to jump straight into bed.

It had been decades since Isla had last had a man. Self-discipline and hard work made it easy to quash desires. *The change* reinforced her state of celibacy. There was simply no point in starting a relationship at her age. Not that she wasn't tempted. For years she'd harboured a secret passion for her former boss, but of course nothing ever came of it. While real affairs wrecked lives, fantasies never caused anyone trouble.

Claude played with the empty teacup, turning it on the saucer. For a man his age, he was rather good-looking. Sexy, if that was what you liked.

Her inner thermostat verged on meltdown. 'More tea?' She grabbed the jug, turned on the cold tap and let the water run over her wrists. Her cheeks were glowing, but her back was towards him so she avoided shame.

At length he broke the silence. 'You might as well make some use of me. Got a lawn mower?'

The heatwave passed and she relaxed a little. 'It's pretty old. I'm not sure if it'll start.'

'Then I'll fix it. Lead the way.'

They went downstairs to the galvanised iron shed beneath the house. She unhooked the padlock. As the door opened, the pong of chicken-shit fertilizer burst out. Curtains of spider silk hung from the roof; the floor was crunchy with dead insects.

'Sorry, I don't come in here much.' Isla swatted down the cobwebs.

'Will you please stop saying *sorry?*'

She shrugged. 'Sorry.'

'Arghh! You did it again!' Brushing past her, he began moving cartons, buckets, newspapers, and tools until he found the mower and a jerry-can of fuel. In the yard he checked the blades, cleaned the spark plug, filled the tank, primed the motor and pulled the cord. It started first time.

'Who usually does the lawn?' He pumped the gauge up and down. The mower coughed out a wad of smoke then settled into a solid roar.

'My neighbour on the corner. When the grass is up to my knees, he comes to the rescue. I usually make him a fruit cake in return.'

Claude hooked on the catcher and took a run across the yard. As the mower munched through the tall paspalum, the scent of chlorophyll filled the air.

Perched on the stairs, Isla watched with the critical eye of a subject mistress. He was *doing a good job*, an A-plus without a doubt. Before she could stop herself, she'd called out to him. 'Great work, Claude.' When would she stop behaving like a damn school teacher?

In half an hour he was finished. The ground was a bit patchy now, but with rain and fertilizer the lawn would thicken up by spring. What the garden needed was regular attention. Perhaps this Claude thing was a good idea after all.

She brought out a jug of water with lemon wedges and they sat on a silvered bench beneath the bougainvillea.

'It looks better already,' she said. 'I'm afraid I'm not much of a gardener.'

'I'm not much of a gardener myself. Guess I had enough of it as a kid. That's how I earned my keep after the old man shot through.'

'Then why did you offer to do this?' She opened her arms, indicating the yard.

'I didn't know how to start.' He caught her hands and held them in his.

'Oh … I see.' She sucked in her lip. *Be like Maddie and go with the flow,* she told herself. Easy to say; hard to do.

'Would you rather we ended this … *arrangement*?'

She extracted her hands and interlaced her fingers.

Rashness was not in her nature. She needed time to think. On the lawn a magpie was pecking for dinner. In the paperbarks, dozens of green and crimson parrots were engaged in an orgy.

'I ought to go.'

'Sorry, I didn't mean to be rude.' She picked at her woollen jumper. 'Maddie's my oldest friend. I've always heeded her advice.'

'Let's take it one day at a time.'

She cast her eyes about the overgrown garden and sighed. 'Do you have many … um … clients?'

'A few.'

'I want a proper answer. What *exactly* are your services?' She turned to face him. A lifetime of excuses for being late, missing class and not doing homework had honed her lie-detection skills to ninety-nine percent accuracy.

In a matter-of-fact tone he replied. 'Within reason, I'll do anything.'

Her eyes widened. 'What do you do for Maddie?'

'That, my dear, is between me and my client.' A smile curved his lips.

'Then here's a proposal: I love to cook and, if I'm not mistaken, you love to eat. Next Tuesday, you do the garden and I'll do a nice roast.'

'Deal! See you next week.' He kissed her cheeks before sauntering along the path to the driveway where the ute was parked.

She followed a short distance behind, stopping at an oversize rosemary bush that hid her from the street. Already she was worrying where this might lead.

Go with the flow, Isla.

In the ute, he waved and sped away.

16

The portrait

Thirteen months ago: winter

On the first Tuesday of July, winter struck with a vengeance. The sky turned the colour of steel and drizzle set in. After spending most of Monday night at the King's Arms, Claude slept late. His SP bookmaker mate, Lefty Long, had been celebrating his sixtieth birthday the way he knew best: with the lads and a skinful of grog.

With a headache the size of New South Wales, Claude sat on the bed and pulled on his work boots. The last thing he needed was a day of endless cups of tea and idle chit-chat, ending with a mow of Isla's lawn.

Most of Claude's clients were easy. All they wanted was a shoulder to cry on and a good screw afterwards. For a few hours each week he delivered happiness and release. They felt better; he felt better. No strings attached. Everyone was a winner.

But not Isla. Complex and hard to read, her shell was as hard as a turtle's. Yet inside that rigid exterior, she was a mush of insecurity. According to her, life was one big disappointment. Her problems needed to be brought to the surface, but he had neither the skill nor the patience to do so. More than most, he knew the damage that old wounds could cause. The pain never went away. Insidious and unseen, it ate you from the inside like a cancer. The more you pretended it didn't exist, the worse it became. He touched his abdomen where the scar was—courtesy of his good-for-nothing father—and bit back tears.

After lighting a cigarette, he tied his shoelaces. Smoke curled into his eyes.

He and Isla had made an agreement and he was a man of his word. He'd deliver his end of the deal until Maddie came back. He was certain she would; none of her previous relationships had lasted more than two years. Besides, Isla did cook a brilliant lamb roast. That alone was worth his while.

In his cramped kitchenette, Claude made toast with Vegemite. He forced himself to eat half a slice before taking two painkillers. It was lucky he'd left the party at midnight and didn't kick on until two when the bar closed. And he'd stuck solely to beer, while the rest of the lads got into rum chasers. He was getting too old for this; his body was letting him down. He rinsed out his mouth with water and then drank an entire glassful.

It was getting late. Should he ring Isla first or blame the traffic? A sharp pain speared his eyeball. Bugger the phone call. He'd take his chances.

When he opened the back door, a blast of freezing air smacked him in the face. He took his oilskin jacket from its hook on the porch. Holding it umbrella-like over his head, he stumbled down the path to the street where his ute was parked.

Inside the cabin, the windows were opaque with condensation. With his shirt sleeve he wiped a patch to see through, turned the key, pressed the accelerator. The engine made a sick whining noise, ticked over once, then rumbled into a silent death. Seldom did Shirl let him down.

It was the final straw, the sign that today was not meant to be. He reached for the phone in his pocket and called Isla.

Straight away she answered. 'What's up?'

'I'm a bit crook and the car won't start. Mind if we give it a miss?'

'Fine by me. Good thing I haven't put on the roast.' There was a trace of relief in her tone. Or was it elation? She sounded younger and more alive than usual.

'See you next week then?' he said.

He half-expected her to say *don't bother*, but she agreed without hesitation.

For a few minutes he sat in the driver's seat and smoked. The headache was starting to clear and he had an entire day to himself. As he wound down the window to toss out the butt, his phone began to buzz. He glanced at name on the screen: Maddie. As far as he was aware, she was in Dubai with her new man.

'To what do I owe the pleasure?' he said with some apprehension. A call from Maddie usually meant bad news or a whole heap of work for him to do.

'Before you start with the chatter, *dahling*, I need to tell you that it's four o'clock in the morning here. I'm tired and cranky.'

'What's up?' He massaged his brow; the headache was coming back.

'I need to ask a favour, *dahling*. I tried calling last night but you didn't answer.'

'Unlike some people, I've got a life.' If only it were true. Lefty Long's birthday bash at the King's Arms was no competition for Maddie's luxury lifestyle.

'Okay, don't get your knickers in a knot. I'm worried about Isla. Last night we talked on Skype and she seemed very low. Are you going to see her today?'

'Maybe.'

'Is that yes or no?'

'Geez, Maddie. Give me a break. I called her just now and said I wasn't going because I have headache, which is the truth. I can't call her back five minutes later and say I'm better.'

'How did she sound?'

'Fine. No, better than fine. She sounded happy.'

There was a pause on the other end of the line. 'All the same, would you please drop by? It'd set my mind at ease.'

'All right. I'll text you.'

The line went dead. Either she'd hung up or the call had dropped out. There was little point in ringing her back, so he called a mechanic he knew about the ute.

An hour later Shirl had a shiny new battery and her engine was purring with gratitude. On the way to Isla's, Claude dropped in to Mac's corner store for a meat pie: best hangover cure in the world. Isla wasn't expecting him so there'd be no hearty meal in the oven. He washed the pie down with a carton of chocolate milk, wiped his lips and belched with contentment. The combination of fat and sugar always worked. Another cigarette and he felt his usual self, ready to do battle with emotional issues and long grass alike.

At 53 Mayfield Avenue he went directly to the door at the back. It was shut. He peered through the bannisters to the garage beneath the house and saw that her car was gone. Downstairs he walked towards the under-house shed where she kept the mower and assorted gardening equipment. Her mangy grey cat, lurking beneath the bushes, lashed its claws at his ankle as he passed. He aimed a light kick and missed. The creature squeezed under the fence and escaped to the neighbour's yard.

Near the laundry tubs was an artist's easel, set up with a large canvas board and a stool. The board was facing away from him; all that was visible was the brand on the back. Curious, he wandered closer. A wooden palette, smothered in glossy colour-curls, and a long-handled brush lay on the stool. It was as if she'd been painting one minute and was vaporised by aliens the next. A familiar odour, a mixture of linseed oil and turps, permeated the space. The smell reminded him of his father's workshop long ago, before the family catastrophe. He choked back tears and hardened his jaw. Although he was there alone, he needed to wear the wooden mask of indifference day and night lest he crumble.

To get a preview of the artwork in progress, he stepped around the easel. What was on the canvas stopped him dead in his tracks.

He was face to face with a life-size image of himself.

Naked.

His mouth fell open in shock. Not once had she seen him like that. And it was not for the lack of trying. Never had she given a hint of being interested in him, apart from as a workman who kept the yard tidy and ate her tucker as payment. Sometimes he caught himself wondering if she was a man-hater or a lesbian. But this ... this could change everything.

He took a couple of steps back from the picture. The various colours and layers of paint all blended together so that the subject sprang to life. The *image* of Claude was more real than reality. Its hair was thicker, its features more chiselled, its muscles more defined. And its manhood, nestled in a soft bed of fur down below, was nothing short of magnificent.

He began to chuckle, which rolled into a belly laugh. How wrong could he have been! He'd been on the verge of giving up the ridiculous arrangement thrust on him by conniving Maddie, but now he was having second thoughts. Not that he was in love with Isla. Far from it. But he had to admit she intrigued him, due in part to her very reticence. Mysteries were meant to be cracked and this painting was the first clue. Quickly, he snapped a photo on his phone and legged it out of there before Isla returned.

Later he texted Maddie in Dubai. *Isla's fine. Stop worrying.*

She responded with one word. *Thanks.*

17

Secret confessions

Saturday 15 August

Early Saturday morning, Seth woke with a head like a balloon and a body that had been used for batting practice. He was in a strange bed, which for a former foreign correspondent was not that unusual. Judging by the soprano singing in the shower, he was also with a strange woman.

He rolled onto his back and shut his eyes, hoping to go back to sleep. Alas, his body ached so much that he couldn't get comfortable. Tossing in bed was enough to crack a couple of ribs. His tongue was glued to the roof of his mouth; his throat was like sandpaper. Disoriented, he groaned to his feet and stumbled down the hall to the powder room. The loo-water was the colour of the ocean. Leaving the door open, he eased himself onto the warmed contoured toilet seat and began to ponder his predicament.

A pink cloud floated down the hall: Maddie in a pink silk kaftan and nothing else.

'Passionfruit yoghurt or left-over pizza?' Shamelessly she stood in the open doorway with her hands on hips, waiting for his answer. Her hair was styled into a shoulder-length bob; not a lock was out of place. She was so perfectly groomed that she could have stepped straight out of a fashion magazine.

Seth mumbled something about black tea and aspirin, but didn't think she heard.

Before he could repeat himself, she'd vanished into the dazzling blaze of morning in an all-glass apartment.

He showered. In the mirror he examined the damage of the night before. His entire left side was a massive bruise. Some parts were yellow; some were green; others were different shades of purple. The worst, south of his left nipple, was a crescent the size of a man's boot. The events of Friday evening came flooding back. The banter, the passion, the rude encounter with a pair of steel-caps.

Feeling slightly more human, he tucked a towel around his waist and went in search of Maddie. In the kitchen she was hovering over an espresso machine that was gushing with aromatic vapours. Two red cups were positioned beneath twin nozzles. While she waited for the coffee to come, she slid a milk jug up and down the steam wand. The way she moved her hands was sensual and arousing. When the coffee was ready she added the milk. The final touch was a heart made of froth.

'Get that into you, *dahling*.'

He inhaled. The coffee aroma was so strong and smooth that he could imagine an entire Jamaican plantation distilled into a single shot. This was truly the nectar of life. The caffeine went straight to his head and kicked him from nowhere to tomorrow.

At last his brain began to work. He tried to recall last night's argument between Maddie and the intruder while he was cowering beneath the low-slung furniture. All that came to mind was the awful gagging sound of a woman in the throes of being strangled to death.

'Who *was* that man?' Unconsciously he touched his ribs.

'Andrew. Ugly bastard, isn't he?'

'Your husband?'

'Ex,' she corrected. 'He must have found my farewell note and caught the next plane out of Dubai. He's the sort who won't take *no* for an answer. Thank God Claude turned up.' Immediately she pressed her lips together, as if she'd let something slip.

'Who's Claude?'

As if stalling for time, Maddie dug a tablespoon into a tub of yoghurt and ladled it evenly into two glass dishes. Yoghurt was not his favourite food at the best of times. Today the stench was reminiscent of stale vomit. He pushed the dish away and helped himself to a slice of cold pizza.

'He's my personal handyman, *dahling*.' She said it with supreme confidence, as if a handyman were a common household item, such as a fridge or a washing machine.

'At the time I seem to recall that you were being strangled and I was stuck under the coffee table. How did this *Claude* get into the apartment?'

'With a key of course. He has keys for all his clients. Look, he's a good man. I'd trust him with my life.'

'Let me get this straight. You called a *personal handyman* in the middle of the night to come and break up a fight between you and your ex-husband after your ... ahem ... *friend with benefits* was attacked?'

It was clear she was uncomfortable with this line of questioning. She licked yoghurt from the tablespoon and dropped it in the sink. 'It's not what you think.'

'And that is ...?'

'You think I'm a high-class hooker. Well I'm not! I happen to like men and they like me ... most of the time. Admittedly I've been unlucky in my choice of husbands, but it's *not my fault*. Claude is the only man I can rely on.'

'So what *is* your relationship with him?'

Her eyes were moist. Hugging herself, she padded to the breakfast table with the multi-million dollar view over the river, the chunky steel structure of the Story Bridge, and the city skyline beyond. She sat down and dropped her head in her hands.

'I was his Tuesday girl, had been for years,' she said. 'When I went to Dubai, we agreed that Isla would take my timeslot. She needed help. He was the best person I knew.'

Seth raised his hands quizzically. 'What exactly did she need?'

'Do I have to spell it out?'

'Quite frankly, yes.'

'Do you know that song called *Handy Man*?'

'James Taylor?'

She nodded. 'What Claude can fix is the same as the song. He's good at it too. Lord knows, I've had my share of troubles with three useless husbands ... and now my best friend. When Isla lost her job, she lost her reason for living.'

Maddie's lower lip was quivering but she continued. 'Her death has taken its toll on me too. The police interrogation, the autopsy, the speculation about whether it was murder or suicide. It's been appalling. Simply appalling!'

Her voice was now a tiny squeak. 'Now she's gone ...'

The dam had finally broken; her tears became a waterfall.

Seth left her alone to have a good cry. All that grief and guilt needed to come out.

He took the pizza onto the balcony, rested his elbows on the glass barricade and breathed in air, dewy from the night. Two CityCats curved across the river, passing each other mid-stream between Mowbray Park and New Farm. Their wakes fanned across the water in graceful swirls. Ten storeys below, a man was walking his dog on the boardwalk that stretched all the way from Sydney Street to the northern end of the CBD.

How the city had changed since he was a youngster! From the *big country town*—as it was once known—to *BrisVegas,* a sprawling metropolis trying to be hip.

A short while later, Maddie brought him another coffee.

'*Dahling*, I'd forgotten how lovely the view is,' she said. Her eyes were a little swollen but she seemed to be in control. 'If you want to talk to Claude, here's his number and address. Please don't mention me. Not to him, not to anyone. And *please* don't identify me in your article.'

He took the note and gave her a kiss. 'You have my word. Look, I'd better be going. I'll call you later.'

*

That afternoon, Seth drove to the house where Claude lived. Beneath a tree outside was a blue tradie's ute with a personalised number plate. SH1RL. A flash of *déjà vu.* Not long ago, he'd seen that very same vehicle parked beneath a different tree. He stroked his chin and tried to wind back the memory tape. For the moment it was blank.

Surreptitiously he snapped a photo on his phone.

In the garden of the house in question was a wiry man of around sixty. He wore a broad-brimmed hat, blue singlet, and shorts. On seeing the Jeep, he straightened and lit a smoke. His arms and legs were covered in tattoos.

Seth made a half-salute and walked to the fence. 'G'day, mate. I'm looking for a fellow by the name of Claude Fabergé.'

'Who wants to know?'

Seth introduced himself and said he was doing an article on unusual jobs. 'If my information is correct, Mr Fabergé is a personal handyman.'

With an expression of visible relief, the man gave a lopsided grin. 'You'd better come in.' He dropped his voice to a whisper. 'Don't want any sticky-beaks to overhear, if you know what I mean.' He nodded towards the neighbouring house.

'Do you know Mr Fabergé?'

The man put a finger to his lips. 'We can talk inside.'

He led the way up the front stairs. The cottage was one of those post-war dog-boxes built in haste and without design to accommodate an army of returned servicemen. The entire street was full of them, all the same apart from the colour of the paint and the shrubs in the yard.

On the top step was a scruffy grey cat which slinked away at first sight. The man kicked off his work boots and beckoned Seth inside. They passed through a tiny lounge room with a well-worn couch and an oversized TV to get to the kitchen-cum-dining room at the back.

'Want a beer?'

'Only if you're having one.'

He rummaged in a fridge that looked at least thirty years old. Freckles of rust spotted the door. But something else caught Seth's eye. Pinned to it with a smiley-face magnet was a business card embossed with a logo of a gold cat. He'd seen that logo before, when he was surfing the internet for tattoo parlours. While the other man was occupied, Seth he snapped a pic of the card on the fridge.

Two tinnies of lager slammed onto the table. 'In answer to your question, yes I do know Claude Fabergé.'

'And *your* name is …?'

'Call me Frank.'

'Haven't we met before?' said Seth.

'Don't think so. I've read your articles in *The Morning Post* of course. You write some interesting stuff.'

'Thanks. How well do you know Mr Fabergé?'

'As well as I know myself.'

'Can you tell me about his occupation?'

Frank proceeded to ramble on about the life of a personal handyman as if he'd had first-hand experience in the business. According to Frank, there were literally thousands of lonely middle-aged women who wanted nothing more than a reliable male to do odd jobs and provide comfort in matters of the heart. For this his friend charged a small fee, barely enough to cover expenses. What Claude Fabergé did, in his opinion, was nothing short of an essential public service. He was an unsung hero who helped clients through tough times and rescued them from the depths of depression. 'In fact,' Frank concluded, 'Claude should be nominated for an Australian of the Year award.'

To Seth, he sounded like a hybrid of Mr Fixit and a poorly-paid gigolo.

'Could I speak to some of Mr Fabergé's clients?'

Frank choked on his beer. 'Fuck no! Everything's strictly confidential.'

For such an innocuous question, the reaction seemed rather extreme. A tender spot had been touched. Something untoward was going on that might involve the mysterious Claude or some of his clients. Was there a chink in the armour of lies?

Seth pressed on. 'Actually one of those clients gave me this address. If Mr Fabergé lives here, can I speak to him in person?'

Frank was starting to sweat. 'Look mate, I'm gunna have to call it quits. It's Saturday night and I've got myself a date. Can't keep a good woman waiting.'

Seth stood up to leave. 'Thanks for your time, Frank. Mind if I call again later?'

'No trouble at all … *mate*.' The last word was muttered through clenched teeth.

In the Jeep, Seth jotted down the gist of the conversation in his notebook and made a sketch of the cat logo on the fridge in case the phone camera hadn't worked. He didn't have much to go on but he was certain that Frank wasn't telling the truth about his so-called friend. He also had a niggling impression that they'd met before. The memory was kind of hazy, perhaps from a long time ago. Possibly they'd had a conversation in a bar when they were both a bit under the weather.

The central figure was the elusive Monsieur Fabergé, by all accounts a noble character with a free-wheeling lifestyle. Had Maddie confused their addresses? He thought not. Frank's over-reactive behaviour had the distinctive odour of a rat.

Seth slid his hand into his jeans pocket and touched the scarlet key; it was cool and smooth against his skin. That key had opened a Pandora's box in the suburbs.

Suddenly the lightbulb went off. Tattoos! That was the connection! Although he was tired and his ribcage was beginning to ache, he had to find out for sure. He Googled *tattoo parlours* again, scrolled through the results for the cat logo. There it was, along with an address in Goongulli. Surprisingly he knew the stretch of road well. His second-favourite caffeine supplier was located near the Goongulli train station. He must have walked past the studio dozens of times without noticing.

Late on a Saturday afternoon, the industrial suburb was deserted. The Jeep cruised down the strip by the railway tracks and stopped outside an old-world shop with an awning, a horse-trough and hitching posts.

On the opaque glass window was the gold cat logo, the same as the card on Frank's fridge. Beneath the business name was a tag-line: *tattoo art and psychic healing.*

It might be a long shot, but it was better than no shot at all.

18

Gone to GOMA

Thirteen months ago: winter

Isla stepped back from the canvas and examined the unfinished portrait of Claude with a critical eye. Some parts were pleasing—no, they were downright fine—but others could have been painted by a chimpanzee. The scale was good, the face was animated. His expression was one of mild surprise, as if startled by an intruder as he stepped from the shower.

But the hands! They were awful! Two clumsy bunches of bananas with no shape or form. The manly bits were far too pendulous and out of proportion. The overall impression was a sleazy seventies porn star.

Slamming down the brush in disgust, she ran her hands through her hair. She took a mouthful of tea made an hour ago which was now icy cold. Six weeks of toil and this was the best she could do. How utterly disheartening! Had she learnt nothing from teaching others about colour and balance and texture? The conclusion she'd reached all those years ago was right after all. *Those who can do, and those who can't teach.*

In a fit of pique, she moistened a rag with turps and scrubbed off the banana-fingers. Tomorrow she might redo them. Or perhaps she'd cross-hatch the canvas so that the face became the focus of the picture. Or maybe she'd simply trash the lot and give up on this dismal attempt at resurrecting an art career.

Slowly she screwed the caps on the tubes of oils, rinsed the brushes in turps, wiped them clean, stretched cling wrap over the palette so that the paint wouldn't dry. Outside the temperature had taken a dive as the rain came in. Dreary skies compounded her bleak mood.

Upstairs she paced several laps of the lounge room, its walls a testament to her favourite artists. Most were prints of famous pieces by Cezanne and Matisse: impressionist work full of colour and movement. Two were originals by talented students, one of whom was Antoinette Collier. Three were hers: two landscapes featuring the local creek and a portrait of Venus copied from a photo.

She sighed into the sofa, let her eyes drift from one picture to the next and back again. Compared to all the others, her paintings were wooden and boring. Even the student work showed flashes of brilliance that were missing in hers. Perhaps she'd been trying too hard or was expecting too much. Perhaps she should seek inspiration in the world of the living instead of trying to emulate dead masters.

Pull yourself together, she told herself. *Go out. Do something different.*

It had been years since she'd visited the Gallery of Modern Art. What better place to break the mould and get fresh ideas? GOMA turned art on its head. Literally. The massive bronze sculpture on the grassy riverbank was an elephant in a headstand, a manoeuvre that brought the pachyderm eye-to-eye with a tiny marsupial rat. At GOMA, art came in many forms. The materials and techniques ranged from experimental to downright silly. In particular, some of the young Asian artists were creating things that broke every rule.

That was what *she* must do: cast away her preconceived ideas and start anew.

After a snack of week-old stew on toast she showered, changed into her blue winter suit, and set off in the Toyota Camry. Mid-afternoon on a weekday, the carpark at the State Library was usually deserted and today was no exception.

The open-air walkway from the carpark to the modern concrete-and-glass cube with the high-flying roof was wet and slippery. Her folding umbrella afforded little protection against the driving rain. With each gust, it flapped like a fish in a bucket. Several times in that hundred-metre dash, it turned itself inside out. Going out in this weather was madness!

The cold blast of air conditioning hit as the sliding glass doors opened. Soaked to the skin as she was, she'd probably catch her death. Still, she was there and had already paid fifteen dollars to the carpark attendant. She might as well make the most of it.

After checking in her umbrella at the counter, she hastened to the ladies room where she dried off under the hand blower. Feeling warmer, she fixed her hair and smoothed her skirt before entering the voluminous space of the gallery.

The feature piece was an enormous 3-D installation by Cai Guo Qiang, showing dozens of life-size animals gathered at a waterhole. A second installation by the same artist was an arc of air-bound wolves, crashing into a glass wall. The detail and the craftsmanship were superb; the scale was monumental.

In awe she wandered amongst the sculptures and paintings, wondering how she could apply the same out-there creativity to her own work. Lost in thought, she didn't notice that a piece of living art was standing beside her.

'Awesome, don't you think?' said a familiar voice.

Isla turned. The woman's head was shaved at the sides; a two-inch crest of hot pink hair stood at attention down the centre. A tattoo of ivy with red roses climbed out of her pullover and wound up the back of her neck.

'Antoinette!' Isla gasped.

'That's me. You seem surprised.'

A blush warmed Isla's cheeks. 'I was a million miles away.'

'Hey, you want a coffee? My treat.'

'Sure.'

They made their way downstairs to the goldfish-bowl café that usually had a sweeping view of the city buildings across the river. Except today the cityscape was shrouded in grey mist. The coffee bar was without customers; the attendants were cleaning up for the day.

Antoinette ordered two takeaway cappuccinos and Isla claimed a table by the window. Rainwater streamed down the glass like tears.

Coffee was not Isla's favourite beverage but only old ladies insisted on tea. To counteract the bitterness of over-roasted beans, she poured in three sachets of sugar and licked the chocolate froth from the spoon.

'I thought you'd have paid us another visit,' Antoinette began. 'You seemed rather taken with Jet.'

'I've been busy,' Isla lied.

'Doing what?'

'Oh, you know …'

The younger woman looked Isla square in the eye as if expecting a better explanation. In the months since their last encounter, Antoinette's appearance had grown more bizarre. For some unknown reason, she seemed hell-bent on replacing the pigment in her skin with a confusion of graffiti of the type you'd see on abandoned buildings.

Ordinarily Isla avoided people with tattoos and punk hairstyles. Yet here, in her neat tailored suit with a woman from another galaxy, she felt oddly at ease. She glanced around the café. The barista was busy cleaning the equipment and the waiters were stacking chairs outside. The two of them were effectively alone. If she didn't talk about what she was going through, she'd either explode or be sucked into a black hole of despair.

'Okay, Nettie, here's the truth. I'm not doing anything. Being without a job is dreadful. Nobody wants to employ an old ex-teacher so I tried doing the charity thing: Meals on Wheels. What happens at the end of life is utterly depressing. Nothing about old age is pretty. You get more and more dependent on strangers for your basic needs. From then on, it's a long, slow, miserable slide into the grave. Every time I did a shift, my own mortality stared me in the face. So I gave it up and started painting again. But that's more depressing. I'm washed up, finished, useless.'

Antoinette reached for her hand, but she pulled it away.

Isla continued. 'I don't know how to get out of this pit. That's why I came here to GOMA. I thought it might spark me up. Sorry, I don't mean to be morose.'

'You need to get this out. Otherwise you'll be like those old people, watching life pass you by until there's nothing left. Jet can help. He's turned my life around.'

Isla said, 'How?'

'I can't explain exactly, but I guess it's like exorcism. When he lays his hands on you, the pain comes out of your heart. Somehow he catches it and turns it into a tattoo. It sounds crazy, but you don't need to tell him what happened or why. He has the gift of second sight. He just *knows*.' She pushed up the sleeve of her jumper, revealing a tattoo in the style of a Japanese scroll. 'See this koi fish?'

Isla put on her reading glasses. The orange fish was done in a traditional oriental style: clean and precise with an elegant curve to its fins.

Antoinette said, 'The koi fish is a symbol of courage and determination. It represents my struggle to fulfil my dreams. Every time I see it, I'm inspired to push on.' With her forefinger she stroked its glistening head. 'Beautiful, isn't it?'

If it were on paper instead of skin, Isla would have instantly agreed. Her mindset against tattoos held her back from expressing enthusiasm. 'How many do you have?'

'Tattoos? More than I can count. My skin illustrates my life.'

Isla nodded. 'And you say this has helped overcome your problems?'

'Absolutely! As you know, I had a tough childhood. Without you, I wouldn't have made it past fourteen.' She pushed up the other sleeve to reveal Japanese characters done in blue ink. This is for you. It means *wise teacher to whom I'm indebted*.'

Tears misted Isla's eyes. She fidgeted with the empty cardboard cup, squishing the rolled rim between her nails. For a while they didn't speak.

Light rain pattered against the windowpane. The clouds were breaking up. In the eastern sky, a rainbow curved above the office towers. Was it a sign?

At length, Isla broke the silence. 'Thank you, Antoinette. You helped me too, and in more ways than you'll ever know.' An idea was brewing.

Antoinette's mobile phone made a wolf-whistle and she checked the screen. 'It's Amber. Gotta go. I'm so glad we had this chat. Promise you'll come and see me and Jet?'

'Yes, I will.' This time Isla meant it. If she'd been drowning, she'd just been thrown a life-ring. All she had to do was have the courage to turn her idea into action.

Like mother and daughter they hugged goodbye.

To an outsider they would have been the stereotypical contradiction: the ultra-conservative parent attempting to understand the whims of her tearaway offspring. Such was the way of the world.

For Isla, all that was about to change.

19

An attempted rescue

Nine months ago: early summer

The cure that Jet provided was better than any pill. Whenever Isla lay on the recliner in his studio, all doubts and fears disappeared. They communicated not by voice but by some sort of silent telepathy. When he placed his hands on her, he was able to step inside her mind. His hands drew out her deepest emotions and implanted them on her skin. The whole thing was so irrational and unbelievable that Isla gave up trying to understand.

After several sessions of 'Jet therapy', Isla had become more at ease with herself and the world. The crushing weariness that had haunted her for the best part of a year persisted, but now she had taken control. To her mandala on the corkboard she'd added another word. *Live.*

Live each day as it comes.

No longer did she have to worry about student assessments or work schedules or lack of progress toward goals. All those things were self-imposed. Manifestations of a past life. That was what Jet, her psychic healer, had said and she trusted him completely. Liberated, she began to reach out to friends who were battling demons of their own.

First there was Maddie. As an expat in a foreign land, Maddie's life sounded like a living nightmare. Her expectations and the reality had proven to be poles apart. Travel brochures showed Dubai as a sleek modern city, dotted with man-made islands in the shape of palm trees. The hype belied how hard it was to live there as a woman, where women had no rights.

'I couldn't believe it,' Maddie said in one of their regular Skype conversations. 'I went to the bank to open an account but they wouldn't give me access. I had to get my *husband* to create the PIN number ... for *my* account!'

And then there was the fashion thing. Maddie liked to wear low-cut tops and skirts that barely covered her knickers. In Dubai, neither was tolerated. In the marketplace old women, blanketed in black, spat at her.

'What's the matter with this place?' Maddie said. 'If nice clothes can only be worn inside your house where nobody can see them, what's the point? What's worse, I think Andrew actually enjoys my suffering. He's become a bloody chauvinist like the rest of them. And he's hardly ever home. The other women in the compound are busy running after kids so there's no-one to talk to. I get so lonely.'

'But what an *adventure*!' Isla gushed, wishing she was as courageous as her friend. 'Make the most of it. Maybe you could write a book, a variation on *Eat, Pray, Love*.'

'I wish! Anyway I'm a doer, not a writer,' was Maddie's response. 'Eat is the only part of *Eat, Pray, Love* that matters to me. Throw in a few bottles of wine and I'd be happy, but we're not allowed to drink either.'

'You're not going to leave, are you?' said Isla.

'To tell you the truth, if I last another six months it'll be a miracle.'

Second there was Claude. As the Tuesday substitute, Isla knew she was no match for Maddie. Often he would turn up with bleary eyes and the smell of alcohol on his breath. Over the months he'd lost a few kilos and was looking a bit haggard. She was sure the only thing that kept him going was the good square meal she cooked him once a week. The rest of the time he seemed to survive on greasy takeaways.

Not only was he drinking too much, but he was also frequenting the betting shop in Corella. With her own eyes she'd seen him there, thumbing through a wad of betting tickets. He swore he wasn't a gambler. Yet when he was flush with cash, he'd bring her flowers. Other times he'd carry on as if he didn't have a cent to his name.

Her greatest concern was that he never spoke about himself or his family. The more she tried to find out, the more he clammed up. It was clear that something bad had happened long ago. If childhood experiences shaped the rest of your life, Claude's must have been truly horrible.

The first Monday of summer was a year to the day since Isla lost her job. In her schedule as an early retiree, Monday had become baking day. While the electric mixer beat butter and sugar into a lovely thick cream, she pondered Claude's predicament. In her hand was an egg, ready to crack against the side of the bowl. On the benchtop were two cups: one of flour and the other of milk and vanilla. Later, when she'd iced the cake, she'd deliver it to the

Corella branch of Meals on Wheels. Their longest-serving member was turning ninety.

After her first therapy session with Jet, Isla decided to re-join Meals on Wheels, this time on her own terms. No longer would she be a lackey, delivering hospital-style dinners door-to-door. Old people deserved nourishing food with lots of flavour. She took a sample of her beef and burgundy pie to the interview and a week later she was 'hired' as a cook.

In no time, word spread through the octogenarian community that Corella Meals on Wheels provided mighty fine tucker. Clientele doubled and with it came additional funding. Win-win all round. Cooking was what she loved and her food brought pleasure to others.

Isla added the flour and milk alternately to the mixing bowl. Little by little the batter expanded and thickened. The cake pans were ready. The oven was coming up to speed: one hundred and sixty degrees and rising.

When the thermostat clicked off, a devious plan clicked on in her head. Suddenly she knew how to help Claude.

Lifting her blouse, she placed her hands on the gauze bandage around her chest. Beneath it, the skin was tender but in a restorative way. Ten years had passed since the surgery. Her mother had been claimed at an early age so when Isla found the lump, she knew what to expect. When she was discharged from hospital, both her breasts were gone.

Not once had she regretted her decision to have them removed, but she missed her curves and nipples. Sometimes, when she caught her naked reflection in the mirror, she wept. No longer a proper woman, she felt destined to live the rest of her days alone.

Now, thanks to Jet, she'd regained her courage. The secret was known only to him. Beneath that gauze bandage was a beautiful work of indelible art: blue lotus flowers and arabesques.

The blue lotus symbolises the ability of the spirit to control the physical world, Jet had said. *Mind over matter, if you will.*

Glancing at the mandala on the corkboard, she realised that she'd already achieved most of what she wanted. *Conquer, dare, create.* And the new addition: *live.* Whether the cancer was beaten no longer mattered. Her fear of it was gone.

Such was the power of blue lotus flowers.

Such was the power of Jet.

Before she could change her mind, she reached for the phone and called Claude.

20

Jet Ink

Nine months ago: the same day

When Claude answered Isla's phone call, he was lazing smugly in a deckchair on his back porch. It was late Monday morning and the neighbours were all at work.

Minutes before he'd read an entire week of newspapers, delivered while he was away. It'd been ages since he'd had a holiday. Now that he was retired from the public service, with its assured fortnightly pay and a flex-day every month, he had to mind his pennies.

Lola Molloy was the person responsible for the mini-break. In fact she'd insisted. Four of her greyhounds were entered in the biggest meet of the racing calendar: the Golden Bone at Dapto.

Lola had arranged everything. 'We'll take my LandCruiser and the trailer. If we leave around one on Tuesday afternoon, we'll make Port Macquarie by nine. A friend of mine can put us up. That gives us plenty of time to get to Dapto and for the dogs to recover before the races.'

According to her, Hot Tamales was a shoo-in for the Golden Bone. The other three dogs were showing good promise but hadn't had much exposure to the track. If all went well, she stood to make several thousand dollars in prize money alone. And there were the side bets with the bookies that Claude would make on her behalf.

On race day, not only had Lola's dogs lived up to expectations, but Claude had also made himself a packet. Blue Suede Shoes, a hundred-to-one outsider, had shot to the lead in the fifth and won by a whisker. What a lovely break it had been! Lola herself was always fun to be around and her

118

greyhounds were the best animals in the world. It was an anticlimax when she dropped him off Sunday night at his dark, lonely house in the outer western suburbs.

On the phone Isla was in a terrible state. 'You're the only one I can turn to, Claude. The burner in my oven is on the blink and I have to make cakes for an important event this afternoon. The Goongulli oven shop has the part but they can't deliver. At this rate I'll never finish in time. Please, can you help?'

Usually on a Monday he'd be at Rita's but she'd gone away to Thailand. With no other commitments, he agreed. Any luck and she'd give him a home-baked treat as a reward. That woman was the best cook he'd ever met.

Isla wept with gratitude and promised to make it worth his while. Inwardly he smiled. Perhaps the favour might crack the ice at last.

She gave him the name and address of the oven repairs shop.

On the internet he located the Goongulli industrial zone abutting the interstate train line. It was not the most salubrious of locations. He could barely remember the last time he'd been out that way. It must have been thirty years ago. His recollection was a couple of iron 'igloos', relics of the Second World War, standing in a paddock by the railway tracks. The Google pictures showed a patchwork of shops, workshops, and showrooms. It seemed the army igloos had long gone.

Half an hour later, Shirl turned into Innovation Drive. The street looked nothing like the name suggested. Stagnation Drive would have been more apt. A row of tired shopfronts—a hairdresser, nail salon, video shop, café— was covered in graffiti. Further on were sheds for light industry: panel beating, spray painting, engineering.

Bun in the Oven repairs was right at the end.

Claude did a lap of the block then parked near the station. On foot and up close, the locality was even seedier than from a distance. It was easy to imagine drug deals being done beneath the railway bridge or in a run-down Chinese restaurant called *Chow Long* that had no staff or customers, despite it being nearly lunchtime.

In the midst of the decay was a quaint shop with a curved iron awning, an old-fashioned horse trough, and a set of hitching posts. Unlike the other businesses along the strip, it was a stand-alone building. It was older than the rest, built maybe in the late eighteen hundreds. On the window was the logo of a cat. Whatever went on inside was a mystery, for the glass was black and opaque.

As he was about to move on, the door opened. A slim man wearing a black t-shirt and red bandanna came out and leant against the wall. He was bearded and heavily tattooed. Folding his arms in a proprietorial stance, he looked directly at Claude as if expecting him.

Caught like a burglar on CCTV, Claude didn't know whether to stop or keep walking. He stood his ground and lit a cigarette.

The tattooed man spoke. 'I knew you'd come, Claude.' His accent had a touch of Eastern Europe.

Claude backed away. How could he possibly know his name?

'Please come in.' The man opened the glass door as if it hadn't occurred to him that his prospective customer might decline. 'I'm Jet. Welcome to the new world.'

Without question Claude obeyed. The first thing that struck him was the smell of phenol. Involuntarily he winced. The odour brought memories of pain that was not only physical.

In the entry area, the front desk was made of carved wood. The walls were decorated with pictures of tattoos. He'd never been to a tattoo parlour before, though he'd sometimes wondered what went on there. A vivid imagination, combined with the scare tactics of the media, made him believe they were at the heart of the drug trade and bikie wars. Tattoos were not for good honest blokes like him.

Although his gut reaction was to turn and run, he was soon overcome with a sense of calm. His mind felt free; his body felt light. For the first time in years he was at ease.

Jet led him behind an oriental screen that separated the entry space from the workspace. Instead of a dungeon with torture implements, the room was shiny and bright. Ceramic tiles, stainless steel implements, recliner chairs, and a flat-screen TV on the ceiling gave it a sleek modern look.

'As you can see, I take pride in my studio.'

As intense as diamonds, Jet's steel-grey eyes drilled into him.

For a moment they held each other's gaze. A mind-to-mind connection was made and an understanding passed between them. For Claude it felt like enlightenment, as if the mental blockages of the past had been lifted, showing him a new way forward.

'Will this take long?' Claude barely recognised his own voice.

'It depends.' A cryptic expression crossed Jet's face. 'Sometimes it comes quicker than others.'

'Okay, let's begin.' Claude's spirits began to rise.

'Every tattoo has a story, Claude. Today is a turning point in your life.'

'How do you know my name?'

If Jet was taken aback, he didn't show it. 'She thinks about you all the time.'

'Who?' Claude frowned. This was getting weird.

'Angel.' The shadow of a smile. 'Your lady with the lotus flowers.'

Claude had no idea who Jet was talking about. He didn't care. It made perfect sense in an illogical sort of way. Everything in the last fifteen minutes had been so surreal he might have been tripping. Yet he hadn't taken drugs in years and his last drink was the day before yesterday, when he and Lola celebrated the big win at Dapto with a bottle of red wine.

'Make yourself comfortable.' Jet indicated one of the padded recliners. As if under hypnosis, Claude immediately sat in the chair. Without realising, he'd also unbuttoned his shirt and dropped it on the floor. He eased back; the chair moulded snugly to the shape of his body.

Jet perched on a stool beside him and prepared the equipment. There was no conversation, no discussion about design or where it should be placed.

Claude caught sight of himself in the mirror. His hair was grey and the once-impressive abdominal six-pack had become a small keg. Reason screamed *you crazy bastard, you're old enough to know better.* But he could not overcome the feeling that his entire future depended on this moment.

He shut his eyes, prepared himself for the needle.

'Lean forward.'

His head rested on a pillow as soft as a whisper. Two strong hands smoothed across the blades of his shoulders. On the sore spot to the left, Jet drew a circle with his finger.

'Here.'

A machine began to buzz. Seconds later, the wasp stung his back.

'Hey! I haven't told you what I want.'

The machine stopped.

'That's not how it works here.' Jet's voice was quiet but commanding.

Claude sat up, opened his mouth to speak. What came out was a long and resounding belch.

Those steel-grey eyes bored right through him. The tattoo gun was poised. 'If you want out, say so or forever hold your peace. What's it to be, Claude?'

'I want a rose. On my chest.'

Jet laughed.

'But I'm the customer.'

Jet shook his head. 'You ink virgins have no idea. This is the moment of rebirth. What you get is determined by what has gone before. In my studio, you do not choose the tattoo. *The tattoo chooses you.*'

Claude swung his feet to the floor. 'This is fuckin' crazy!'

Jet held up his hands. Tattooed on each palm was an eye: one blue and one green. 'Through these I see your past. I see your present and I see your future.'

Keeping Jet and the tattoo gun within his line of sight, Claude let his body sink back into the chair. Instantly the spell of tranquillity returned.

Jet continued in an even tone. 'When I place my hands on your body, I see events, people, emotions you've supressed for a very long time. They appear as symbols, visible only to me. As the image is tattooed on your skin, you relive the experience. That is the first step towards healing and forgiveness.'

The explanation was bizarre, based on faith or fear. Yet in his mesmerised state Claude thought it sounded plausible.

'Can you *really* erase my past?'

'You've heard of *wearing your heart on your sleeve*. That's what happens. The pain comes out and stays out. Every tattoo has a story.'

Claude let the information sink in. On balance there was little to lose and a lot to gain. He said, 'It seems I've come here for a reason.'

He resumed his position with his shoulder exposed and his head braced against the pillow. The needle found the spot on his left shoulder blade. A buzzing machine started and his skin was ripped apart. He shut his eyes and clenched his jaw, determined not to flinch. Before long, the sting lessened and the pain switched from his hide to his heart.

Suddenly his body jerked as if hit by a high-voltage wire. Wondering if he was dead, he tried to wiggle his fingers. They moved. He went to sit up but Jet held him fast.

'Lie still. This will pass.'

Reassured, Claude forced his muscles to relax. Presently his mind began to wander, back to an episode from the dim dark past.

It was the day life as he knew it disappeared forever.

21

An ugly end

Summer 1961

When Frank Low was six years old the unthinkable happened. It was late afternoon at the end of his first year at school. That day he'd walked home with his brother Jake, who was four years older. As usual the front door was unlocked. Inside, the house was as quiet as a graveyard.

Jake dumped his bag on the floor, took an apple from the bowl, and loped into the back yard. Through the open window Frank saw him pick up the half-paling that was their cricket bat and spin-bowl an old tennis ball against the wall.

Usually Mum would be bustling about with home-baked biscuits and glasses of milk. He never knew how she spent her time while they were at school. Probably she scrubbed the floors, or watered the lilies in the garden, or fired up the copper to wash the sheets, or gossiped with the old lady next door.

Some days the special glasses from the cocktail cabinet would be in the sink. Those days, backyard cricket would be banned and the boys would have to play as quiet as mice because of her *thumping headache.*

Today the kitchen benches were bare and no afternoon snack was on the table. On the floor were a bundle of clothes and the shattered shards of her best china.

'Mum?' Frank called as he wandered from room to room.

Jake's ball thunked against the weatherboards.

His little legs took him to the laundry with the copper boiler and concrete tubs. He returned via the living room with the plump couches,

123

swirly rag rug, and the wireless in the corner. In the bathroom with the primrose tub and matching basin, the medicine cabinet was open. Lots of brown-glass pill bottles were lined up in neat rows. In the middle of the shelf was an empty space.

His stomach was starting to hurt. He ran to the room he shared with Jake. She'd made their single beds with matching purple chenille bedspreads. On the shelf their collections of rocks, bird-nests, and glass marbles had been straightened.

Only one room remained. The forbidden room, on pain of the strap.

The door was shut. He put his ear to the wood and listened.

Whop went Jake's ball against the house. *Howzat!*

Softly he knocked. 'Mum? Are you there?'

His hand was shaking as he cracked open the door. The drapes were drawn. At first it was hard to see but he could smell the sickly sweet odour that he knew too well. Whenever he smelt it, there was trouble.

She was asleep on the double bed with the sheet pulled up to her neck. Her mouth was open and her head was at an angle. She was pale and very, very still.

'Mum?' His voice came out as a squeak.

He touched her cheek; it was as cool and waxy as plasticine.

'Mum. Wake up!' He shook her arm.

That was when he knew. Something was horribly wrong.

He tugged at the sheet and pulled it right off the bed. His mother was wearing her favourite frock with white flowers. It was twisted around her like rope. Beside her was an empty liquor bottle. White pills were scattered across the bed.

There was something else. Something too shocking for a little boy to comprehend.

Blood had pooled between her legs. Blood by the bucketful. In amongst it was a globule of pink jelly, as fragile as a partly-formed chick inside an egg.

Frank screamed at the top of his lungs and bolted outside.

It was the last time he saw his mother and the last day they lived in that house.

*

In the studio Jet said, 'It wasn't your fault, Claude … or should I call you Frank?'

Claude shook his head. 'I stopped being Frank the day I turned sixteen and left the orphanage. No-one but Jake knew what I'd seen. It was years until it made any sense.'

Jet held up a hand-mirror so that Claude could see his new tattoo: a red heart with white lilies. 'The feelings you have about your mother, good and bad, are all there.'

Overwhelmed, Claude closed his eyes. The room was whirling. He felt as if he were a helium balloon floating to the ceiling. From above he watched his earthly form in the chair weep like a child. Whatever Jet had done had changed everything. The sense of release opened the floodgates as he realised that this mother had been as much of a victim as he was. She'd had no choice. In the 1960s, that was how things worked. At last he could let go of the anger. She'd tried her best but that was not enough.

Claude rested his head on the pillow and slept.

When he woke, the tattoo was covered with gauze, his shirt was folded on the chair and the tattooist was nowhere to be seen.

In a state of confusion, he stood up and left. Outside in the sun, Shirl's metallic paint sparkled like a million sapphires. She might be nearly ten but the old girl was just as gorgeous as the day he'd brought her home.

A breeze sent lunch wrappers scudding across the footpath and lifted a white paper beneath the wiper blade. He snatched the parking ticket off the windshield and stormed along the footpath, squinting at the hours on the parking signs. They were so complicated they might as well have been written in code. All, except the one next to Shirl. The big white letters on a red background were as easy to read as a stop sign.

Loading zone, fifteen minutes.

The ute had been there at least an hour. His impromptu tattoo was going to cost a shit-load. He stuffed the parking ticket into his pocket. Despite the win at the Dapto Dogs, his bank account wasn't all too flash. Muttering every swear word he knew, he slid into the driver's seat. He was about head off when he remembered the reason he'd gone there. He cut the engine and trudged to *Bun in the Oven* spares.

With the new gas burner tucked under his arm, he dashed back to the ute and stepped on the gas before the parking shark returned. You win some and you lose some. His shoulder blade was stinging like crazy but he knew the battle scar would make him stronger. All in all, despite the costly setback, he felt as if a weight had been lifted.

At Isla's he didn't say a word about his new acquisition, or the parking fine for that matter. In fact he didn't say much at all. While Isla fretted over the state of the cake batter, he set to work replacing the burner. In five minutes it was done. He tested the oven to make sure it worked. As soon as the thermostat clicked off at one hundred and eighty degrees, he made an excuse and departed before she could draw him into a conversation he wasn't ready to have.

He was still reeling from the morning's events. During that brief interlude, Jet had read his innermost thoughts and touched the root of his pain. What power the man had!

Every tattoo has a story.

Beneath the bandage, his skin was burning and itching at the same time. But that was nothing compared to the abscess that had festered inside for decades. Through his shirt he touched the tattoo. The red heart and white lilies epitomised how he felt about that awful day.

It's perfect, he whispered to himself. *Absolutely bloody perfect.*

22

Antoinette

Saturday 15 August

The sun was dipping into the western ranges. Soon daylight would be gone. Outside the tattoo parlour Seth glanced at his watch. It was after five and the place seemed deserted. As he hesitated, the door flew open and a man in a black leather jacket barged out. Thick chains clanked against his thigh. His head was shaven and every square inch of skin was tattooed.

'Watch it, bro.'

Seth stepped aside to let him pass.

Without a grunt of acknowledgement, he thundered on his way. The skull-and-crossbones patch of an outlaw bikie gang was on the jacket. The back of his head was tattooed with a face, an exact replica of his own. The artistry was so good that it was hard to tell which way he was walking.

Seth pushed on the door and went inside. At the counter, a youngish woman in a vintage frock was sketching on tracing paper. Her breasts spilled into the low neckline; her skin was a riot of ink. Her electric-blue hair reminded him of Andy Warhol's *Marilyn*. A tattoo in the shape of a necklace revealed her name.

Antoinette: the name of Isla's foster child.

His mind flashed back to the day of the funeral. While he'd been trying to extract information from a grieving Maddie, Cate had tackled the younger tattooed set. Had Antoinette been one of them?

Until now, Seth had been working on the theory that Antoinette was the victim of the crime. Yet here she was, larger than life, working in a suburban tattoo parlour. The name was unusual but not unique. Did he have the right person?

To attract her attention, he knocked on the desk.

With a flick of her eyes, she took him in from his Converse sneakers to his burnt-orange shirt.

'Is Jet in?' he said.

In another room, a tattoo gun was buzzing.

'Sorry, we're fully booked today.'

Brushed off like a piece of fluff, he tried a different approach. 'Hello, Antoinette. Haven't we met before?'

She flinched. 'That's the oldest pickup line in the book.'

Inwardly he smiled: he'd confirmed her name. 'No, I mean it.' Now for the riskier part. 'At Isla Bright's funeral, I seem to recall.'

She put down the pencil and looked him in the eye. The intensity of those baby blues made him go weak at the knees. All of a sudden they filled with tears.

He bit his lip. He hadn't meant to be cruel, but as usual his hunch was right. 'My condolences,' he said gently.

'She was like a mother to me.' Black eyeliner was beginning to seep down her cheeks. She blotted it with a tissue then blew her nose. 'What's your name?'

By way of introduction, Seth gave her a business card.

A frown crossed her brow. Without another word, she turned on her heels and disappeared behind a screen.

Throughout a muffled exchange the tattoo gun continued to buzz.

Returning she said, 'Take a seat. Jet is expecting you.'

How could that be? His decision to come was on impulse. Or had Frank/Claude cottoned on and phoned ahead? If the conversation with Jet drew a blank, Antoinette could be a handy backup. But he'd have to be careful. Already she was wary of him.

Seth sank into a chair by the door. On the coffee table was a stack of glossy magazines. *Tattoo Weekly* was on top. He picked it up and absently leafed through picture after picture of tattoos, piercings and implants. One showed a person who'd transformed his face into a deer's: black nose, cleft lip, whiskers, horn buds and pointy ears. Overcoming a reaction of slight queasiness, he flipped to the centrefold.

Aussie artist aces Amsterdam was the headline. The double-page photo showed a tattoo of angel wings that swept down the model's back from shoulder blades to hips. Outlined in blue and vibrant with colour, the tattoo had an otherworldly quality that suggested a purpose more mysterious than decoration.

He rubbed his eyes.

It was her! Angel Tattoo of sleepy suburban Corella.

With a fingertip he traced the outline down the page. He skimmed the article about the creator of the masterpiece. The tattooist was cast as an enigma with no backstory. The article suggested that his talents included not only the artistic flair of da Vinci but also the gift of second sight.

The photo must have been taken immediately after the tattoo was finished. The model was draped elegantly across a bed with her back toward the camera.

'Oh my God!' he breathed. Only a few hours later, she was taken by the Angel of Death. Surely Jet would have known. Reports had been all over the news. Why hadn't he come forward and spoken to the police? And out of respect, why hadn't he withdrawn his entry from the tattoo competition?

A shadow fell across the page. Seth glanced up. Jet caught him reading the story.

'A courageous woman. The photo captures it, don't you think?' Jet said.

'Congratulations on your win.' Seth stood up and met the other man's eyes. They were the colour of a stormy sky.

'Those wings were meant for her. I've never done a set like them and I'll never do another.'

'Surely they're not all one-offs.'

'I never use a template, not even for the simplest pieces. Sometimes the differences are subtle. If you examine them, you'll see that each of my tattoos is unique.'

While they were talking, they'd somehow wandered into the studio. Seth sat in a recliner chair, while Jet perched on a stool.

'I knew you'd come here today. You want to ask about her, don't you?' said Jet.

'Who is she?'

'Haven't you already worked that out?'

'Maybe I have; maybe I need confirmation. As you know I'm a journalist, not a cop. If we do this off the record, only the two of us will ever know what was said. If you don't want to talk, tell me to leave and I will.'

'All well and good. I'm an artist and psychic healer and I happen to work with tattoos. There is a pact of confidentiality between me and my client that cannot be breached. In this case, as we both know, that pact is impossible to renegotiate.'

Inwardly Seth gave himself a pat on the back. He'd been confident that Angel Tattoo and the model in the magazine were one and the same. Now he was certain. 'Then can I ask some general questions about your work?'

'Fire away.'

In the next hour Seth learnt more about tattoos than he ever imagined.

Over a lifetime, Jet had studied various forms of the craft. In particular he was a devotee of Japanese styles which went back thousands of years. The ink was made in the traditional way, by hand-grinding Sumi sticks and mixing the powdered pigment with water. His speciality was full bodysuits, featuring tigers or phoenix combined with ancient symbols of power, strength or compassion. The decision to get a bodysuit was a big undertaking, Jet explained. Its execution was done in stages and it could take up to five years, not to mention the excruciating pain and the cost.

'Some people come to my shop wanting a fashion statement. I don't do that.'

'What *do* you do then?' said Seth.

'My hands see what is inside and so can heal the past. Every tattoo has a story.'

To demonstrate he rested his palms on Seth's arm. The warm tingling sensation was not unlike sunburn. Suddenly his body grew heavy with an oppressive fatigue. His muscles loosened, his mind drifted.

In the twilight zone between wakefulness and sleep, Seth heard a familiar voice talking about the horrors of military service in Vietnam. The unknown enemy, the innocents slaughtered, the constant threat of land mines, the whop-whop-whop of the choppers. And the rain. Torrential rain that hammered combat helmets and filled their boots with mud. Rain that soaked through their tents and seeped into their brains. Relentless, driving rain that drove trained soldiers mad.

Suddenly the ramblings stopped and Seth's arm went cold. He opened his eyes, found he was safe and dry in a fresh-smelling studio. He turned over his arm, half-expecting to find a tattoo. The spot where Jet's hands had been was pink but the skin was unblemished.

'What happened just now?'

'Your deepest memories were coming to the surface. If you'd have wanted, I could have inked them onto your skin. But I know you are not ready. I don't force myself on anyone, Mister VerBeek.'

'Tell me about Angel.'

Jet smiled patiently. 'As I said before, that is between her and me.'

23

Barbed wire cross

Five months ago: autumn

Claude Fabergé returned again and again to Jet Ink. Each time, he walked out with a new tattoo and a sense of calm and wellbeing. In three months since December he'd collected nine tattoos, all of which were associated with the traumas of his youth. Today's visit would tackle the crossroads: the make-or-break chapter of his former life as the victim of a fractured household.

In Jet's studio, he took off his shirt and lay on his back so that the abdominal scar was exposed. Already he knew that the physical pain would be excruciating. The abdomen was a sensitive place, but he expected the internal torment to be worse.

Each time he'd received treatment, his reactions had surprised him. Fears that had seemed insurmountable as a kid were trivial as an adult. Conversely, what had little impact on him as a boy now hit him with the force of a tsunami. Emotions, he concluded, were hard to predict.

Jet finished mixing the ink and silently placed his hands on the scar. All at once the gates opened and Claude's fury gushed out.

*

Not long before Frank's mother died, his old man shot through.

At the time, the gossip was that Mick Low had knocked up a barmaid from *The Swan*, a pub he frequented. At the age of six, Frank didn't know

131

what *knocked up* meant. When he found out later, he vowed to kill his father with his bare hands. In fact, he and Jake made a pact. If they ever saw the drunken bastard again, they'd let their cricket bat do the talking.

The day after their mother died, Frank and Jake were packed off to an orphanage controlled by nuns who detested little boys. How he hated that place! He and Jake were put into separate dorms, each of which held twenty bunks that were lined up on either side of a central corridor. The mattresses were lumpy and stank of pee. There was never enough to eat. After a meagre dinner, the boys would fight over wash-up duty so they could eat the scraps floating in the dishwater. By day they toiled in the vegetable garden or the woodworking shop to pay their keep. Schooling consisted of rote-learning prayers in Latin and counting the cuts of the cane. Most misdemeanours were punishable by a thrashing. It was not unusual to be beaten for simply being in the wrong place at the wrong time. If Frank would've had an opportunity to leave in exchange for forgiving his father, he would have grabbed it without hesitation.

Sadly, the old man never once showed his face.

The day Frank turned sixteen, he packed his meagre possessions: his Sunday shirt, a comb, toothbrush, and two pairs of underpants and escaped through a loose paling in the fence. His destination was the train station. From time to time he cast a glance over his shoulder, anxious that Father Doherty would come in the black Austin and take him back to the orphanage. It was only when he was safely on the train that he could breathe easy. The chug of the stream locomotive was as comforting as a mother's embrace. He had no ticket and no money but he could taste freedom.

A new life demanded a new name. On the train, he ran through all the film stars and famous people he could think of. He'd always liked *Claude*: it sounded aristocratic and French. Yes, that would do nicely. But the surname was proving more difficult.

A passenger sitting opposite was reading *The Morning Post*. On the back page, and right before Frank's eyes, was a black-and-white photo of a fabulous jewelled egg. Alongside the pic was an article about some fusty antique shop. Neither the shop nor the egg caught his attention. It was the name: *Fabergé*.

Claude Fabergé sounded as smooth as caramel and epitomised the sort of man he wanted to be.

After getting off the train in the Valley, he walked up the hill to the Spring Hill boarding house where his brother was renting the attic. With each step he practiced his new name. By the time he reached the run-down boarding house, he could say it as if he'd been born a Fabergé.

To pay his board, he took a job as a grease monkey in a mechanical workshop. At night, he slept on the floor beside Jake's single bed. Young Claude had a hunch that their father lived nearby. From the window of the attic, he kept watch over the main thoroughfare. He had little idea of what his father would look like these days. The last time he'd laid eyes on him was ten years earlier, the day he walked out on them all.

Throughout the winter he went to the rugby league matches at Lang Park, where he'd scan the stands for a forty-eight-year-old drunk called Mick Low. Often he'd miss the on-field action in his quest for retribution.

When it came to his father, the word *forgiveness* was banished from his vocabulary. For two-thirds of his lifetime, he'd been imprisoned in a reform school for innocents where he'd been brutally stripped of his childhood.

Then one evening Claude saw him—at least he thought it was him—coming out of the Wallaby Hotel. The old man was bandy with booze, wobbling all over the footpath. He stumbled up against a hedge that bordered the railway tracks and opened his fly.

Claude had just finished work. Grimy with sump oil, he doubted anyone would recognise him. Slowly he sauntered by, trying to get a squiz at the man's face.

It was a mighty long pee. Long enough for him to spot the familiar sailor's tattoo on the age-speckled forearm. Although the man's face was in shadow and the hairline had retreated across his pate, there was no doubt that this was Mick Low.

Claude swallowed his disgust and walked on. Although he wasn't yet fully a man, he didn't have it in him to bash a defenceless drunk. Instead he'd watch the fellow, observe what he did and where he went. Then, when the time was right, he'd kill the bastard.

On his way home, Claude couldn't decide whether to tell Jake. If his brother was angry about what the old man had done, he rarely showed it.

Later in their attic, Jake told him the news. His number had come up in the lottery for National Service. Soon he'd be off to Puckapunyal for twelve weeks' military training and then on to Vietnam to fight a war.

That night, for the first time in years, Claude cried himself to sleep.

Claude never told Jake about his encounter with the drunk. After Jake left, he stayed on in the attic. The winos, crazies and dropouts who lived in the cockroach-infested rooms below became his friends and confidantes.

Late one night, in a fit of self-pity, he told Wally the Yugoslav the story of his father, his mother, and the orphanage. Alone in the decrepit kitchen, they were sharing a tall bottle of lager. Although Claude was not yet the legal drinking age of twenty-one, he had plenty of willing suppliers.

It felt good to talk to someone who knew what it was to be an outcast. The beer fired his bravado, and before long he'd built up a head of steam that drove words into action.

Wally took a flick-knife from his sock. 'You go, you take knife.' He pressed the weapon into Claude's hand.

Claude knew where his father would be. Wally said he'd stay close and back him up if needed. His English wasn't great but Claude thought he'd understood perfectly.

In the pale light of the full moon, the pair walked west along the Terrace. They crossed the bridge over the railway lines and stopped outside the Wallaby pub. It was close on ten o'clock closing time. Inside, the bar-flies would be swilling last drinks.

On the footpath Claude positioned himself in the deep shadows of a spreading fig tree. The publican stood at the door, ushering out the stragglers.

Mick Low was last to leave.

Claude's heart was pounding so fast he could barely breathe. The flick-knife was hard and reassuring inside his sock. Swallowing his fear, he stepped into the moonlight, blocking his father's path.

'Remember me?' said Claude in the most menacing tone he could muster.

Mick stared at him without comprehension. He stank of rum and sweat.

'Waddaya want?' he slurred.

Claude spat at his feet. 'To make you suffer as I have.'

'Who *are* you?' The old man's hand shifted to his belt. Moonlight flashed on a metal blade.

'You filthy scumbag! Don't recognise your own flesh and blood!'

'Jake?' he said uncertainly.

'Wrong! I'm the other son you abandoned.'

Mick lowered his eyes. 'Times were tough.'

'Too right they were, especially after what you did to Mum. If you'd killed her with your bare hands, it would have been kinder. What she had to do was criminal. Criminal! Now it's your turn to pay.'

Claude thrust his weight against him.

Mick took the first punch without retaliating. He stumbled backwards into the fence that bounded the embankment. Then he began to push back. Their horns were locked: the young buck against the old. Mick's wiry build belied his strength. In a swift move, he spun Claude around and slammed him hard against the fence.

Winded, Claude doubled over. In his sock was the flick-knife. He took the chance and grabbed it. But before he could get a hold, there was a sharp pain low down in his belly. The next second he hit the ground. Someone was running. He shouted to Wally.

The night closed in.

When he came to, he was lying on his back on the moist grass. Above were a million fireflies; the full moon was hovering in the west. His body was shivering out of control. He had no idea of where he was or how long he'd been there.

He tried to roll over. Pain ripped through his guts.

Gingerly he touched a spot down low on his abdomen. His hands were reeking of blood. Blood was everywhere; he was wallowing in it.

As he lost consciousness, one terrible thought entered his mind.

Mick Low—his own father—had left him there to die.

*

In Jet's tattoo studio the reverie came to an abrupt end. Claude said, 'I don't know what happened to my old man. And I don't care.'

'Do you mean that?' said Jet.

'I'll never forgive him for what he did to Mum and Jake and me. But, thanks to you, I've lost the urge to smash his fuckin' face in. With any luck, he's already dead.'

'That's an improvement.'

'What do you mean?'

'The needle snapped while I was doing the tattoo. Sometimes it happens. An avalanche of strong emotion can do amazing things.'

Claude looked down at the scar on his abdomen. Now in its place was a blue tattoo: a barbed-wire cross and a banner held by two little doves. The image was so apt that it took his breath away. He began to weep. Great soul-wrenching sobs of remorse. And yes, a touch of forgiveness.

Tears cascaded down his cheeks onto his chest, onto the chair. The tattoo was as sore as the lick of a whip, but the ache in his heart was gone.

24

Pieces of the puzzle

Saturday 22 August

The best day of Seth's week was Saturday. Saturday was an excuse for a long lie in bed, followed by coffee and croissants at the farmers markets at New Farm. There he'd buy bread, meat, and vegetables for the week, and maybe a treat or two. Later he'd stretch out under the jacarandas and read the weekend papers. If he fell asleep, it didn't matter. If he had more coffee than he should, it didn't matter. Saturday night he'd go out to dinner, maybe with a woman, maybe not. If he was feeling lazy he'd get take-away and wash it down with a bottle of red in front of the tele.

Yep, Saturdays were special.

Except this Saturday he was in the midst of an investigation that wasn't coming together. Since six in the morning, he'd been hunched over his laptop in his sunless living room. The oil heater was humming and he'd wrapped himself in a blanket to keep warm.

Outside, a wild wind howled. With each gust, snapped-off branches thrashed the window panes. He needed to make a start on the feature article. His editor was hounding him. It was due by the end of the week. The only thing he was pleased with so far was the working title: *the mystery of the scarlet key.* If he ever found time to write a novel, he'd use it for sure.

So far he'd organised the information into chronological order. The result was inconclusive, more of a grab-bag of random events and unanswered questions than a proper analysis.

Out aloud, he read the list.

Elderly male brings envelope containing red key and address.
Key opens back door of 53 Mayfield Avenue, Corella.
Unknown female—tattoos, pink hair—is dead in the bathroom.
House owner—Isla Jean Bright, retired teacher—is also deceased.
Key courier brings a second tip-off about Isla Bright's funeral.
Madeline Hilton-Byrne—best friend—swears Isla has no tattoos.
Antoinette—one-time foster child of Isla Bright—works at Jet Ink.
Who is Claude Fabergé/Frank Low really?
What else does Jet know?

It had more holes than a sea sponge. Critical to it all was the identity of the elderly male who was the bearer of the key. Who could help him find out?

The first answer that sprang to mind was Cate Bradshaw. News-hungry and energetic, she had the one quality he didn't: female intuition. These past few months she'd been lying low, working on a big-time investigation. To him, a case of disappearing cats didn't sound like a big deal at all. Cats strayed all the time. Independent and fickle, they'd hang around anyone who offered a meal and a warm bed. Yet Cate seemed determined to complete the assignment and had told him only yesterday that she might have a breakthrough at last.

In addition, she was the only one who'd actually seen the key courier. Could she identify him? At present, he had three likely suspects: Jet, Claude, and Frank.

Despite Jet's recent win in the Amsterdam tattoo contest, there was not an image of him to be found. As for Claude Fabergé, it was doubtful that it was a real name for he appeared on neither the internet nor the electoral roll. All Seth had on Frank was a picture of his rusty fridge. He also had a strong suspicion that Claude and Frank were the same person anyway.

There was another explanation: the key courier was somebody else entirely. Perhaps he was a relative, or a friend, or a psychopath who stole Isla Bright's house key. In a city of two million people, that left a lot of leg-work to do.

The other thing that bugged him was Cate's odd reaction to the address. She knew Mayfield Avenue. Why did she want to keep it quiet? Had Isla Bright, much-loved teacher who'd taught half the suburb, been harbouring a sordid little secret?

Seth checked the time. Seven a.m. was too early to call Cate on her day off.

He shut down the laptop and stretched his spine. Breakfast. Saturday was a celebration, which called for a feast. Bacon, eggs, tomatoes, mushrooms, toast. He wasn't much of a chef, but he had to admit the aroma was divine.

While he worked, he turned on the TV for the news. Another terrorist attack. Another village reduced to rubble. Another wasteland of human tragedy.

He muted the volume and brought the steaming plate to the table. For once he was impressed with his culinary skills. The entire meal looked appetizing; not a skerrick of burnt stuff amongst it.

When he looked up again at the TV, it was showing footage of greyhounds on a training track. In the background was a bank of wire cages with small creatures inside. Animal rights activists in yellow t-shirts raced in and bombarded the trainer with abuse. The picture juddered as the cameraman ran towards the lure. Attached to it was a bloodied bundle of fur. Suddenly it moved; the poor thing was still alive.

Seth turned up the volume.

'Police are questioning a man and a woman in relation to the alleged use of live cats to train greyhounds.'

Before he'd finished the mouthful, Cate's number was flashing on his phone. He hit the answer button.

'I was just going to call you,' he said.

'Have you seen the news?' She sounded deflated. 'They've beaten me to it.'

'The cat story?'

'Got it in one. I'd been watching that trainer for months. I *knew* something was going on. There's more to it than unscrupulous training techniques but they've probably beaten me to *that* as well.'

'Give it a few days and it'll blow over. Anything planned for today?'

'No.'

'I need your help, Cate. Can I tempt you with a nice lunch afterwards?'

'You'll have to do better than McDonalds.'

'Name your price.'

Without hesitation she said. '*Le Poisson*, that new seafood restaurant by the river. It's been getting rave reviews.'

He whistled. 'You don't come cheap.'

'In case you hadn't noticed, it's Saturday. Penalty rates apply.' She laughed.

'Okay. Meet you at the office in an hour.'

At Newspaper House, Seth updated her about the Angel Tattoo story, including his hunt for the elusive Claude and his extraordinary visit to Jet Ink. He avoided mentioning Maddie. Some things were best left unsaid.

He pressed her for a description of the elderly man who'd delivered the scarlet key.

Cate said, 'I didn't get a good look at his face. Honest, the whole encounter was over in a flash.'

'What about the second time?'

'He left the envelope with a security guard.'

'Is there anything at all you remember?'

'Sorry boss, I've got nothing.'

Seth pushed back the chair, folded his arms and sighed. If she wasn't going to co-operate by prompting, he'd bloody-well ask straight out.

'What aren't you telling me, Cate?'

The epitome of guilt, she chewed her lip and studied her fingernails.

'You knew Isla Bright, didn't you?' he persisted.

'A lot of people knew her.'

'C'mon Cate, I didn't come down in the last shower.'

'Okay, okay. I interviewed her once when her cat went missing. It turned up alive, by the way.'

'Well, that's a mighty relief!' His sarcasm was hard to conceal. 'Grey, was it?'

'How did you know?'

He tapped his nose. 'Elementary, my dear Cate. Go on.'

'Isla told me she'd seen a man dump a suspicious-looking sack in the creek. We went down there together and pulled it out. It was totally disgusting: full of animal carcasses. Later, the police came and took it for testing. I've asked and asked but they won't tell me the results.'

'I've got a few contacts. Do you want me to try?'

'Yeah, thanks.'

'Anything more?'

'Isla said the man's ute was kingfisher blue with lots of chrome.'

'Did he see her?'

Cate shrugged.

'Motive for murder, do you think?' On his phone Seth located the photo of the blue ute with the numberplate SH1RL, taken outside Frank's house.

She studied it closely. 'That could be it.'

'A few years ago I investigated dubious practices in the greyhound industry. I wonder if there's any connection,' he said.

Cate said, 'I've been keeping an eye on a trainer called Lola Molloy. She has a nice setup at Greenfield but sometimes appearances are misleading. I have pictures of all the cats that were reported missing. Four were held in cages at her property.'

'You broke in?'

'No, binoculars.'

Seth grinned. 'Your proficiency as a spy is impressive.'

'At least I didn't get caught. Until I spoke with Isla, I'd been working on the theory that the cat thefts were associated with a pet shop racket. She was a lovely lady and I was genuinely shocked when she died.'

Seth was packing up his papers. 'Sorry if I was a bit belligerent.'

'That's okay, boss. I should have told you.'

'You hungry?'

'Not yet.'

'Fancy a drive to Greenfield before lunch?'

'Sure. Let's do it. We could get two stories for the price of one.'

25

A birthday gift

Five months ago: autumn

The day Antoinette turned thirty-six, Isla planned to surprise her with her specialty: a chocolate mud cake. As a teenager, Antoinette practically lived on chocolate. Chocolate milk, chocolate spread, chocolate ice-cream, chocolate anything. No matter how much chocolate there was, she'd always come sniffing for more. Once, when Isla was at her wit's end trying to get her to eat vegetables, she'd coated the Brussels sprouts in chocolate. Straightaway the girl wolfed them down without realising what she'd eaten.

Nostalgia: mooning over rose-coloured memories.

Isla smiled. Amongst all the conflict and teenage angst, there had been days that were pure gold.

In the kitchen, Isla selected a medium-sized saucepan and lit the burners. Over a low heat she combined dark chocolate pieces, butter, milk, sugar and vanilla, stirring until it was smooth. She removed the pan and waited until it had cooled before adding an egg, flour and cocoa. The joy of baking was mixed with sadness that this cake could well be her last.

The oven had reached the right temperature. After pouring the cake batter into the tin, she lifted the spoon to her lips. The smell of the chocolate made her stomach do a backflip. Dropping the spoon, she raced to the bathroom and was sick. It was the second time this week. Clutching a pain in her side, she phoned the doctor.

Late in the afternoon Dr Barnes came to the front door.

Isla was curled up on the couch, her stomach as tight and round as a basketball. 'Come in,' she called weakly.

The doctor did the usual poking and prodding, took her pulse and blood pressure, and looked down her throat. When he pressed on her belly, she yelped and had to race to the bathroom again.

Apologetic, she returned.

'Any other symptoms?' said Dr Barnes.

'Just female stuff … itchy skin, hot flushes.'

'How long have you been like this?'

'About three weeks. At first, I didn't think much of it.'

'I'll give you an injection to settle your stomach. Make an appointment to see me at the surgery next week. In the meantime, stay hydrated and get plenty of rest. No parties, no alcohol, no rich food.'

Isla forced a smile. 'I'll try to behave.'

The next day Isla felt slightly better, well enough to have Antoinette over for the birthday morning tea. As expected, she was delighted with the mud cake and cut herself a generous serve. Meanwhile, Isla nibbled on a dry cracker biscuit.

'You're the best cook in the universe.' Antoinette wiped her lips with a napkin. Today her hair was turquoise and red. 'Aren't you having some?'

Isla patted her distended abdomen. 'I need to watch my weight.' Behind her back she held an envelope.

'Thank you for remembering. Nobody else did.'

'Not even Amber?'

'Since she moved in with her boyfriend, she doesn't give me a second thought. Ungrateful toad.'

'Just like *her* mother.' Isla nodded sagely. 'At that age, you couldn't wait to lead your own life either.'

'You're right, as usual. Thank you for putting up with me.' Antoinette reached across the table and gave Isla's arm a squeeze.

Before tears began to fall, Isla took a deep breath and launched into her little speech. 'Today is not only to celebrate your birthday, but to tell you how much happiness you've given me. Our relationship hasn't always been easy, but I guess no parent-child relationship is. We don't share the same genes but, in my eyes, you are my daughter and I'm proud of you.'

Antoinette's eyes were glistening. 'That's so lovely!'

'I'm not finished yet.' Isla slid the envelope across the table. 'Happy birthday, Nettie. May you relish whatever life brings.'

Antoinette opened the flap, took out a pretty card with a hand-painted picture of a cat. Inside the card was a voucher for a return flight to Mexico and three thousand dollars in cash. 'Oh my God, Isla! Are you sure? I don't know what to say.'

'*Thank you* would be fine.'

Antoinette threw her arms around Isla's neck and kissed her cheeks. 'I've always wanted to go to Mexico. Frida Kahlo, the Aztecs, Mexico City. Pinch me. I can't believe it's actually going to happen.'

'Don't worry about taking time off work. I've already cleared it with Jet. This time next month you'll be having the time of your life.'

The younger woman's face was shining with delight.

Isla stood up and put on the kettle, thrilled with the success of her gift. Now was not the time to mention that it came with strings attached.

Although deviousness wasn't in her nature, on this occasion she had no other option. To carry out her plan, she required an accomplice.

For many reasons, Antoinette was the obvious choice.

26

Show and tell

Five months ago: autumn

'You got another one, didn't you?' In the kitchen, Isla poured Claude's tea.

He gave her a sheepish grin. Since his first visit to Jet, tattoos had become his obsession. The more he got, the better he felt. Whatever magic Jet had at his command, it was potent indeed. Even the nightmares that had plagued him since boyhood had morphed into tolerable dreams.

Before he discovered Jet Ink, Claude would relive the nightly horrors of creaking floorboards and squeaking leather shoes that paced the corridors. Fat hands would grasp his skinny body and drag him struggling to the boys' shower room. There he'd be pinned against the wall. Although he'd clench his teeth and force his mind go blank, nothing would lessen the brutality. The stench of old-man sweat. The alcohol breath, hot on his neck. The crucifix slapping his bare back. Usually the ordeal was over quickly. He'd count the number of thrusts and pray for the pig-grunt that signalled the end.

Now he slept as he should have slept as a boy: deep and sweet. Mornings, he woke refreshed instead of disgusted and sore.

Proudly he unbuttoned his shirtsleeve and showed Isla his latest tattoo: a red dragon wrapped around his forearm. 'It symbolises strength and good fortune. You should try it yourself.'

Her lips curled into a smile. 'What makes you think I haven't already?'

He laughed. 'You're not the type.'

'What's that supposed to mean?'

'You wouldn't *dare*.'

Whatever he'd said pushed the button to end the world. Her eyes popped out and her face turned a deep shade of puce.

'You don't know the first thing about me!' She slammed her fist on the table.

'Whoa! Isla, I meant nothing by it. Just sayin' you're a smart woman with class.'

'Tell me this: how did you first find Jet?'

Claude thought back to the day he'd stumbled across the tattoo studio. 'Actually, he found me. I was going to the oven spares shop to get you a burner. Jet started talking to me outside.'

'And *who* sent you on the errand to Goongulli?'

He stared at her in astonishment.

Before he could gather his wits, she'd unbuttoned her dress and let it slip to the floor. For the first time he saw her naked. To his shock, her upper arms, shoulders, and torso were wallpapered in tattoos.

Her bra was plain white cotton, no frills or lace. The sort boys used to call an *over-shoulder boulder-holder.* Reaching behind, she unclipped it. With a soft thud, it hit the floor upside down: a pair of bleached clams.

Beneath the padded bra, Isla was as flat as a man. Where her breasts should have been was a tattoo of blue lotus flowers and arabesques.

The show wasn't over. Slowly she turned. On her back was the outline of angel wings. Intricate and graceful, the tattoo extended across her shoulder blades and down the curve of her body to her buttocks. It was so fresh that the ink was barely dry.

'Every tattoo tells a story,' she said. 'These are mine.'

'I had no idea!'

She retrieved her clothing from the floor. 'We all have secrets we don't want to share. Bottled up inside, they kill us. I learnt that from Jet. Now at last, I've found peace.'

Claude's eyes misted with tears. He put his arms around her and drew her close. Returning the embrace, she moulded herself to his body and laid her head on his shoulder.

For several minutes they held each other like lovers. Venus came in and slinked around their legs, purring for attention, demanding to get in on the act.

'Tell me what they mean.' Claude lifted her chin and kissed her lightly on the lips.

In a matter-of-fact tone she said, 'I have cancer.'

He held her and their tears ran together.

'Years ago my breasts were removed and I went into remission. Now it's back.'

'When did you get the diagnosis?'

'I haven't ... yet.'

'Then how do you know for sure?'

'Jet can see it growing inside me, eating me away. He started the back piece last week. Two more sessions and the wings will be finished. And I will be too.' She kissed his cheeks. 'Will you help me, Claude?'

'Of course. What you want me to do?'

She took his hand and led him to the bedroom. The curtains were drawn against the morning light. On a desk in the corner, a laptop softly whirred. Venus, voyeur in a fur coat, followed them to the bed.

Isla removed her panties, exposing the full extent of her secret ink. It was hard to believe such a plain, straightforward person could have such an outrageous core. Although the reasons differed, her skin was the same as his: a canvas of pigment and pain.

He took his time and was gentle, for the wings on her back were still raw.

Afterwards, they lay in each other's arms. She sighed. 'It's been more than a decade since I did this. Most men think a woman with no breasts isn't a real woman. Does it bother you dreadfully?'

'Not a bit! You are *you*. That's all that matters.'

'Thank you. You mean the world to me.'

Not to be outdone, Venus walked up the doona and touched her moist nose to Claude's. *Urgh!* He sat up and pushed her away.

'No, Venus!' Isla shooed her off the bed.

Defiantly flicking her tail, the cat sprang onto the computer desk. The sudden movement woke the laptop. A blaze of brilliance lit the room. The screen was facing the bed; the content of the website was unavoidable.

Claude focussed his attention on the screen. It was tattoo central. There were tattoos of every type, style and colour. Tattoos were shown on every part of the body: the eyes, the toes, the penis, the soles of the feet.

'Amazing, isn't it?' Isla said. 'I thought I was alone but there's a world-wide community.' She rolled off the mattress, groaning a little from the effort. 'Look at this.'

She manoeuvred the mouse to the log-in box and entered a codename. Dozens of thumbnails appeared, set out like postage stamps in an album. All her 'friends' were tattooed. The locations where they lived ranged from Chicago to Edinburgh to Auckland.

'We're all artists. Because of the different time zones, we can chat any time of the day or night. I never feel alone.'

At last the veil of delusion fell from his eyes. The woman he'd regarded as a wonderful cook but an otherwise boring individual grew larger than life.

In the last two hours, his heart had been rent open. To lose her now would be too much to bear.

Later in the day, she cooked him spaghetti with pork ribs, tomato, oregano and red wine. While he wolfed down two large helpings, she picked around the edge of her plate. Halfway through the meal, she excused herself. Although she shut the bathroom door, he could hear her retching.

When she returned, she poured a glass of lemonade and sipped it slowly. Her robust figure was shrinking; her skin was too big for its frame. Her complexion had a tinge of sickly grey instead of the usual healthy pink.

As he rose to leave, she gave him a key. 'This is for the back door. I want you to keep it. Use it whenever you need to. I trust you completely.'

The sparkling key in the cup of his hand was the colour of blood. 'I'll take care of everything, Isla. I promise.'

With mixed emotions they embraced. Then he broke away and plodded slowly down the stairs.

27

Gone to the dogs

Saturday 22 August

Cate guided Seth through a maze of back streets onto Greenfield Road, an unsealed gash of red dust through the flat coastal scrubland. Spindly trees, starved for nourishment, struggled to reach full height. Sparse clumps of paspalum bristled from the stony ground. Ahead, a huge Moreton Bay fig tree towered above the plain. Sunlight glittered on silver rooftops.

'We're there.' Cate told him to park behind a stand of lantana where they'd get a good view of the Molloy property without giving their position away.

Seth took in the rows of kennels, the sheds and the training circuit. The outbuildings were freshly painted and in good condition. The house itself was a 1920s Queenslander, set low to the ground with a wide front verandah. A dirt track divided the residential side of the property from the business side. Something was faintly familiar about the place.

He whistled softly. 'Nice setup. How many dogs does she keep?'

'It varies. As many as eighty, or as few as twenty. As well as being a trainer, she's a registered breeder.'

'Where are the cat cages?'

Cate produced a pair of field glasses from her tote bag. She positioned them to her face and adjusted the focus. A moment later she groaned. 'They're gone! They *were* behind the kennels but they're not there anymore. Here, can you see them?'

Through the field glasses he made a full sweep of the property. The only cages he could see were the exercise runs for the dogs. 'Either they've

148

moved fast or the footage on the news was out-of-date. You never know with these activist groups. They aim to show everything at its worst.'

Cate said, 'Right, we need to get in and get answers. I'll ask her about the cat cages and live baiting.'

'I'll ask about the bloke with the ute.'

'And what happens to underperforming greyhounds,' Cate added.

'Okay. Let's do it.'

Simultaneously they opened the Jeep doors then walked along the fence, thick with prickly lantana, to a chain-wire farm gate. A sign on it warned *beware savage dogs*.

'I'll go in first.' said Seth. 'Wait here.'

After checking for marauding canines, he unlatched the gate and went in. Despite the bravado—mainly for Cate's benefit—he was shitting himself. In small doses dogs were nice, in particular the lap-sitting variety and certainly nothing larger than a poodle.

The distance from the gate to the house was further than anticipated. With every step he prayed that the *savage dogs* sign was an empty threat to scare off door-to-door salesmen. In this part of Greenfield, miles from neighbours, a scream or a shout for help would go unheard. One wrong foot and he could end up a dog's dinner.

Finally he climbed three steps to the verandah. The door was shut; the melodramatic sounds of a TV soapie filtered through the chamfer boards.

He knocked.

Inside, paws scuttled on the floorboards. A couple of barks and a growl. Despite the chill of the day, he was sweating. Should he cut his losses and run?

A female voice commanded, 'Sit!'

The door cracked open. The woman would have been in her sixties. Overweight and grey-haired, she wore faded track pants, sheepskin boots, a brown pullover and no bra.

'What do you want?'

Seth introduced himself and said he was looking for the owner of a blue ute with the numberplate SH1RL. 'I believe you may know him.'

'Haven't we met before?' She scrutinised him from head to toe. 'Yes, of course! A couple of years back you wrote about my two beauties.' Beneath the pullover her breasts were moving like two oversized papaws in a sack.

For a moment Seth didn't know what to say. His mind was whirling through hundreds of old interviews for the bones of their previous encounter. Then it occurred to him that she was referring not to her anatomy but her animals. Mentally he smacked the heel of his hand to his forehead. 'Ah yes, the greyhounds!'

'Here they are.' The door yawned open. Two ageing dogs sat patiently on the mat. 'Bessie and Freeman are twelve now and still beautiful, don't you think?'

'Sorry I didn't recognise you, Mrs Molloy.'

She inclined her head and smiled. Her ruddy face became younger and a spark of wickedness lit her eyes. 'Call me Lola.'

'Pleased to see you again, Lola. The dogs are looking well. Actually I'm on an assignment about the tattoo industry. Claude Fabergé may have some important information.'

'Claude's here every Wednesday. That'd be the best day to get him.'

'So he works for you?'

'He does odd jobs. Lovely bloke. All heart. He's not in trouble, is he?'

'No, not at all. Out of curiosity, does he have any tattoos?'

'Yeah, heaps. Got the first one a year ago and now it's turned into a friggin' collection. Why anyone gets tattooed is a mystery to me. Bloody awful things.'

'He has a friend called Frank. Do you know him?'

Lola began to chuckle. 'You don't know Claude very well. Claude Fabergé isn't a real name. Good heavens no! *And* he's not really French. That's a trick to get the ladies.'

'He *is* Frank, am I right?'

'You got it. Frank Low. Bang, bang. Like two sharp punches. Nothing exotic about *that* name. Hey, you want a cup of tea? I'll put the kettle on.' Lola peered beyond him, to where Cate was leaning on the gate. 'Oh, I see you've brought your lady friend. Ask her in. The more the merrier.'

Seth was about to say she was a colleague, then thought better of it. In the past, working as a couple had helped them uncover surprising material. Informants were more relaxed when Cate was there; she took the hard edge off a conversation.

At the gate he quickly sketched out the situation. 'You're my girlfriend, okay?'

'Sure, why not.'

While it was probably bending the rules, he had no qualms about the little charade in the interests of getting the story. Lola already knew he was a newspaper reporter and that, in his opinion, was sufficient.

As it turned out, Lola loved company and a good chat. Instantly she settled into a comfortable banter that centred on her beauties. In a scrapbook she'd kept a clipping of Seth's previous article about greyhound racing as well as write-ups about all her wins at the track. As he flipped through the pages, Bessie sidled up to him and dropped her head in his lap. He fondled her silky ears while he listened to her owner talk about the business of breeding and training greyhounds.

'When my dogs are no longer competitive, I find them new homes. Greyhounds make wonderful pets. As you can see, they're as gentle as lambs.'

The cat cages, Lola explained, had been an experiment in holiday boarding to boost her income. The venture proved to be a dismal failure, mainly because all that yowling at night upset the dogs. Months ago, she dismantled the business and sold the cages. According to her, the news report about live baiting was *complete and utter bullshit*, and probably a scheme by a rival trainer to ruin her reputation.

'There's no chance I'd treat an animal that way,' she said.

Seth was inclined to believe her.

Two hours later, Seth and Cate had most of their answers. Lola insisted on giving them a guided tour of the facilities, probably to prove a point. Last stop was the isolation room where sick dogs were housed.

That was where Cate casually baited the trap. 'Do you ever put dogs to sleep?'

'Sadly, yes. In this game, serious injuries happen all the time. Wayne, my vet, isn't always available, so I keep a supply of drugs on hand.' She unlocked a steel cabinet. Inside was an array of bottles, jars, and tubes.

Lola continued. 'Before I started this business, I was a veterinary nurse. Actually I used to work for Wayne. If an injury is beyond treatment, I give the dog a shot of this.' She showed them a phial of clear liquid, marked with a long chemical name. 'I can't stand to see animals suffer.'

'Do you dispose of the bodies here on the property?' Cate looked as wide-eyed and innocent as a child.

'No, no, no. That'd bring bad luck. They go to a pet crematorium.'

'Would Claude take them there?' said Seth.

'Yeah. He does anything I ask.'

The trio fell into an uncomfortable silence, as if paying respects to dearly departed greyhounds. At length, Seth said they had to go and thanked Lola for her hospitality.

In the Jeep he said, 'What do you reckon?'

'Plausible explanations but I *know* there's something more. The drug in the phial was pentobarbital. You have to be a vet to administer it, which she isn't. Small misdemeanour I know, but there's not much else to work with.'

'How much would a dog cremation cost?' said Seth.

Cate consulted her phone. 'Holy moly! We're looking at upward of two hundred dollars per animal. The sack we pulled out of the creek held three carcases. That's six hundred dollars. I'll bet that went straight into Frank Low's pocket. Not bad for an hour's work. My boss is a mastermind!'

'All in a day's work, my dear Cate.'

'What should we do now?'

An impish grin crept over his face as he reached for the scarlet key.

28

The Secrets of Mayfield Avenue

Saturday 22 August

At Mayfield Avenue the police crime-scene tape had been removed. Isla Bright's house looked decidedly abandoned. Yellow dandelions sprouted from the unmown lawn; the perennials along the fence were either wilted or dead. Being a winter Saturday, the playing fields swarmed with girls wielding hockey sticks. Parked cars lined the street. Seth finally found a spot more than two blocks away.

It was going on three o'clock and they hadn't had time for the promised restaurant lunch. He'd suggested going to the *Best Bloody Burgers* store but they were both keen for the leg-work to be done and to have the rest of the day off.

Feeling a little light-headed from lack of food, Seth went ahead to open up.

Close behind him, Cate said, 'I wonder what happened to Venus.'

'Who?'

'Isla's cat. The one I rescued from the drain.'

'The grey moggy.'

'*Latvian Grey*, if you don't mind.' She grinned. 'That's what her snooty friend said when she gave me the tip-off. I know now it was a lie.'

The scarlet key slotted easily into the lock. As he pushed on the door, memories of that first time came flooding back. The ominous wind-chimes, the odour of death. Now the house was fragrant with eucalyptus.

'You check the bedrooms. I'll do the rest,' he told Cate.

153

Confidently she strode down the hall. He reminded himself that she too had been there before. If only they'd worked together the day he got the key. By now they'd have the puzzle solved. Instead, they'd been picking away at two separate stories that now seemed interlinked.

The bathroom—the former crime scene—reeked of eucalyptus disinfectant. All traces of Angel Tattoo had been thoroughly scrubbed off. The black-and-white tiles around the washbasin sparkled. Even the grout was perfectly clean. The only indication of what he'd discovered was a dusting of fingerprint powder on the tub.

He stared at the spot where she'd been. In his mind she was still there, partly covered by the doona, the wings folded across her back. The image was so strong that he reached out a hand to touch her.

'Hey boss!' Cate's voice crackled with excitement.

'Just a sec.' He glanced up. The spell was broken. When he looked down again, the ghost on the tiles was gone.

'Calling Mister VerBeek,' Cate sang.

Cheeky cow.

In the main bedroom, he found Cate sitting on the floor with a photo album open on her lap. She turned it around and held it up for him to see. The page was covered in holiday snaps taken at the beach. *Mooloolaba, Christmas* read the caption. It showed a younger, slimmer Isla and a girl of about fifteen.

'Antoinette?' Cate said.

Seth took the album and examined the photos through a magnifier from his wallet. The girl in the picture was attractive and slender. Her long blond hair was parted down the centre. Judging from the skunk stripe, her natural colour was dark brown. The way she draped her body across the beach towel was downright seductive. No-one could have called her a classic beauty: her forehead was too wide, her mouth too large, her eyes too far apart. But the combination was simply stunning.

Now, her hair was blue or pink or green—depending on the whim of the day—and her skin was even more colourful. There was no doubt in his mind that this was the Antoinette who worked at *Jet Ink*.

Cate retrieved the album and scanned the photos into her phone.

Seth left her in the bedroom to rummage through the other closets and chests. In the sleep-out he found bookshelves heavy with magazines and art materials. Beneath the casement windows was a two-drawer filing cabinet. He tugged on the top drawer and with a clunk it trundled open.

Starting at the front, he flicked through scores of manila folders tucked into suspension hangers. Isla Bright must have harboured a secret ambition to be an accountant. All her paperwork was labelled and notated and filed in order. It bore no resemblance to his shoe-box stuffed with random receipts that he sorted out at tax time.

At the back of the drawer were the bank statements, clipped together in date order. Accounts were held at three different banks. The first showed ninety-two dollars credit. The second—a term deposit—was fifty thousand.

The third had him rubbing his eyes in disbelief.

The account had been opened on the twentieth of March, six years ago. The opening balance was two million dollars. Round figures, no notation, no explanation. Where in the world would a school teacher get that sort of cash?

He flipped through the statements. The only transactions were the monthly interest deposits and weekly withdrawals of one thousand dollars. Page after page was the same. On through the years they went, from that first extraordinary lump sum to the last statement, dated one month ago.

Seth's fingers raced through the rest of the files. Surely she would have kept something that told of a two million dollar windfall.

Was it an inheritance? A lottery win? A property sale?

Half an hour later he'd gone through every folder in the cabinet and was none the wiser. His back ached and his stomach was about to devour itself. As he was packing up, Cate came in carrying a large grey envelope.

'Look at this!' There was a catch in her voice.

'I've found something too,' he said.

'You go first.'

He told her about the money but she scarcely raised an eyebrow.

When he was done, she opened the envelope and tipped the contents onto the floor. There were CT scans, ultrasounds, x-rays, medical photographs.

'All the evidence is here,' said Cate. 'She was dying.'

He picked up a report. It was all statistics, percentages and terms he didn't understand. It might as well have been written in Swahili for the sense it made.

He held up an x-ray to the light that streamed in through the sleep-out windows. He could identify a pelvis and a couple of ribs. Apart from that he had no idea what he was looking at. Medical things always gave him a headache.

'According to this, the cancer was misdiagnosed as a benign cyst. Several years later she had a double mastectomy and then refused chemo.' Cate slammed her fist on the pile of documents. 'She didn't give herself a chance! Breast cancer doesn't have to be a death sentence.'

'Breast cancer,' Seth echoed.

'She didn't die of breast cancer.' Cate handed him a letter, dated two months ago. 'It says that the cancer had metastasised into the liver. *That* was the death knell.'

'How do you know all this medical stuff?'

She shrugged. 'It interests me. My first degree is in bioscience.'

He couldn't quite picture the spectacular Cate in a white lab coat and horn-rimmed glasses, hunched over a microscope. Nevertheless, his admiration of her abilities escalated from awesome to superhero.

In silence, they sat on the floor surrounded by a patchwork of reports, transparencies, and colour glamour shots of various internal organs.

After short while Seth said, 'That doesn't explain everything. The autopsy showed an illicit substance in Isla Bright's body. And then there's the matter of two million dollars in the bank and a generous living allowance. How did she get the money and what did she spend it on? From all appearances she lived a frugal life.'

'Painkillers perhaps?' Cate stretched and moved to the window that overlooked the street. 'Not all medication is covered by health insurance.'

'But a thousand dollars a week?'

'Perhaps her drug of choice wasn't legal,' suggested Cate.

'Or she could have been a gambler.'

'Or she was supporting a relative or lover.'

Seth's imagination began to wander. How would *he* blow a cool grand every week? The possibilities were endless. If only …

'Do you reckon there's any connection to Jet?' said Cate.

She could be onto something. It was bizarre that a conservative middle-aged woman would get all those tattoos, yet take such pains to conceal them. Not to mention the cost. Would that account for a thousand dollars per week? If Jet really did have psychic powers, he'd have known about her failing health … and her treasure chest. Was his studio a front for drug dealing or some other sinister operation?

Seth returned his attention to the files. There had to be a clue somewhere.

Cate was at the window. 'Shhhh!' She lifted a blade of the venetian blind. 'I think we're being watched.' Ducking into the shadows, she let the blind chink into place. 'Cop car, ten o'clock. Thank God we're not parked right outside.'

'Listen, I'm already up to my neck in this. You go. Cut across the park. Take the track to the Reedy Creek bridge. I'll pick you up if I can get away. Otherwise head home.' He shepherded her into the hall.

Carrying her shoes, she scampered to the kitchen. A moment later he heard the backdoor latch click closed.

Working fast, Seth stuffed the files into the cabinet. The medical records went back into the grey envelope, which he hid behind the curtain. He was scratching to invent a plausible excuse for being in a dead woman's house.

In a flash of brilliance it came. Through the window he saw two cops—one male and one female—at the gate. He hurtled down the back stairs and nicked under the house. His plan was only half-formed; he had to think fast.

Near the laundry was a metal garden shed. He jiggled the handle; the door swung open. He grabbed a spanner and the lawnmower and tipped it on its side.

Squatting, he began to remove the cutting blades. One of the bolts had come loose when he glimpsed two blue-uniformed forms flickering between the battens.

'Hey you! What are you doing there?' said the male cop.

'Trying to fix this heap-of-shit mower.'

The cop sauntered to the doorway at the foot of the stairs. On his belt was a Taser; his hand hovered ready. 'This house is vacant and the owner is deceased. Who are you?'

'Jack Jones, the gardener. She paid me three months in advance.' It sounded reasonable.

'Is that so?' The cop wore a poker face. 'To be sure, I'll keep you company while my colleague looks around.'

Seth stood up, way too fast for his empty stomach. The house was spinning. He shut his eyes and caught the side of the shed for balance.

'You're in pretty bad shape for a gardener,' commented the cop.

Meanwhile the policewoman had climbed the stairs. She turned the knob of the ripple-glass door. With a long ominous squeak it swung open. 'Don't let him go, Rick.'

Sweat trickled down Seth's spine. In his haste to get out, he'd forgotten to snib the lock. Now he was doomed. A conviction of break and enter or trespassing wouldn't look good on his CV. For the sake of his job, he'd always pushed the boundaries, and until now he'd never been caught. He kicked himself for becoming sloppy in his old age. At least he'd saved Cate's hide.

Seth wiped his palms on his pants and turned to face his captor.

The cop was about four inches taller and about thirty years younger than him. His eyes were as unforgiving as a bullet. He looked the epitome of an officer with a strong sense of duty and a promising career ahead.

There was no chance Seth could sweet-talk his way out of this one.

'Okay mate, now tell me the *true* story.'

29

What they do with dogs

Two months ago: early winter

Wednesday was Lola's.

Always had been, ever since Claude left his boring office job for a racy new profession he invented. On the long drive to Greenfield, he surfed the radio stations for the news about the government inquiry into the dog racing industry. Somewhere between the football commentary and a toilet paper ad, he caught the word *greyhound*.

The commission had finally released its report. The two main issues they addressed were live baiting and the treatment of non-performing dogs. Neither was new to Claude, however this time the government's response would be both swift and catastrophic. That morning at a press conference, the Premier had vowed to shut down the entire industry by year's end.

In disbelief, Claude pulled over to the side of the road.

Poor Lola! This would break her. The dogs were her life; her financial survival depended on breeding and training them. Hundreds of thousands of dollars had been sunk into the business, not to mention her blood, sweat and tears. Selling the purpose-built property in the current market would be practically impossible.

He lit a smoke.

The radio news turned to happenings overseas: another vessel of refugees in the Mediterranean, another suicide bomb in France, thousands left homeless after an earthquake in China.

While reports of other people's miseries droned on, Claude's pondered his own predicament. This personal handyman gig was grinding to a halt.

First he'd lost Maddie. Since returning from Dubai, she'd only called him once to bust up a fight between her two lovers.

Then Rita had sent him a text from Thailand to cancel his services. She'd decided to stay on for at least a year, maybe longer.

And then there was Isla. Who knew how long she'd survive. From the sound of things, her days were numbered. The thought of losing her brought tears to his eyes. Of all his women, she'd become the favourite.

A few days ago, she'd told him of her plan. *The Dutch solution*, she'd called it. *Except I'm not going to Europe.*

She'd also told him of her gift to Antoinette, whose return flight from Mexico was due early this morning. Isla was driving to the International Airport to pick her up. If all went to schedule, they'd be on their way home by now.

He hoped that Antoinette had done her bit. Part of him was worried. Reality shows such as *Border Patrol* showed people being caught and interrogated at airports for bringing in contraband. Steep penalties applied for smuggling drugs, produce, or animals into Australia. The sleeping pills that Isla had asked for sounded safe enough. But when it came to customs officers and sniffer dogs, nothing was certain.

It was getting late. Lola would be worried. Had she caught the morning news about the end of her lifestyle career? He lit another smoke, nudged the gearstick into first, rolled the ute onto the bitumen and tramped on the gas.

Beyond the outer band of sleek new townhouses, the road to Greenfield dived into sparse scrubland. Claude's phone began to buzz. He took the call.

It was Isla and it was clear that she was upset. 'She didn't get it.'

'Where are you?'

'At home. I need to talk to someone. Do you mind?'

'Not at all, my angel. Tell me what happened.' His eyeballs hurt.

'Mexico's cracked down on prescriptions for foreigners. Supply has gone underground. They're asking black market prices and there's no guarantee the drugs are genuine. Antoinette didn't want to take the risk so she came back empty-handed.'

'Oh, Isla! I'm sorry.'

'There's no denying I'm disappointed. But there is a Plan B.' Her voice brightened.

'Which is …?'

'Where you come in.' Isla went on to explain.

Without hesitation, Claude agreed.

At her property in Greenfield, Lola was pacing the verandah and biting her nails. As soon as the ute came up the drive, she waddled down to meet him.

Through the driver's open window, she threw her arms around his neck. 'Thank God you're here, Claude.'

He gave her a kiss and asked what was wrong, expecting a tirade about the Premier's sudden announcement.

'It's Lightning Flash again. She has a tumour. Wayne gave her painkillers and took a biopsy but the outlook is grim.'

'Poor pet. When do you get the results?'

'This afternoon. Even if it's operable, I doubt she'll ever race again.'

He stroked her arm. 'Can I see her?'

'She's in sick bay. I was about to go up and check on her.' She patted his hand and gave it a little squeeze. 'You're a good man, Claude. Don't let anyone say otherwise.'

Hand in hand they walked towards the night kennels. After an unusually dry spell, the grass was like straw and the air was thick with dust. Claude sneezed. Once, twice. His nose was itching, his eyes were streaming. He washed his face under the garden tap.

When Lola opened the gate to the exercise yard, the other greyhounds ran up. Their tongues lolled out and their faces were lit with expressions of joy.

'Later, doggies,' she said. 'Go! Chase!' She clapped and they raced along the fence to the far end of their runs.

In sick bay, Lightning Flash whimpered and twitched in her sleep. Behind her left ear was a nasty-looking lump the size of a golf ball.

Lola opened the metal cabinet on the wall and sorted through the various containers until she found a syringe and a phial of clear liquid.

'What are you giving her?'

'Painkillers.'

She took out another plastic phial and showed it to Claude. It was marked *POISON: Veterinary Use Only*. 'If the diagnosis is what we expect, this one will see her out. I'd rather do it here at home than take her all the way to Wayne's surgery.'

She prepared the painkillers and opened the dog's cage. Lightning lifted an eyelid and gave Lola's hand a lick. She kissed the dog on the nose then turned her attention to administering the injection.

Claude, who had a weak stomach for needles, hung back. He was standing against the wall beside the medications safe.

Lola stroked Lightning's ears until she settled. 'When it's done, will you take her?'

'The usual?'

'Yes. I'll give you some cash before you go.'

Lola packed up the drugs and relocked the cabinet.

With a leaden heart, Claude went about his chores, cleaning the kennels and grooming the dogs. All the while he was pondering the difference between animals and people at the end of their lives. Animal suffering was not tolerated. The humane thing for incurably sick animals was to put them to sleep. Yet human life was considered so precious that people were kept on life support when there was no hope of survival. Even when minute-to-minute existence was torture and the patient pleaded to go, all that the law allowed was to disconnect the machines and pray for a quick, merciful end.

The final chores on Claude's job list were to whipper-snip the weeds and trim the hedge. After giving Lola a goodbye hug, he climbed into the ute.

Tomorrow, he expected, she'd call and ask him to take Lightning away.

Tomorrow, he'd do what he was paid to do.

Now there were more pressing matters. As he turned left onto the highway, he touched the small plastic container in his jeans pocket. Although it was wrong to steal, especially from a client, he thought Lola would understand.

He stepped on gas and switched on the radio. Wagner. *The Ride of the Valkyries*. It was all he could do to keep Shirl on the road.

30

Preparations

One month ago: mid-winter

Stage two of Isla's angel tattoo was complete. Each feather now had an outline and was shaded in blue. Raw as her skin was, she couldn't help but admire Jet's work. The execution of those wings was impeccable; she envied him his artistic gift. The third and final session was scheduled for Monday the following week.

In preparation, she'd been sorting through her paperwork, paying bills and taxes, reviewing her will, writing letters, and generally tidying up her affairs.

Venus had scarcely left her side. As well as nine lives, that cat had a sixth sense. If Isla had a choice, she'd definitely come back as a Latvian Grey. She pulled her dressing gown around her and squatted to stroke the best little friend she'd ever had.

'My dear puss.' Scarcely had the words left her lips than she had to race to the bathroom. The frailer her body became, the more violent was the retching. Sometimes she thought she'd crack a rib. Breathless and clutching her side, she took a fresh morphine patch from the medicine cabinet, peeled the spent one off her arm, and patted on the new. Sitting on the toilet seat, she waited until the chemical relief kicked in. Every day it took a little longer and masked the pain a little less. The end was coming and she was glad.

Purring, Venus slunk around her legs and gazed adoringly into her weary eyes.

At last Isla gathered the energy to creep into the kitchen and put on the kettle. While the tea was brewing she wrote to Maddie. Normally they communicated by Skype, but this was too important to trust to cyberspace. She wanted to set everything out logically, without embellishment or interruption, while she was able to write it.

When she finished, she read it through. The letter was cool and businesslike: more a list of instructions to a solicitor than a goodbye note to a friend.

'Never mind, it'll have to do,' she said to Venus as she poured the tea. She didn't have the strength to rewrite it. Later she sealed it in an envelope and addressed it to Dubai. Today was Tuesday: Claude's day. If he caught the evening mail, Maddie would get it next week. The timing was perfect.

At ten, Claude bounded in with a big smile and a bigger bunch of red roses. As soon as he saw her, he took a backward step.

She returned the smile and gave him a kiss. 'They're beautiful! Roses are my favourite. Be a dear, there's a vase on top of the cupboard. Fill it with water for me?'

While she arranged the flowers, he poured a cup of tea and helped himself to store-bought ginger nut biscuits.

'Did you get it?'

He took the plastic container from his pocket and placed it on the table.

'What would I do without you?'

He sighed and folded his hands in his lap. His bottom lip was trembling. 'I don't know what *I'll* do without *you*.'

Morphine from the patch coursed through Isla's body, muffling the pain. Every breath was precious. To her ears every word was poetry. She showed him the mandala, pinned to the corkboard.

Conquer. Dare. Create. Live.

'I've achieved them all,' she said proudly. 'The circle is complete.'

They fell into the comfortable silence of old friends and lovers. He held her hand as if it were as fragile as an egg.

At length she said, 'Can I ask another favour?'

He nodded.

'Post this to Maddie.'

He took the envelope. 'Is that all?'

'No. I've left the hardest until last. Will you look after Venus?'

For a second he hesitated. Then he said, 'I'd be honoured.'

'You're a wonderful friend, Claude. Now, take me to bed.'

As if she were a small child, he scooped her into his arms. On the double bed they lay together, their naked bodies touching. Sexual desire had deserted her. Just to be close, to hear him breathing, to feel the warmth of his skin was all she wanted.

She must have drifted off.

When she opened her eyes, the room was dark and Claude was gone. In the shallow indentation where his body had been, Venus was curled up asleep.

She called him. No answer. The electric clock announced it was half past six.

In the bathroom was a packet of hot-pink hair dye, bought especially for the occasion. She opened it and read the instructions while she ran the water for a bath.

'I'll go in a blaze of colour,' she said to Venus as she worked the dye into her hair.

Later she sat by the computer, scrolled the newsfeed on the *Tattoo Lovers* website. Found a photo of blue-haired Antoinette showing off her latest kewpie-doll tattoo.

Exhausted, she fell onto the bed.

31

Discovery

Tuesday 4 August

When Claude went to Isla's house the first Tuesday of August, he knew in his heart that it was done. At the back door, Venus was running frantically back and forth across the porch. As soon as she spotted him, she tore down the stairs and wove around his legs. In all the time he'd been going there, she'd only had eyes for Isla. Now she was his. Cats were such fickle creatures, good for nothing except catching rats. He doubted Venus had caught a single rodent in her entire pampered life.

He rubbed the stubble on his chin. A sense of dread percolated through his veins. Not so long ago, the door would have been open and the aroma of delicious cooking would have floated down to greet him.

Today the door was shut and an air of desolation hung about the house. He grasped the handrail, powdery with old paint, and plodded up the steps. The cat's food bowl had been licked clean and a dusty scum had settled on her water.

He knocked. The house echoed like a coffin.

Venus mewled and eyed him expectantly.

'Are you hungry, puss?' Talking to a cat was as dumb as talking to a shadow. As if in response, she turned her back and sharpened her claws on the mat.

Claude rattled the doorknob and put his ear to the glass. No sound from inside.

In his pocket was a set of keys. One for his house, one for Shirl, one for Lola's, one for his shed, and one for 53 Mayfield Avenue.

He slotted the scarlet key into the lock. As the door opened, the cat pushed between his legs to get in. The first thing he noticed was the emptiness, as if the house had been suddenly vacated and left to its own devices. The air was chilly from the previous night. The sunlight was shut out by the blinds. The only sounds were whoosh of the westerly wind and the squabble of mickey birds outside.

The kitchen benches were spotless, not a pan or a cup was out of place. On the table was the vase of roses he'd brought last week. Their withered heads were bowed. Red petals had dripped onto the lino and pooled like blood.

Alone in her house, he felt like a thief. He was debating whether to stay or go when Venus took off at a gallop down the hallway. Outside the bathroom the cat flattened her ears and dropped to a crouch. Her tail flicked from side to side. All her attention was focussed on something in that room.

Claude's throat went dry. His pulse hammered in his ears as he crept down the hall towards the bathroom. His heart already knew what to expect.

On the black-and-white tiles, a naked Isla was lying on her side, as still as a statue. She was shoe-horned into a space between the glass shower screen and the washbasin with her feet pointing towards him. Although her face was hidden by shocking hot-pink hair, there was no mistaking her identity. Sweeping down her back were the magnificent wings. The tattoo was complete, weeping in its colourful glory. She looked at peace, as if she'd found freedom from pain at last.

He squatted and felt for a pulse. Her skin was cool and the texture of plasticine. Although he wasn't a religious man, he mumbled a prayer of sorts.

Venus slunk in. Her button nose touched Isla's and remained there for a moment, as if checking for vital signs. The diagnosis complete, she backed away and sat down. Her eyes never once left her owner.

'What do I do now?' Claude dragged his hands through his hair.

The cat made a mournful yowl. Although she was just a dumb animal it was clear she knew and was grieving in her own way. He left them there together.

In a daze he wandered through the house. The lounge room looked exactly the same as it always was. An impression of her body dented the cushions of her favourite armchair. On the side-table was an art magazine, open with an empty teacup beside it.

In her bedroom, the block-out drapes were drawn making the room as dark as night. He snapped on the light. The bed was a tangle of sheets and pillows. The fluffy white doona on the floor looked like a fallen cloud.

A blue light on her laptop pulsed as bright as a navigation beacon. On the windowsill behind was a row of boxes covered in gift-wrap. Odd that he'd not noticed them before.

He picked one up, tipped up the lid. The stink of rubber wrinkled his nose. He opened the box fully and his eyes almost popped out of his head.

Inside was a purple dildo.

At that moment, Isla's laptop burst into life. Her favourite website, *Tattoo Lovers,* was open. On the screen were dozens of images of men; all were facing the camera and all were stark naked. The male members were impressive indeed. Then it dawned on him that the name of the site was a double entendre. The purpose wasn't to share your love *of* tattoos but to get lovers *with* tattoos.

'Isla, you wicked girl!' He chuckled as he put the dildo back into the box.

Until now he'd thought that Isla had few friends and no lovers. In fact he was rather flattered with the idea of being the only man in her life. How wrong could he have been!

The weight of knowledge pressed against his chest, making it hard to breathe. Tears seeped from the corners of his eyes, trickled down the furrows of his skin. Her presence was in the room, watching him, waiting for his reaction.

What he should have done was phone the cops. But that would have exposed them both. Her disease-ravaged body, the tattoos, her sordid secret, their relationship, his dubious profession. There'd be reporters and headlines and speculation. He could hear the neighbourhood gossips already, whispering over fences.

Did you hear about Isla Bright?

Who'd have thought!

She was so quiet ... so plain ... so ordinary.

The air was thin and he began to panic. He wasn't meant to be in her house, in her boudoir. No-one but Maddie knew about the arrangement. And Maddie was in Dubai.

As he massaged his chest, the tears became a torrent. His body was shaking all over. There was no time to waste. He had to get out.

If he were found there, the cops would ask questions he didn't want to answer. Suspicions would be raised. Before long, he'd be the chief suspect. In his experience murder investigations ended in the arrest of the person who called the police.

No, it was simpler to walk down that hall and shut the door behind him. But, on the chance he'd been seen, he also needed to establish an alibi.

In a flash of genius it came. He'd go to the King's Arms and have a few beers with the lads. It was nearly lunchtime and the usual crowd would be drowning their sorrows in beer and bullshit. Nobody would notice when he arrived; all he had to do was fit in.

The bunch of keys in his pocket clinked against his leg. He took them out and removed the red one. He intended to leave it on her desk but then changed his mind and slipped it into his shirt pocket. To protect her reputation, he shut down the laptop and put the sex toys into a plastic bag. He'd work out what to do with them all later.

Before leaving he returned to the bathroom to say goodbye. Her tattoos and hot-pink hair made her look like a hooker. His conscience wouldn't allow him leave her like that.

Not thinking straight, he retrieved the doona from the bedroom floor and in his haste knocked over a bowl of lavender. Purple buds exploded across the floor. There was no time to clean it up; he had to get out. He dropped the doona over her like a shroud, grabbed the plastic bag and the laptop, and raced down the hall.

Geezes, the cat! He'd made a promise.

He took a can of food and the bowls from the porch. Lastly, he clamped Venus under his arm. She yowled and struggled and he began to sneeze.

What was he going to do with a bloody cat?

Loaded to the eyeballs, he trudged down the path and flung everything into the cabin of the ute. If he was lucky, he'd get away unseen.

He pushed the gear-stick into first, released the handbrake. As the vehicle rolled down the incline, he eased off the clutch. The engine ticked over. He pumped the accelerator. Shirl farted once then zoomed away.

32

The alibi

Wednesday 5 August

Wednesday morning an internal jackhammer woke Claude from a restless sleep. His clothes reeked of onions and stale beer; his lips were crusted with saliva. While last night's events were a bit of a blur, he'd succeeded in getting his alibi. It was iron-clad, backed up by none other than Lefty Long, luckiest SP bookie on the north side. But best of all, it was in writing. On the back of a beer coaster, Lefty had scribbled the times and odds for the mid-week gallops at Randwick.

Rolling over on the bed, Claude squinted at the digital clock. Nine thirty-five.

Shit! He'd be late for Lola.

Way too fast he stood up. His stomach was burning like battery acid. He belched a couple of times, took a few quick breaths. If only the room would stop spinning! His bladder was bursting. Seven steps would get him to the bathroom. He blundered into the hallway. The floor was a rollercoaster. He clung to the door frame to stop it swaying.

A quick dash then eighty bucks of booze went straight down the toilet. He rinsed out his mouth, splashed water on his face, staggered into the kitchen.

On a chair, Kat was curled up with her tail wrapped around her. Her nose was buried in fur. She was purring in her sleep. On the bench was an open can of Whiskas with a knife sticking out like a lonely flagpole. On the rim a blue-arsed fly squatted and rubbed its legs together. Claude had no memory of what happened past eleven o'clock last night, but he was glad Kat hadn't gone hungry.

He opened the fridge. It didn't look promising. Bread crusts, four eggs, half a bottle of milk, a jar with three pickled onions, a six-pack of lager.

Bread was the safest. He slotted the crusts into the toaster and trawled through the pantry for Vegemite. The combination of salt and caramel and tar was exactly what was needed. The miracle cure fixed every misery known to man. Had done since he was a youngster. It was best over thick slices of butter. Sadly he'd finished the butter a week ago and hadn't remembered to buy more.

The familiar yellow-and-red jar was right at the back behind bottles of sauce and cans of baked beans. He moved them around the shelf like chess pieces. Just when it was within reach, he caught a whiff of smoke.

Flames were leaping from the toaster. In the one movement he ripped out the power plug and dumped the toaster in the sink. His stomach did a backflip. Deep breath … deep breath. The wave of nausea swelled and ebbed.

Meanwhile Kat raced to the door and began plucking the flywire with her claws. In yesterday's panic he'd forgotten about kitty litter. He opened the screen to let her out, wondering if she'd ever come back again.

He was doing his best. He hoped Isla would approve. The image of her lying on the bathroom floor flashed into his mind. He bit his bottom lip to stave off tears. She'd achieved what she intended and he'd had the privilege of playing a small part.

Lord, how he'd miss her!

His head was aching, his stomach was roiling. The old sailors' remedy might fix it. Although he wasn't an old sailor, he knew plenty of blokes with salt in their veins. Every last one had the constitution of an ox. From the fridge he took a can of lager and gulped it down like medicine. At first it was touch and go. After a few hiccups his gut settled into a precarious equilibrium and he began to feel better.

One day at a time, he'd learnt at AA. *One day at a time*. The day he must get through now was Wednesday.

Wednesdays were Lola's.

She was expecting him and he wouldn't let her down. He showered, shaved and splashed his face with citrus cologne. In the mirror, his cheeks were drawn and his eyes had dark rings. Nothing a decent night's sleep wouldn't cure. Stepping back, he scrutinised his physique. For his age, he was in good shape. His chest was muscular and his waist was fairly trim. The tattoos complemented his tan but they were more than mere decorations.

Every day they reminded him that his past was past. His future could be whatever he made it.

Create. Dare. Conquer. Live. Her words gave him hope.

He dressed, grabbed the keys and locked the house. Kat was outside on the path, sunning herself and looking as if she owned the place. If she was there when he returned, he'd keep her, at least until he found her a kind home.

Shirl was parked on the street. Her metallic paint sparkled like the ocean but something wasn't quite right. She seemed lopsided: up at the front, down at the back. Bloody neighbourhood punks must've stolen her wheels again. That would make three times this year. Fuming, he trotted down the driveway.

Up close, the problem was immediately obvious. The front wheels were on the footpath and the back wheels were in the gutter. Had he driven home last night or had one of the lads done him a favour?

He checked the duco for dents, fur, blood. Found nothing. His luck was holding. Easing into the driver's seat, he started her up and bumped the front wheels onto the bitumen. Lola's place was more than twenty kilometres away: a long distance in his fragile state of health. If the cops pulled him over, he'd blow the breathalyser off the scale. He'd best stick to the back streets.

The route passed by the turnoff to Isla's place. The reason for last night's binge came flooding home. Was she still lying on the bathroom floor? What if she wasn't found for a week? A month? A year? There'd been terrible cases shown on TV. People with no-one in the world to mourn them.

Although Isla wasn't a recluse, was it likely someone would find her?

He'd already gone past her street. Only a coward would drive on without checking. He swerved onto the verge and tramped on the brakes. The wheels skidded; dust floated in through the air-con. With the indicator ticking, he lit a smoke.

Feeling calmer after a second cigarette, he was ready to face his fears. Outside number 53, two plastic-wrapped newspapers lay on the lawn. The letter box bristled with junk mail. The casement windows down the northern side were half-open as they always were. And in the mud on the driveway was a perfect mould of Shirl's tyres. *Geezes!* After taking all the trouble yesterday to exit without a noise, he'd forgotten to cover his tracks.

From all appearances no-one had been to the house. Isla would still be on the floor. Apart from crime shows, his knowledge of the human decomposition process was scant. What he did know tied his stomach in knots.

Why hadn't he called the cops yesterday? He would have had ample time to get out and find a place to go to ground.

Taking a shovel, he smoothed the tyre prints from the driveway. He was the gardener-handyman for chrissake. If anyone had a right to be there, it was him. When it was done, he made a U-turn and drove back to the main road.

Awful possibilities bounced around his mind like toxic billiard balls. Although he'd deny everything, he was up to his neck in shit. Who could he trust?

His phone rang. Lola. He was late. Very late.

'Hey, are you coming today?' she said.

'Can we give it a miss? I wouldn't be much use anyway.'

'Big night?' It was more a statement than a question.

'Yeah, got a stinker of a headache.' Technically he wasn't lying but he wasn't about to tell her the whole truth either. In a small way she too was implicated.

'You should've phoned sooner.'

'I'll make it up next time. Forgive me?' The performance was well-practiced.

'Okay. See you next week.' Abruptly she ended the call.

He puffed out his cheeks and blew through his lips. Every way he was doomed. His head dropped to the steering wheel. Whether he confessed or kept the secret, whether he stayed to face the consequences or vanished without a trace, he was lost.

Out of nowhere came a small voice of inspiration. Instead of the cops, he'd tell the press. He'd go to a reporter who'd take him seriously and treat Isla's death with respect. Seth VerBeek of *The Morning Post* had once written a balanced story about Lola and her greyhounds. Anyone else would have taken the easy route and turned the live-baiting evidence against her. There was another reason to choose Seth. According to Lola, his childhood had been tough. Of all the journos, he would understand life on Struggle Street.

Claude rummaged in the glovebox for a pen and paper. All he could find was a blunt carpenter's pencil and envelopes. He tore off the flap and in his best handwriting wrote the address. He wrapped it around the scarlet key and sealed it inside another envelope. He knew he should drop it in the post. But what if there was a delay? What if Seth VerBeek didn't get it until next week?

He'd do it himself. Hand-deliver it to Newspaper House. Leave it anonymously at reception. Yes, that's what he'd do. First thing tomorrow morning.

*

Thursday night at six o'clock, Claude took a takeaway box of pepperoni pizza and a can of beer to his lounge room for the TV news. A young woman with short bleached hair and dark eyebrows was delivering her report outside a suburban house.

'A body has been found in this gracious Queenslander in Corella. According to police the woman has been dead for several days.' The hostility in her voice was intense, as if she were accusing an entire community of domestic violence or worse. The camera walked with her along a side path, bordered by agapanthus and hippeastrums.

The monologue continued. 'Neighbours saw a dark blue ute, possibly a Ford, parked near the victim's house. Police are investigating tyre marks found on the road.'

Claude's mobile was ringing. He let the call go to message bank.

The camera panned Isla's yard, taking in the massive mango tree, the driveway along the southern side and skid marks on the bitumen. A picture of a ute identical to his flashed onto the screen.

'If you've seen this vehicle, call Crime Stoppers immediately.'

The wedge of hot pizza dripped cheese onto his lap. His appetite had vanished.

The dragnets were out. He'd have to run faster than a Dapto dog to avoid being caught. Should he go bush until the whole catastrophe blew over? He could go to the Gulf, pitch a tent, live off the land and the sea. In the Gulf, no-one asked questions. Blokes like him went there to escape their wives, or underworld retribution, or bad debts. Some sought to dodge the taxman or the immigration department. He had enough cash to cover expenses for six months. With a bit of paid work he could string it out for a year. All he needed to buy was fuel and grog.

The other option was to turn himself in. All he was guilty of was love and compassion. Isla's death was her own doing, pure and simple. Had she been of sound mind? You betcha!

He could never commit murder, though once he'd come close. Even then, when he had the chance to get his father, he couldn't bring himself to do it.

Murder. A shocking word for a shocking act.

In the news reports, the M-word hadn't yet been used but it was only a matter of time. Pondering his situation, Claude finished the beer.

Later he dialled message bank for the missed call.

It's Lola. Call me. It's urgent.

Unlike others he could name, Lola never phoned unless there was an actual crisis. A dozen scenarios sprang to mind as he waited for her to answer. Finally she picked up.

'Claude—the six o'clock news—the ute—the tyre marks. It was you, wasn't it!' The accusation stung like a slap.

'Hold on, Lola. I can explain.'

She took a breath then babbled on faster than before. In no uncertain terms she told him where he should go and what he should do when he got there. The last suggestion would have been extremely painful and a physical impossibility anyway.

Claude yelled through the phone. 'Listen, Lola! I didn't kill anyone!'

The other end went silent.

'Did you hear me?'

'If you *knew* about this, why did you do nothing?'

He had no answer, other than being scared shitless that he'd end up the scapegoat.

That was what always happened. The cops would push on and on until they made an arrest. Not necessarily the guilty party, but some sucker who'd carry the can.

Until now, he'd thought he'd held it together and everything was going fine. But now an innocent death was being twisted into a horrific crime. The public would be baying for justice. Without a suspect or an arrest, police careers would be on the line. In the absence of actual evidence, the media would make up a story. A private tragedy would be blown into an outrage the scale of a school massacre or suicide bombing.

'Okay, okay. I'll go to the cops, I promise.'

Long after the call ended, Claude stared at the phone. During that brief interaction, Lola had made him feel as dirty as a paedophile. He'd made her a promise, and promises were meant to be kept.

Lola was a smart woman. Even in this vast sprawling city, his sapphire-blue ute with the shiny chrome trim wouldn't stay unnoticed. For the first time he regretted the personalised numberplate: SH1RL. Named in loving memory of his mother, it advertised his whereabouts to the world. The police would set up road blocks and go door-to-door until they tracked him down. Already he was being depicted as the bad guy. Giving himself up might turn that around. More than anything he wanted to prove he was a good guy.

Yes, he'd do it. First thing tomorrow, he'd drive Shirl to the cop shop and clear his name. The decision lifted a weight from his shoulders.

At dawn on Friday he woke at peace with the world. Barefoot, he padded to the kitchen and switched on the electric jug. The lino was as cold as a sheet of ice. In his best blue mug he made coffee with an espresso bag. While it brewed, he swept back the curtains. Outside was a pall of white. Although the fog was too thick to see Shirl in the carport, he could feel her glaring at him.

Why fix it if it ain't broke? she seemed to say.

He opened the window. Doubt floated in on the foetid air. His determination to fulfil his promise to Lola began to waver. His head was aching. A cigarette was what he craved but he'd finished the pack last night. Although the corner store was only ten minutes away, it would be stupid to drive.

The coffee cup was on the table. Wisps of steam curled up and evaporated. If only he could do that now: evaporate without a trace. Not that he'd ever admit it, but deep down he was a lily-livered wuss. Any less backbone and he'd be a jellyfish.

He rested his head on the table and wept.

33

The letter

Sunday 23 August

Sunday morning Seth sat on the balcony of his apartment with notepad and pen trying to tie together the various threads of the story.

By some minor miracle, he'd escaped charges of trespassing and interfering with police evidence. This was due in part to a certain senior detective who'd vouched for his honesty and in part to his silver tongue. After yesterday's fiasco, Cate had caught a bus home and was still mad at him for dumping her. *You owe me big time*, were her parting words when he called her afterwards.

Ping went his phone.

The text was from Maddie. *Meet me at ChocoLatte New Farm 11 o'clock.*

After the previous episode at Maddie's apartment, Seth never expected to hear from her again. To be honest, it was a relief. Some might have called her precious, but in his experience she was a full-blown princess.

Attractive and seductive were also on the list of descriptors. But the word *relationship* was out of the question. Quite simply, she wasn't worth the effort.

From a professional perspective, however, she could be critical to the case. Whether the information she had about Isla Bright was enough to unravel the mystery was yet unknown. Instinct told him that meeting her at the café was not only risky but probably a complete waste of time.

Cautiously, he texted her back. *What's it about?*

Straight away she responded. *Isla sent me a letter.*

OK. See you there. As he pressed the *send* button, he hoped it wasn't a decision to regret. His ribs were still sore after the last encounter with the jealous ex. Maddie was persuasive and hard to refuse. He'd need to keep his wits about him, and that meant absolutely no alcohol.

Sunday morning in up-market New Farm was the busiest day of the week. All along the café strip couples and families were gathering for brunch. Brunch: that in-between meal of pancakes, or bacon and eggs, or smoked salmon and avocado, served anytime between dawn and mid-afternoon. A lazy meal for a lazy day. Seth himself was a devotee.

Two blocks south of the cinemas, he parked and walked back along Bowen Terrace to *ChocoLatte*. As expected, the place was packed. The queue to buy pastries stretched right along the footpath. Getting a table for brunch would be impossible and getting served would be even harder.

Dressed in cream culottes and a low-cut burgundy sweater, Maddie waved and ran across the road. On one arm was an expensive-looking handbag and on the other a carry box from the bakery. '*Dahling*! Let's get out of here. It's madness!'

He kissed her cheek; she smelt of roses and cinnamon. 'Nice perfume.'

'Why thank you. It's called *Boudoir*. A cheeky little scent, don't you think?'

'Good to see you, Maddie.' Despite his reservations he meant it. 'New Farm Park?'

'Absolutely! The gardens are glorious this time of year.' She patted the carry box. 'While I was waiting, I bought us some treats.'

The vast leafy park was as busy as the café strip. People of every age, race and colour had congregated for barbeques and picnics. Kids were running around, playing with kites, Frisbees, and balls.

Seth parked beneath a spreading jacaranda tree whose leaves were turning gold. Come October, it would be a spectacle of purple blossoms.

'Shall we go down by the river?' Maddie said with a sly smile.

'Whatever you say.' Was his charm irresistible or was he just an old fool?

She took his hand as they strolled beneath the foliage. Under the clear winter's sky, the brown river had turned blue. On the far bank were the sleek architect-designed homes of billionaires. Pools, private jetties, luxury yachts. A different world from the ordinary working-class people in the park: people who played soccer with their kids and ate sausages with tomato sauce on white bread.

In the shade of a Moreton Bay fig the pair sat down on a park bench. Neat lawns rolled down an embankment to the river walkway. A flock of pelicans, wings wide, skidded like seaplanes into the water.

Maddie opened the box from *ChocoLatte*. The buttery aroma was irresistible.

'I'm supposed to be watching my weight,' said Seth.

'Go on. One little treat won't hurt.'

'Temptress.'

She laughed. 'I'll take that as a compliment.'

He chose a chocolate éclair. The pastry was so light it could have floated away. In two bites it was gone. 'Did you bring Isla's letter?'

'Yes, of course. You can borrow it if you like.' She gave him an envelope with a Dubai address. It had been redirected to her apartment in New Farm.

'I'm surprised you're still living there.'

'Andrew and I are officially separated, but he's letting me stay there while he's overseas. On one condition ...' She paused and made a girlish giggle.

'Which is?'

'That I don't take any more men home. Ha! Can you imagine? Try telling a lioness not to hunt.' Hastily she added, 'Of course I agreed.'

Seth got the impression he might be next on the menu. As long as that man-mountain was in a different country, it was probably safe. He helped himself to another pastry. She was watching him with dusky bedroom eyes.

'Have you been behaving yourself then?' He was headed for dangerous territory but he couldn't stop himself.

'What do *you* think?' She moved closer on the seat, removed the pastry from his hand, eased his face towards hers. Her lips brushed his cheek, his neck, tickled his ear. When her tongue flicked a crumb from the edge of his mouth, he could resist no more.

Hungrily he ran his hands over her body and kissed her deeply. Her mouth tasted of vanilla and chocolate. What a combination! She threw back her head and moaned with delight. Seconds later her hand was working into his jeans pocket, searching for the keys. 'No-one will ever know, *dahling*.'

Ten minutes later, they were inside her riverfront apartment, in the sumptuous bedroom with views over the city. Not that he noticed until they were done and she lay dozing in his arms. She was a lioness all right. She'd caught his scent, tracked him down, and gone in for the kill. He hoped the killing part wasn't literal.

Suddenly she opened her eyes and turned to him. 'You know this can't go on, this *thing* between you and me. There is no future in it.'

'I wasn't exactly looking for a partner.'

'Well if you were, you deserve better. You're a nice fellow, Seth VerBeek.'

'Thanks, but I'm old enough and ugly enough to take care of myself.'

She laughed. 'Don't say you haven't been warned.'

He cupped her breasts and pressed his lips to them. Like a python she wound her naked body around him. They made love again, this time without the haste. Sensual, slow, and easy. The promise of no strings attached suited him fine.

Later, in his Clayfield apartment he read Isla Bright's letter. Partly a goodbye note and partly a list of tasks, it was clear that she was winding up her affairs. Her courage and attention to detail were impressive. He found himself wishing that he'd known her in life.

At the end Isla listed the web accounts she wanted shut down. Most were the usual suspects: Facebook, Twitter, Instagram. Others he'd never heard of.

He opened his laptop, typed in the web address *inked.com*.

If you were into tattoos, it was a treasure trove of body art, ranging from the crass to the sublime. He entered her name in the search engine. Nothing came up. Then he thought about the spread of wings on her back and did a search for *angel tattoo*.

There they were, sparkling with colour. Some pictures showed the progress of their creation over three stages. The first was the blue outline. Even as a sketch Jet's skill was remarkable. While the wings were anatomically correct, they were drawn with the sensuality of da Vinci. The second stage gave depth to the vanes, the barbs, the tips of the feathers. The third stage was the colour.

One of the photos he'd seen before, in a magazine in Jet's waiting room.

No wonder he'd won an international competition. The image was atmospheric and otherworldly, as if it were of a real angel. In some ways, he supposed, that was true.

The user identity at the top of the homepage was *brightangel*. He thought of how he invented his own usernames and passwords. There were so many that he kept a coded list in his desk drawer. Usually he chose variations of his name or events in his life. *Bright* was Isla's family name. Was it significant that she chosen the word *angel*?

If Maddie was to shut down the accounts, she'd already have all the passwords. For his purpose it didn't matter; it was not his business to interfere.

Using the pseudonym *brightangel*, he searched the *Tattoo Lovers* website. There she was again, this time in all her colourful naked glory.

The website was exactly what it suggested—tattoos and lovers—with some of the hottest bodies he'd ever seen. All the pics were suggestive or erotic; some showed couples or trios. Tattoos were the main focus of course. But this was no arty photo site. This was verging on porn. He navigated to a page that promised 'live action'. It required him to open an account and pay.

Normally he would have exited. Porn wasn't his thing. In a lifetime of travel to exotic ports, he'd seen just about everything anyway. But this was legitimate research. It could solve the mystery of Isla Bright's demise. While all the signs pointed to self-administered euthanasia—the word *suicide* didn't do her justice—a few questions remained unanswered.

On *Tattoo Lovers* he registered as a heterosexual male, aged 50, and provided his credit card details. Instantly an array of thumbnail shots of women spread across the screen. Big breasts and small. Young, old, middle aged. White hair, black hair, red hair, blue hair. Take your pick. For the sake of research, he clicked on one at random.

In an eye-blink, she was up close and personal on his screen. As she removed her shirt her tattooed boobs swung like melons. 'Waddaya want, babe?' she cooed.

Taken aback, he said, 'What're you offering?'

'Check the menu at the bottom. Give me a poke when you're ready.'

Seth scrolled down the page. Apart from actual penetration (obviously a physical impossibility), he could get whatever a man could desire. It was a voyeur's paradise. For a price, she'd do anything … *with* anything. He'd never seen a site like it. He clicked the 'poke' button and she returned to the screen.

Fifteen minutes later he'd received the education of a lifetime and was two hundred bucks out of pocket. Not in his wildest dreams had he imagined a woman doing things like that with an ordinary bowl of fruit. Never again would he be able to look at a grape without cracking a smile.

34

Confession

Monday 24 August

The station was less than a kilometre from Claude's house yet he seldom went anywhere by train. Queues, delays, and whinging snotty-nosed kids had long cured him of public transport. But today it wasn't safe to drive. Not with everyone on the lookout for the infamous blue ute with the numberplate SH1RL.

Under a cold leaden sky, he jammed on a baseball cap and pulled up his collar against the drizzle. At the station, he stood in a queue behind a whinging snotty-nosed kid and bought a ticket to Goongulli. So far the experience was meeting expectations. The railway clerk told him to get off at Central and change platforms for the connection. He pointed out the route on a diagrammatic map. The network was a multi-coloured spider whose legs stretched up and down the coast and west as far as Rosewood.

Five minutes later the train wheezed into the platform. On schedule. Inside, the carriage was clean and air-conditioned. Although crowded, there was plenty of room to spread out his legs without people tripping over them. He settled into a padded seat and prepared to be jolted and juddered over the switchbacks. Instead he was lulled by the smooth whirr of the wheels on the track. This was not at all what he'd imagined.

His last train ride was more than forty years ago, when passengers crammed into hard bench seats that ran right across the smoky carriages. For air, you had to drop down a window. The frames were made of solid hardwood. When they fell, they became guillotines for fingers. The

181

windows in the train to Goongulli were shut and sealed; fresh air circulated inside a capsule of comfort.

At Central, Claude ran down the stairs to an underground tunnel and then climbed another heart-breaker flight against a tide of passengers. The alarm sounded and the doors were starting to close. He took a flying leap and managed to get inside the carriage without being snapped. Puffing, he took the nearest seat. Unlike the first leg of the journey, this train was practically empty. Four other people shared the carriage: a mother with a baby asleep in a stroller, a high-school student, a bearded man with a walking stick.

The train eased into the tunnel between Central and Brunswick Street. The ancient brick walls were infused with black soot, just as he remembered as a little boy.

Years ago, he would lean his head against the glass and listen to the chug of the steam locomotive. In pitch darkness, he'd watch for the arch of light at the end of the mile-long horizontal shaft. His teeth would chatter in time with the rattle of the window pane. The acrid odour of decades of soot would reach through the cracks in the wall and choke him. That tunnel seemed to go forever. As the carriages rolled around the bend, the passengers would sway like wheat in the wind. Before the train burst from deepest night into daylight, the whistle would blast, the signal to shut his eyes against the dazzle.

Today the tunnel seemed shorter. There was no charry smell, no rattle and roll, no whistle blast at the end. In three minutes, the quiet cocoon sighed into Brunswick Street station. All in all, it was an anticlimax.

Four stops later, Claude stepped onto the rain-drenched platform at Goongulli. On the eastern side of the tracks was the familiar row of decrepit shops. What if Jet wasn't there?

For a moment he regretted not phoning first. A niggle of suspicion had warned against it. Trusting his instincts had always served him well. He crossed the railway bridge and strode down the line of businesses to *Jet Ink*.

An hour later, Claude emerged with a new tattoo on his wrist. It throbbed like the sting of a blue-bottle. In the process he'd made a promise to keep Jet's identity secret. If the cops learnt about his psychic powers, they'd be onto him. He had hundreds of clients from both sides of the tracks. What he knew would fill a courtroom for a year. In the tattoo business, dob-ins came with guarantees of pay-back. Self-preservation drove Jet to keep a low profile, an instinct that Claude knew well.

In no time Claude was at Roma Street. The criminal justice end of the CBD was surrounded by courthouses and offices leased by lawyers and judges. Instead of changing platforms for home, he took the pedestrian tunnel to the bustling main thoroughfare. There he smoked his last cigarette. Police headquarters was directly opposite. He forced himself to keep moving before he completely lost his nerve.

Outside the cop shop, he hesitated. Through the glass doors he could see them, dressed in blue military-style uniforms, going about their business of solving crimes.

The sliding doors hissed open. A youth with an orange Mohawk, shredded jeans and Docs sauntered out. Before he was on the footpath, a cigarette was between his lips. A match flared. As if he were a drowning man, Claude gasped for the second-hand smoke. He'd made it this far; he couldn't turn back.

At the counter he told a young female cop about his blue Falcon ute and that he was a friend of the tattooed lady. She wrote down his name and told him to take a seat. Shortly after, a crusty sergeant took him to an interview room. Claude answered the questions the best way he could and took care not to mention Jet.

'Where's the vehicle now?' said the sergeant.

'In the yard at home.'

'Righto, let's take a look.'

In the cop car, two portly officers sat in the front while Claude was relegated to the back like a criminal. They sped along the western arterial, through the poorer suburbs where timber shacks perched on tall steel stilts to escape floodwaters.

When they pulled up outside Claude's modest weatherboard cottage, he took comfort that the lawn was mown and the edges were trimmed. A lot could be said about a man from the state of his yard. Pity about the house: the paintwork was blistering like a bad case of sunburn.

He led the cops along the driveway to the carport at the back.

After unlocking the ute, he sat on a stump to keep an eye on them. Rainwater had pooled in the boggy patch near the banana grove. The drone of a million ravenous bloodsuckers set his teeth on edge. The mosquito repellent was in the glovebox which was out of bounds for the present.

With gloved hands the cops examined every nook and crevice of the vehicle. Samples were taken from the tyre treads, the windows were dusted for prints, the back tray was vacuumed. One took photos of the grid-shaped dent on the passenger door, caused by a run-in with a shopping trolley outside Coles. Each piece of evidence was sealed in a plastic bag, labelled, numbered and filed in a box.

When they were done, the sergeant said, 'Depending on the lab results, you may be required for further questioning. I wouldn't plan on taking any holidays. Do I make myself clear?'

'Clear as crystal.'

The sergeant handed Claude a business card. 'Call me if you think of anything else. We'll be in touch soon.' He hurried towards his colleague who was stowing the evidence box in the boot of their car.

Claude called out after him. 'Are you treating this as murder?'

The sergeant spun around and glared as if to say, *don't stretch the friendship*. Without a word, the pair got in the cop car and drove off.

That was when Claude knew for sure *he* was the chief suspect.

The new tattoo was hurting and he badly needed a drink. Upstairs he opened the fridge for a beer. If he was going to spend his twilight years behind bars for a crime he didn't commit, he'd do whatever he bloody well liked until they dragged him in.

On the top shelf of the kitchen cupboard, he found an oversized tin of roasted cashews that Isla had given him last Christmas. He'd been saving them for a special occasion but these days he didn't get many visitors. After nearly a year, the tin remained unopened.

The lid was covered with dust. The use-by date was a month ago. He broke the seal, popped the lid and dived in. Soft and salty and perfect with beer. He ended up eating the lot.

At six o'clock and feeling as stuffed as a chook, he switched on the TV news. Kat jumped onto his lap and began licking her fur. He tickled her chin and she drooled onto his fingers. Despite his initial reservations, she had proven to be good company, even when he wanted to be alone.

First up were the political shenanigans in the lead-up to another election. Then came an update about the tattooed lady. He pushed up the volume to the max.

'Autopsy results revealed the presence of a prohibited chemical. It has not yet been established whether this was the cause of death.'

The newsreader didn't say what the chemical was and didn't speculate on whether foul play might have been involved. The report continued, showing interviews with random people in the Mall and file photos of a tattoo parlour that doubled as a bikies' den. Few facts and lots of embellishment.

It was only a matter of time before Claude would be in front of the cameras. He imagined himself in handcuffs, shirt over his head, being bundled into the courthouse.

Events were careering out of control. Alone and without anyone to support him, he felt as if he was heading full steam into a brick wall.

35

The feature article

Monday 24 August

First thing Monday morning, Cate danced into Seth's cubicle. In her hand were several sheets of paper. The feature article. She must have worked all weekend to finish it.

'Here, boss. Two thousand of my best words and a couple of excellent pics.' She seemed exceedingly pleased with herself.

The headline was *Live or let die?* He hoped the title wouldn't breach copyright. The opening line was sharp and to the point. He set the cardboard coffee cup on his desk and began to skim through the piece. In the two years since she'd cut her teeth as a uni student, her style had improved enormously. Now she had flair and confidence and could run an argument about the most controversial of topics.

Voluntary euthanasia: how much more controversial could you get?

The two separate investigations he and Cate been working on had finally come together. She'd taken the philosophical route and compared end-of-life decisions for people and animals. While Claude Fabergé had featured in both their investigations, his name wasn't mentioned at all. Neither was Jet's. The final paragraphs summed up the issue beautifully.

> *At law, failing to prevent the suffering of an animal is a criminal offence with a maximum penalty of seven years imprisonment.*

> *For humans, it is the opposite. Even in terminal cases with unbearable pain, the law does not allow one person to help*

185

another to die. In most states of Australia assisted suicide is a criminal offence with a penalty of life imprisonment.

As we approach death, should we have a choice? Should helping a loved one to a peaceful end receive punishment the same as murder?

Email your views to cate.bradshaw@themorningpost.com.

'Great work, Cate. You've nailed it.'

Seth was yet to complete his own investigations. Two elusive pieces of the puzzle were missing: the identity of the key courier and the truth about Isla's death.

He was close. So very close.

A few more days and he should be done.

36

Captured and released

Tuesday 25 August

The watch house was not a pleasant place. In addition to uncomfortable furniture, iron bars, and being treated like a complete fuckwit, the other guests weren't much company. Apart from Claude, there were two others. One kept banging his head against the wall and the other was a raving ice addict.

Claude had already been subjected to a strip search, including a digital examination of every cavity of his body. A thoroughly nasty experience. He'd been fingerprinted, urine-tested, swabbed for drugs. The mug shot they'd taken made him look like a psychopathic killer. The lawyer he demanded to see didn't turn up. Sadly his finances didn't stretch to having a QC on retainer, so his future lay in whomever Legal Aid coughed up.

Late in the afternoon by Claude's estimation—there were no clocks in the cells—a cop opened the grille and took him upstairs to an interview room. It was sparsely-furnished with a table, recording equipment, and several straight-backed chairs. The air-conditioner was set to the temperature of January in Siberia.

A teenager in a black suit was already there. He stood up and shook Claude's hand.

'I'm Matt Hennessy. Pleased to meet you, Mr Low. I'm your legal representative.'

The bubble of hope that he might get a reprieve popped. From the lawyer's youthful appearance, it was highly likely that this was his first ever case.

'Before we begin, I expect you to tell me the complete truth. Otherwise I can't defend you. Do you agree?'

'I'll do whatever it takes.'

Matt Hennessy proceeded to ask lots of questions. Some made Claude squirm. He wanted to know exactly what a *personal handyman* did, the precise nature of his relationship with Isla, and why he continued to visit the house after she died.

Claude managed to answer without telling any straight-out lies. Certainly he didn't volunteer any extra information about Maddie or Antoinette or Jet. Nor did he divulge the secrets of Isla's online tattoo world.

The following day, the miracle happened.

Claude was taken to the same icy interview room and told that all charges had been dropped. Information had been received that absolved him from any crime. He was free to go. They called him a cab and forty minutes later he was back in his Oleander Street home as if nothing had happened.

Except it had.

During those few hours of imprisonment, he'd realised that life was short. Too short to hold grudges and to ache for revenge. Through Jet, he'd finally come to terms with the trials of his youth. He'd forgiven his mother for dying when he was a kid. He'd forgiven the nuns at the orphanage for their cruelty and he'd forgiven Devil Doherty for being a sexual pervert.

One person remained: Mick Low.

He had a vague idea where his father might be. He began with a Google search on his smartphone. A few clicks later, he'd located the address at Mount Gravatt.

On the way there he bought a bunch of flowers: banksia and bottle brush and silvery eucalyptus leaves. His heart was thundering as he turned off the freeway and onto University Road. At the roundabout he took the first exit. After driving through an impressive entrance gate, he stopped to consult the map. The grounds were vast and bustling with activity. Up the hill he crawled at snail's pace and turned left at the chapel. He parked in a visitor's bay and retrieved the man-flowers from the passenger seat.

As he entered the garden, his eyes began to mist. The lawns were freshly mown and the garden beds were fragrant with flowering shrubs. Like a dead man, he plodded along the concrete path. He was walking through treacle; every fibre of his body was pushing against an immobile force.

Crows called to each other across the grounds. *Car-car-carrrr*. By the time he found the place, his eyes were streaming. The brass plaque was black with age.

Michael Patrick Low
10 April 1932—26 September 2005

Claude squatted and laid the sheath of flowers in the garden bed beside the plaque. He bowed his head and tried to conjure up an image of his father the last time he was called *Dad*.

Could he ever forgive the misery that man had caused the family? All of them had been affected. His mother Shirl, who'd supported her young sons the only way she could. His brother Jake, who'd never returned from the war in Vietnam. And himself, who'd spent a lifetime suffering because of what had happened.

In that garden bed were the old man's ashes. Unlike his human offspring, the plants he'd spawned were thriving and strong.

Claude unbuttoned his shirt. Over the abdominal scar was the tattoo of the barbed-wire cross. Falling to his hands and knees, he sobbed with anger and grief and regret.

In the chapel an organ played the funeral march. On the tarmac outside was a black hearse. The uniformed driver was waiting for the attendants to roll out the coffin. Who had attended Mick Low's funeral? Were there many friends? Lovers? Claude envied them the chance to say goodbye.

For him, the announcement his father had passed came via Jet's tattoo.

There was no point in holding a grudge. Dead men made no apologies. The living must set aside their pain and get on with the business of living.

'I'm sorry for what I did.' Claude's voice was cracking. 'I forgive you, Dad.'

He kissed his fingers and touched the plaque.

'Rest in peace, you old bastard.'

37

Smoke and mirrors

Wednesday 26 August

Seth weighed the scarlet key in his hand, wondering what to do next. He thought back to the day he'd acquired it. According to Cate, the courier was an *elderly gentleman*. Now that he knew the main players in Isla's life, he knew the informant had to be either Claude or Jet.

Who should he tackle first?

Goongulli was a short distance away but Claude lived on the other side of town. Convenience won. He turned the Jeep toward the industrial zone. Although it was unlikely that Jet would disclose the entire story, he might drop some clues.

At Innovation Drive, the white arch of the railway bridge towered over the landscape. In the middle of the line-up of shops was the timber store with the curved awning, the horse trough and the hitching posts.

The place looked completely derelict, as if it hadn't been occupied in decades. The iron awning was pitted with rust; sunlight shone through the holes. The chamfer boards were crumbling with dry rot or termites. The windows and door were boarded up.

Seth scratched his head and checked the address.

As if in a dream, he wandered the length of the strip. All the other buildings were exactly as they were last time he was there.

At the end of the street was *Bun in the Oven Spares*. Judging by the weathered signs and the amount of clutter, it would have been there the longest. Surely the owner would know what happened to the only tattoo parlour on the block.

Seth went inside.

A man in his seventies was sorting invoices on the counter. He wore a cap embroidered with the logo of a nearby retirement village. 'G'day, mate. Need any help?'

'I'm looking for a tattoo shop called *Jet Ink*.'

'Well you won't find it here.' The fellow laughed. 'Not this century, any rate.

'Has he moved?'

'Hasn't been here for more than thirty years.'

'You're joking!'

'You mean the place with the horse trough? The bloke must've died or something. It's been empty since the eighties. If you don't believe me, ask around.'

Shaking his head, Seth left the shop. Either it was April Fool's Day or the oven repair guy had a screw loose. To be sure, he glanced at the date on his smartphone; it was definitely *not* the first of April, nor was it 1985.

At the café, Seth asked the same question, received the same answer. In the nail salon, the Asian girls barely spoke English. The hairdresser said she'd never heard of *Jet Ink*.

Had he imagined the entire episode? Was he the one who was losing his mind?

After a good stiff coffee from *Full 'o Beans* café, he felt less rattled. Although the riddle of Jet's shop remained unanswered, Seth was able to convince himself that he was still mentally lucid and a logical explanation would emerge in the future.

His second option was to see Claude. This time he wanted to be certain of the facts so he called Cate and asked her to come along as a witness. It was going on for five o'clock and he still hadn't fulfilled his promise of dinner at that fancy French restaurant.

'No shirking out this time,' she warned.

'Cate, you're the only one who's actually met the key courier. Do you think you'd recognise him in person?'

'Maybe.' She sounded doubtful.

It was worth a shot. 'I'll pick you up from the office in fifteen.'

As he started the Jeep, his phone began to ring. Maddie. That was all he needed. Against his better judgement, he took the call.

'*Dahling*, I've had a *most interesting* conversation with my ex-husband.'

Seth groaned. 'Which one?'

'Don't be a pain, *dahling*. Darren, the lawyer. A knowledgeable man but frightfully dull. Anyway he also got a letter from Isla.'

'Sounds as if she was saying goodbye to everyone.'

'Wait until you hear this! She instructed Darren to change her will. She's left her house and all her worldly possessions—including a substantial amount of cash—to Claude Fabergé. Can you believe it?'

'Well, well, well.' Seth wondered what other surprises today might bring.

'I had no idea she was so fond of him! She never talked about him at all. I thought the extent of their relationship was gardening and food. Quite frankly, I'm speechless.'

'What sort of sum are we talking about?

'A house in that location would be worth heaps, and then there's the damages settlement for misdiagnosed cancer. Maybe three million all up.'

Seth whistled. Another piece of the puzzle slotted neatly into place. 'Who would have inherited otherwise?'

'As you know, she was childless. Antoinette was close but they had a falling-out. At one point she wanted to leave everything to the cat refuge. Now this!'

'Do you think Claude knows about it?'

'Darren said she wanted it to be a surprise. Now that Claude has been cleared of wrongdoing, I daresay he'll get a call tomorrow.'

'He's been cleared? How do you know?'

'Darren can be a prick but he's a very smart lawyer.'

'Look, Maddie, I've got to go. Can we talk some other time?'

'Anytime, *dahling*. Call me.' She ended with kisses through the phone.

After collecting Cate, Seth sped towards the western suburbs. Through the Inner City Bypass the traffic flowed freely, but on the Western Freeway it came to a crawl. Most days in the sprawling city, the so-called *rush hour* started at three and ended at seven.

In the car they discussed the inheritance, speculated on the relationship between Claude and Isla. Of his own admission, Claude was no saint. In fact, he seemed proud of the services he provided to lonely women. Was this his *modus operandi*? Did he prey upon clients in order to feather his own nest? Had he 'helped' anyone else to end her life?

At last they were at Oleander Street. The lights of the house were blazing. Together they walked to the front door. Seth knocked. In his pocket was the scarlet key that began it all.

The light came on and the door opened. Claude was wearing a blue tracksuit and yellow football socks. He looked haggard; the stark floodlights accentuated his age. Behind him a grey cat skedaddled down the hall.

'Whatever you're selling, I don't want any,' he said testily.

'Hey Claude, it's me. Seth VerBeek. This is my colleague, Cate Bradshaw.'

For a moment he didn't seem to comprehend. Then he gave a weary smile. 'You'd better come in out of the cold. They say it'll get down to five degrees tonight.'

In the living room a bar heater was humming. Beside it the cat had curled up on the rug. The TV news was on. Another abduction, another car bomb, another drug bust. The world had gone mad.

'Want a beer?'

Seth answered for the both of them. 'Yeah. That'd be great.'

When he'd left the room, Cate whispered, 'It's him alright. I'd know that drawl anywhere. I don't think he knows who I am yet.'

Claude returned with three tinnies and a glass which he set down on the coffee table. He turned on the lights and snapped off the TV.

'Here puss, puss.' Cate tickled the creature under the chin. Purring, she stretched and jumped onto Cate's lap.

'She's gorgeous. What's her name?'

'I call her Kat. She belonged to a friend of mine.'

'Venus and I have met before, haven't we puss?' Her hand smoothed the soft fur.

Claude's mouth fell open. To cover his astonishment, he put the beer to his lips and took several long swallows.

'I was doing a story about a spate of missing pet cats. After Venus disappeared during a storm, I went to Mayfield Avenue to interview her owner. Isla Bright had seen something that day: the driver of a blue ute who dumped a sack in the creek. We went to investigate and by chance found Venus stuck in a drain. We found something more. The sack was hooked on a branch over the water. We opened it and found grisly remains. Later the police confirmed the animal carcasses were greyhounds.'

The colour drained from Claude's face. 'I never killed any greyhounds. I never killed anything in my life.'

'You'd better explain yourself, mate,' Seth said with a hint of menace. He hadn't heard this story before; his admiration of Cate's investigative skills skyrocketed.

Claude said, 'A client of mine is a trainer. If a dog must be put down, she does it with a lethal injection. Sometimes I dispose of the bodies.'

'You *dump* them in *creeks*?' Cate was beside herself.

Claude gave an awkward shrug. 'I'm not a wealthy man. She pays me to take them to the animal crematorium. Waste of money if you ask me.'

'For the love of God!' Cate snorted.

'Whoa! Keep it down.' Seth's voice was calm. 'Apart from a minor misdemeanour—illegal dumping—he hasn't done much wrong.'

She stuck out her jaw. 'You must hate animals.'

'We all do things we regret.' Claude looked miserable. 'And for the record, I love animals, especially dogs. And in particular, I love greyhounds. They're noble creatures. Intelligent, full of personality. But a dead dog is a dead dog. You have to do something with its body. I helped because Lola was cut up about losing three of her best racers in a week. And if I didn't come up with the cash, Lefty would've had my balls for dinner.'

'Who's Lefty?' said Seth.

'An SP bookie I know.'

An uncomfortable hush fell. The heater clicked and buzzed. Claude finished his beer. Cate's remained untouched on the table.

'And after Isla's death you took her cat!' She wasn't letting go.

'She asked me to look after her. What else could I do? Isla was a good friend. Look, I've never been part of that live baiting caper. Believe me. The very thought makes me sick to the stomach.' Claude clicked his fingers to Kat. Mewling, she ran to him and leapt onto his lap.

Cate lowered her eyes. She seemed to be struggling with herself. 'Tell me this then. Why did you bring us the key? Why didn't you go straight to the cops?'

Claude sighed. 'I thought it'd be an easy way out. I'm sorry if it caused any trouble.'

After a pause, Cate sighed and dropped her shoulders. 'I'm sorry too.' She reached for the tinnie and took a mouthful.

It was getting late. They had to go. To make good his promise, Seth had booked a table for two at *Le Poisson* for seven. He took the scarlet key from his pocket. 'The reason we came here was to return something that belongs to you.'

One glance at the key and tears filled Claude's eyes. 'That was Isla's.'

'And now it's yours.'

Claude shook his head but Seth pressed the key into his hand.

Without another word they left. No doubt, Darren would break the news about the inheritance later. Seth wished he could be a fly on the wall when he did.

Epilogue

Monday 3 August

For Isla's third and final tattoo session, Jet brought the equipment to Mayfield Avenue. By then she was so weak she could no longer travel to Goongulli, not even by taxi. The morphine took the edge off the pain but left her exhausted. It took all her strength to drag herself from the bedroom to the toilet and back. Two days ago she'd stopped eating.

On the bed, she rolled onto her stomach while Jet prepared the ink. He made his own with powdered pigment and sterilised water. Except today Isla insisted that he use a special phial from her medicine cabinet.

On the slab of slate, he mixed blue and red powder with the clear liquid. The tattoo gun buzzed and he started to colour the wings. A touch of pink, a highlight of yellow. He kept saying how beautiful they looked. How those wings would carry her pain away.

He worked his way down her back. The pressure on her skin was light, as if he were using the back of a spoon instead of a needle. Perhaps it was the morphine or the drug in the phial, but the sensation was not unpleasant.

She knew what would happen; she'd planned it to the minute. Her gift to Claude would take him from poverty to comfort. She smiled. He'd helped her enormously; now she could return the favour. The world was good.

Her eyes closed. Consciousness faded. She stretched out a hand, touched the softness of fur. Beside her, Venus was purring. All was ready; she was nearly done.

Later, she was woken by a pain shooting through her jaw. The bedroom was dark; she was alone. Her throat was as dry as a desert. Getting up, she blundered to the hallway.

The house was slowly spinning. She stumbled, fell. As fragile as an eggshell her bones cracked on impact. All the breath was knocked out of

"

her; she couldn't get it back. Blind with panic and numb with fear, she lay helplessly on the cold hard tiles.

Then she remembered the angel wings.

Where would they take her?

Now nothing else mattered. Not the breath, not the pain.

The wings moved and she gently lifted from the floor. Her body became light and the pain melted away.

At last she was free.

Acknowledgments

~ Thank you ~

Brisbane Book Authors for your stimulating ideas, generosity and support

Ruth Bonetti, writing buddy extraordinaire, for pep talks, encouragement and empathy

Lucretia, Marianna and Gert for energy-giving thoughts and validation

The tattoo studios I contacted for letting me peek into an unfamiliar world

Devotees of *Baby Farm* for hounding me to write the next book

Sam, my wonderful husband, for enduring long hours of solitude when my mind was otherwise occupied

Elise, my creative daughter, for the beautiful cover design.

About the author

Debbie Terranova is a prize-winning author of historical fiction and crime mysteries with a conscience. She has been writing creatively for more than ten years and has published novels, novellas, and short stories.

Enemies within these Shores, historical fiction about life, love, and internment in Australia during World War Two, is her third novel.

Crime mystery novels, *Baby Farm* and *The Scarlet Key,* are gripping romps in and around Brisbane, featuring a dynamic duo of journalist super-sleuths, Seth VerBeek and Cate Bradshaw.

Mowbray Bathers, a heart-warming short story about coming of age and brotherly love, was a winner of *One Book Many Brisbanes* in 2011.

Connect with Debbie Terranova

Website: terranovapublications.com
Email: terranovapublications@gmail.com
Facebook: Terranova Books

Other titles by Debbie Terranova

Baby Farm, companion novel to ***The Scarlet Key***
How much is a baby worth?
Politician Vann Willis is on track to find out when a blast rips through her electoral office. Her Inquiry into forced adoptions and surrogacy has uncovered crooked deals so she forms an unlikely partnership with investigative reporter, Seth VerBeek.

Together, they explore the seamy side of Maidenhead, a gothic homestead that was once a hideaway for pregnant teens. Now, its electrified fence suggests the enterprise is far more sinister.

Dark secrets emerge. Vann's life is under threat. One relationship ends while another blossoms. At the heart of it all is the baby farm.

Enemies within these Shores, historical fiction
What really happened on Australia's home front during World War II?
Spring 1939. To appease his electorate, Delahunty orders a police roundup of Italian sugarcane workers. With his marriage failing, he initiates a volatile affair with Amy. What will be her revenge?

Summer 1941. Canefarmer Luigi is a naturalized British citizen, yet he is classified as an enemy alien during the war. Captured and interned for three years, what will he find on his return?

Autumn 1943. Edith is the wife of Tony Zucchero, an accountant and canefarmer. When he is unjustly interned, her father refuses to help. How will a city girl manage the farm alone?

Winter 1945. At Loveday Internment Camp, shell-shocked WWI veteran Ted prevents a breakout and an uprising and oversees secret experiments for the army. After the war, what will he do with his life?

Mowbray Brothers, short fiction
Saturday night, summer of 1920. Mowbray Park is where the local lads go for a laugh, a beer, and a smoke. Eight-year-old Lucky sneaks out of bed to discover his brother and hero has taken a dare that could cost much more than his one shilling bet.

Mowbray Brothers is set in world that no longer exists. An era of gaslight, rattling trams, Saturday night sing-songs, and a sand-bottomed river with a bathing enclosure at its edge. Inspiration came from the author's father and his stories of growing up in Brisbane in the 1920s.

Baby Farm

Sample pages

Tuesday, 18th February

He was back. Steptoe. The rag and bone man whose life story was a question mark. Unmistakable in the same khaki greatcoat, scarlet beanie, and football shorts that he wore summer and winter alike. The coat was unbuttoned, the only concession to the heat of the morning. It flapped about his hairy legs like flying fox wings.

From the front seat of the taxi, Vann watched him lumber up the hill.

Today he carried a grubby green shopping bag, the reusable type you'd get for a dollar from the supermarket to save the planet. Steptoe wouldn't use it to take the groceries home. For him it would be a blanket, or a rain hat, or a groundsheet, or a container for an arsenal of scrap metal. Everything had a vast array of uses. Today's effort must have been heavy, for he held the bulging bundle with both arms against his chest.

His progress through the morning crowd was erratic. In the crush around the railway station everyone conformed to unspoken laws. Like sheep, they followed the leader down the ramp to the platform. They kept to the left—always to the left—the same side as the traffic on the road.

But not Steptoe.

Whatever was on his mind—*if* there was anything on his mind—blinded him to the customs of the flock. People flowed around him as if he was a tree stump in a stream. Except he pushed against them, bumping them away without the usual muttered *sorry* that was part of the etiquette.

Just as the taxi found a space to turn from the driveway onto the road, Steptoe reached the external stairs of the electorate office.

Vann Willis MP Member for Riverdale, the sign read. Beneath in smaller letters, *Minister for Communities*.

As he laboured up the steps, Vann caught a glimpse of his determined expression. His eyes were focussed on the glass door at the top as if nothing would get in his way. What did he want this time? A tremor of foreboding rippled through her mind. For a moment she considered telling the taxi driver to stop so that she could nip whatever it was in the bud. But she was already cutting it fine for an important meeting in town.

She sighed and turned her attention to the papers she'd prepared. In half an hour she would be centre stage for ten precious minutes. In that short time, she would have to sell her proposal to the Premier and her Party colleagues. Compensation for the victims of forced adoptions. She had been chipping away at the 'elephant in the room' ever since she'd gone into politics long ago. Recently she had made progress on the tail of a senate enquiry and a royal commission into other unmentionables such as the treatment of children in orphanages and paedophilia by clergymen.

There was also a down side. Her worthy cause came with a price tag. Sadly, there were no hidden buckets of money in government coffers. Seven years after a global financial crisis triggered a spree of altruistic spending, a dark cloud of austerity had settled over the state budget. It would have been easier to let matters slide, but an election promise was still a promise. For many reasons she was determined to keep it.

The line of traffic outside her office had not moved. Cars were honking a P-plate driver who'd broken down at the lights. With the papers for the meeting on her lap, Vann reached into her satchel for reading glasses. Then she remembered they were sitting on her desk. Holding the page at arm's length did nothing to stop the print from going blurry. Her presentation would be impossible without them.

She glanced at the screen on her phone. Big bold numerals showed it was 9:07 a.m. The traffic was gridlocked. Over the course of five minutes the taxi had gone exactly nowhere. She touched the number for her office.

Freya's bright voice answered, professional as always.

Vann said, 'Can you get my glasses? I'm outside, stuck in traffic.'

'James already noticed them. He's bringing them down.'

'There he is!' Vann waved to her young policy advisor as he trotted toward the taxi. He was smiling, teeth impeccably white, eyes so blue you could swim in them. At twenty-seven he oozed confidence and ambition. If only she were his age again!

Freya's voice dropped to a whisper. 'By the way, Steptoe is here.'

Vann sighed. Of course he was there. Again.

'Oh, and a package just came. Marked to you. Personal,' said Freya.

'It's probably sales stuff. I'll get it later. What does Steptoe want?'

James and the reading glasses had almost reached the taxi.

Freya breathed into the phone. 'I don't know. He's behaving kind of strange. It's as if——'

KA-BOOM!

The explosion rocked the taxi, banging Vann's head against the door.

'Holy crap!' yelled James as he dived for cover.

Glass shards pelted the bonnet like hail. Down the concrete staircase rolled a thunderous cloud of smoke.

Vann's jaw dropped, her eyes glued to the awful spectacle. One minute her office was there; the next it was a raging ball of fire. Surreal, fascinating, incredible. Like seeing footage of the planes slamming into the World Trade Centre all over again. Over the years she must have seen it a hundred times and still it was impossible to believe.

Suddenly she remembered the half-finished conversation with Freya. She lifted the phone to her ear. 'Freya?'

No reply.

'Freya. Can you hear me? Freya!'

The connection was dead. Bile rose up Vann's throat. For a moment she thought she might be sick. Then, swallowing hard, she managed to muster her courage.

Flinging open the cab door, she raced toward the churning smoke. Somewhere inside that mess was Freya, her friend and confidante. This could not be happening! It must be a terrible dream.

Flames licked the entrance to the building. Smoke stung her eyes, burnt her nostrils, filled her lungs. Unable to get within fifteen metres of the place, she retreated to the taxi. Powerless, she could do nothing but hope and pray.

Standing beside her, James was on the phone to the emergency services. In an even voice, he described what had happened and gave the address in Riverdale.

How could he be so calm? His life had been saved by a pair of spectacles. One minute later and he might have been dead. Just like ...

The cacophony of car horns, alarms, sirens, the crackle and crash of fire converged into one chaotic roar. The upper floor of the two-story office block was now alight. Flames lapped the adjoining structure. People scattered like crazy ants. Some who had been struck by glass or debris lay moaning on the ground. Everywhere there was blood.

Numb and sickened, Vann leant against the vehicle. The driver was pacing around the cab, examining the damage to the paintwork. He shook his head and made tutting noises, as if a few dents were the major catastrophe of the day.

A high scream snapped Vann out of her stupor.

The clouds of smoke momentarily parted. Writhing on the staircase was a woman of about forty. Her blouse and skirt were covered in blood. A yellow handbag lay close by, its contents scattered like confetti across the pavement.

Her face was glistening with shards of glass. She began to convulse.

Vann baulked at the sight of all that blood. Then adrenalin kicked in. Swallowing her revulsion, she forced herself on.

The woman reached out her hand.

Vann held it, cold and slimy as a fish.

The woman's breathing became shallow. She was slipping in and out of consciousness.

Vann squatted beside her. 'You're okay, honey.' Her stomach was knotted but her voice was calm.

On the pocket of the blouse was a nametag. *Lara.*

'Lara,' said Vann. 'Can you hear me?'

The eyelids lifted slightly then closed.

'Lara, stay with me.'

The air was thick with a metallic stench. Another wave of nausea rolled over and away. Vann focussed on holding Lara's slimy red hand. The nails were neat and natural; there were no rings. It was the hand of an office worker or a teacher or a librarian. A lover of books, like herself.

'You're okay. You're okay.' Vann repeated the mantra again and again. But in her mind she was screaming *where the hell's the ambulance?* Hot flushes shot up her neck. Her heart was racing.

Only last week the Minister for Health had bragged in Parliament about *his* world-standard emergency callout times. She had a good mind to ring the idiot and tell him exactly what he could do with *his* statistics.

After what seemed like an eternity, the howl of sirens cut through the confusion. Two fire appliances roared onto the footpath. Men in helmets and protective clothing unrolled and fitted hoses. Jets of water gushed into the core of the blaze.

Meanwhile the grip on Vann's hand was loosening. She shook Lara's arms in an effort to keep her awake. That's what they did on TV medical dramas. With no first aid training, it was all Vann had to work with.

An ambulance siren. Finally! She waved to get their attention.

Paramedics came and eased the limp form onto a stretcher. Vann scooped up cosmetics, cards, keys, coins from the footpath, replaced them in the yellow leather handbag. It was an expensive brand. Mimco.

She zipped it shut and put it in the back of the ambulance near the stretcher. 'See you soon, honey.'

'Are you a relative?' asked the paramedic.

'Just a friend. Where will you take her?'

'The Royal if we can get in.'

'Please look after her.'

The paramedic gave her a reassuring smile. 'Of course we will.'

Lights flashing and sirens wailing, the ambulance sped away.

Vann glanced at the screen of her phone. Less than an hour had passed since the world turned upside down. A smoking ruin was where her office used to be. And Freya … she blocked the thought before it could fully form.

Blue-and-white police tape criss-crossed the footpath, marking the boundary between the crime scene and the zoo. Calamities always attracted a motley audience of stickybeaks and do-gooders.

A two-man team from Channel Six News had set up. The reporter, in standard attire of faded jeans and smart navy jacket, was positioned so that the smouldering building was the background. He was interviewing an eyewitness, a young man with short blond hair and a slim black suit.

Vann gazed beyond them at the shell of steel and concrete. It could have been her who'd taken the brunt of a madman's plot. No, it *should* have been her. Something she had said or done must have made Steptoe snap. She rolled back her memory.

Several months ago, before he last disappeared, Steptoe had gone to her for help. He was facing eviction from the ramshackle boarding house he called home, so she'd gone to see the landlord on his behalf.

What she'd found had shocked her. In the backyard was a collection of junk that dwarfed the Willawong dump. Tyres, bicycle frames, ancient fridges, rusty paint tins, machine parts, roofing iron, cracked TV screens, garden gnomes, curls of chicken wire, a wooden ladder with three missing rungs, PVC pipes. Black plastic bags that oozed foul juices. God only knew what they contained and Vann had no inclination to find out.

Somehow she had convinced him to clean it up. He wasn't happy and he told her so. Despite his protests, she arranged for a man to cart it away and paid for it from her own wallet. It was a wonder the Council hadn't condemned the place. Reluctantly the landlord agreed to let Steptoe stay, on the proviso that he stopped bringing home other people's rubbish.

For all her trouble, he did a disappearing act soon afterwards and hadn't resurfaced until this morning.

She should have followed him up, kept a better eye on him. She had no idea where he had gone or why. Perhaps he bore her a grudge for taking away his hoard. For, just like his namesake in the vintage British comedy series, the items he acquired were treasured like family heirlooms.

Whatever his movements had been, she should have been more alert. In hindsight, he had been a ticking time bomb. And now, along with his own troubled self, he'd wiped out at least one other soul.

Vann's attention returned to the TV reporter who was babbling on. Actually, he was grilling the interviewee about the upcoming election. Since when did an eyewitness to a catastrophe become an expert in politics? It was all a bit bizarre. The blond man answering the questions had his back was towards her, but his voice was oddly familiar.

Then it came to her. He was Jake Stone, political rival and endorsed candidate for the People's Progressive Party (PPP). The young upstart was criticising her for ignoring the plight of a homeless man and neglecting her constituents in the pursuit of power.

The very hide of him! Point-scoring at a terrible time like this!

Seething, she balled her fists and took a step in his direction. She was smart enough to know that retaliation would make her look foolish but was too rattled to care.

Before she could open her mouth, a deep voice as smooth as chocolate floated across the crowd.

'Ms Willis, can I have a word?'

She spun around. It was *him* again. Her heart skipped a beat.

'Seth VerBeek, what are you doing here?' she said a little too sharply.

He was a senior reporter from *The Morning Post*. New to this city but not to the media, he'd established his career covering war zones in Europe and the Middle East for a Sydney newspaper. His craggy appearance suggested a man who enjoyed a drink. His reputation as a ladies' man was the worst-kept secret in town. Despite this, his articles were well researched, insightful and even-handed. Besides, he was so easy going it was hard to not like him.

He sidled towards her. 'Good Lord,' he said frowning. 'Look at the state you're in!'

She looked down at her shoes, her skirt, her blouse. She could have passed as an axe murderer. The crisis had passed but the bloody evidence remained. In fact, it was all over her. Until now she'd managed to keep herself more or less in check. She began to shiver. Unexpected tears rolled down her cheeks.

He took her arm, guided her to a quiet corner by the garden wall. Like a gentleman he offered her a clean hanky.

Gratefully she accepted it, cleaned her fingers and blew her nose. 'Thanks, I'll wash it and send it back.'

'Keep it. I'm just glad you're okay.' He sounded genuine. After dipping into his pocket, he rattled a tin of Eclipse mints. 'Can I tempt you?'

The corners of her lips lifted. 'Perhaps another time.' Her mouth was as dry as the Simpson Desert. What she really needed was a good stiff Scotch. On the rocks. Double shot.

He tossed two mint pellets into his mouth. 'You want to tell me about it?' Casually he leant against the wall. 'Off the record of course.'

Vann gnawed her lip, trying to stop trembling. 'I was on my way to town.' With renewed disbelief she stared at the dismal scene and wracked her brain for answers. 'That bomb … it was meant for me.'

'Whoever would do such a thing?' Seth stroked his chin and followed her line of sight to the skeleton of the building.

She looked down at her palms. The creases—the life line, the heart line, the head line—were marked out in dried blood. She rubbed them together and brushed off the sticky red rolls. 'I have no idea.'

In her mind there was only one suspect. But before she exposed him, she had to make sure. Dead, as he most certainly was, he was no longer a threat to anyone.

People never ceased to amaze her, even those she knew and trusted. That was why she loved her work. Her community programs tapped into the vagaries of human nature and sought to mend broken lives. Sometimes they worked, which gave her joy. When they didn't, she rationalised them as *learning opportunities* and moved on. Steptoe was one big learning opportunity. One day he'd be as lucid as a professor, the next he'd be a mumbling idiot. Yet despite his mood swings and curious behaviour, she'd never picked him as a violent type.

One burning question haunted her. Why?

'Thanks for the moral support,' she said to Seth. 'And for the hanky.' Her self-control returned. Without it she'd never have survived a lifetime in the dirty game of politics.

The TV spotlight swept over the crowd and found her hidey hole. The reporter in the jacket was metres away, the cameraman close behind.

'Minister, was this a terrorist attack?' The reporter shoved the microphone under her nose. The scent of cheap aftershave tickled her nose.

With a stern expression, she held up her hands to stop. 'Not a word unless you show respect. I don't want this to look like a bloodbath.'

The reporter nodded his assent. The cameraman repositioned himself to get headshots only. The question about terrorism was repeated.

She looked directly into the camera. 'We'll have to see what the investigators come up with. In the meantime, I appeal to anyone with information to contact the police. My deepest sympathy goes to the victims and their families.' Her voice was steady, unemotional.

'Was your office specifically targeted?'

'Aren't you jumping to conclusions? For all we know, the explosion might have been caused by a gas leak.'

'Is it true you've received death threats?'

'People threaten me all the time. It comes with the job.'

'Witnesses say they saw a man in an overcoat just before the blast.'

'Perhaps they should tell that to the investigators. Now, you must excuse me.'

Outside Café Nero on the other side of Station Road, James was talking to a sergeant of police. Vann threaded her way between vehicles that jammed the roadway. An ambulance was parked across the footpath. At the foot of the stairs, paramedics waited for casualties who might come out alive. The building released a final puff of smoke. Fire fighters began to hack their way in.

'Any news about Freya Ekeberg?' Vann asked the police sergeant. She tried to sound upbeat but in her heart she knew.

'It doesn't look good, I'm afraid.'

Vann nodded. 'Has anyone called her family?' Her lips pressed into a narrow line.

James answered. 'Yeah, worst thing I've ever had to do.'

Against her will, tears again filled her eyes.

Usually James was as unemotional as a hit man in Tomb Raider. To her utter amazement, he opened his arms and drew her into his broad chest. She allowed herself the luxury of one giant sob, then she realised that he too was weeping.

As quickly as he had lost it, he pulled himself together. 'Leave this to me. You should clean up and go to that meeting in town. If you don't, you'll probably regret it.'

Before she could protest, he was on his phone for another taxi.

He was right. She needed to go. If she stayed, she'd only wallow in grief and self-pity and that would achieve nothing. The cabinet session would have long begun and it was a meeting she could ill afford to miss. If she was ever to get support for her proposed *Compensation for the Victims of Forced Adoptions Bill*, it was now. This would be the Holy Grail, the most important achievement of her career. The time was right, the mood was right. All the excruciating evidence had been unearthed, raked over, scrutinised *ad nauseam*. Money for the victims might help wash away their pain.

The taxi arrived. As was her habit, she sat in the front. Egalitarian society, she liked to argue. As the cab turned onto the road, she wound down the window and called out to James. 'I want to visit everyone who was hurt. Get their names and details.'

Again, the shockwaves ripped through her. She was glad of Seth's hanky, which she used to daub her eyes.

'Tough day, luv?' said the cab driver.

'The worst!' The finality of her statement shut down any further conversation. She was free to process her thoughts.

Today's events happened in other countries. International news was full of violence and bloodshed: the Bali bombings, 9/11 in New York, a passenger jet shot down over the Ukraine. No-one did those things in sleepy suburban Riverdale. Who was Steptoe really? The label *suicide bomber* didn't sit comfortably on his shoulders.

At her apartment, Vann quickly showered and changed into a cream suit. In the taxi again, her mobile phone showed two missed calls and three text messages. All were from Lance, her partner. She pictured him in the restaurant he owned with his brother in Paddington. He'd be wearing a white chef's cap, hounds-tooth trousers and black shirt. This time of day he'd be prepping for lunch. She pressed the recall button.

He answered at the first rang. 'Are you hurt, baby? I heard about it on the radio.' There was a quiver in his voice. In the background was the sizzle of a frying pan.

'I'm fine. Can't say the same for Freya though.' Tears again. If she wasn't careful she'd ruin her makeup. There'd be plenty of time for grief tonight, when she was alone in the apartment and Lance was on dinner shift at the restaurant.

At the end of their brief exchange he said, 'Why don't you give this away? We could get that farm at Maleny and enjoy life instead.'

She snapped back, 'I can't. There's a big job to do, and no-one to do it but me.'

'Then you're a misguided egotist!' he shouted and ended the call.

That didn't go as expected. Feeling peeved, she slouched in the seat. The line of jacaranda trees along Coro Drive blurred together as the taxi kept pace with a downstream ferry, laden with students and tourists. On the front deck, a man was taking snaps of his wife and kids against the jagged silhouette of city high-rises. Happy and carefree they seemed, unaware of the horrors of this smouldering summer's morning.

The road spilled into North Quay and the traffic lights lined up green. Vann had five minutes to concentrate on her pitch before entering the dog-eat-dog arena. No doubt the Premier and her colleagues would have heard the shocking news. For a few minutes they'd express support and sympathy. Then they'd debate their policy platform and strategies for the election soon to be announced. The Australian Conservative Party (ACP) needed to get it right, for the balance of power in government rested on the votes of two unlikely independents. The latest public opinion polls showed increased support for the dreaded PPP. If that young upstart Jake Stone were to be elected instead of her, she would never live it down.

At six o'clock in the evening, after many exhausting hours of debate and lengthy briefings, Vann headed to the Royal Hospital to fulfil a promise of a non-political kind. The air was thick with humidity, the twilight clouds glowed bilious yellow, the sign of a brewing storm. Her energy reserve was bordering on empty.

At the desk she asked about the three bombing casualties by name. As usual James had done a thorough job of research. Not only had he emailed her their names but also their home addresses and phone numbers.

'Lara Dainford is in ward 5F. Her condition is stable,' said the receptionist.

From the gift shop Vann bought three bunches of colourful gerberas, put on a bright face and navigated the labyrinth of polished lino and stark fluorescent lights to Ward 5F. The nurses' station was unoccupied, so she sat in the drab grey waiting area for someone to come.

Her only experience of institutions like this had been more than forty years ago, when she'd spent five miserable months in a dorm with nineteen girls. Often she'd wake in the night to the sound of her own weeping. Sensible shoes would click on the floorboards, a hard shadow would fall across her bed.

'Why aren't you asleep like the others?' the old bitch would snarl.

'I can't sleep in this place.'

'It's your own fault you are here. So shut up and don't be a cry-baby.'

Vann shuddered at the memory.

With no nurses in sight, she picked her way along the length of the corridor, checking bed numbers as she went, until she reached the cubicle at the end.

The shoebox was shared by six patients, separated by lime-milkshake coloured curtains, suspended from the ceiling. In the bed closest to the door was Lara, sound asleep on her back with her hands folded across her chest. She wore a primrose hospital-issue nightie. Her chestnut hair was tied back from her face, revealing a line of salt-and-pepper regrowth. Her face was a patchwork of dressings. Tubes and drip-lines attached her to the medical hardware on the wall. On the bedside table was a magnificent bouquet of pink roses and carnations.

For a few minutes Vann stood at the end of the bed and watched the rise and fall of Lara's chest. She was obviously knocked out with strong painkillers. Vann arranged the gerberas in a jar of water and scribbled 'get well soon' on the back of her business card.

The card on the big bouquet was tantalisingly under her nose. Like a thief she glanced around. The coast clear, she lifted it from the plastic holder and turned it over.

Dear Lara,
Hope you make a quick recovery. Best wishes always.
Jake Stone, your next Member for Riverdale.

Vann's mouth fell open. Over her dead body! Bring it on. This was war. The thought crossed her mind to swap the cards. Against the starburst of delicate pinks, her straggly gerberas looked limp and garish. No-one was looking and Lara was off on another planet. Did she dare?

After making the rounds of the other casualties, who also had spectacular floral tributes from Jake Stone, she hailed a cab outside the hospital. Lightning cracked over the western ranges, the air was crisp with the scent of coming hail.

Her last appointment at the Ekeberg residence was going to be tough. The inner strength that had powered her through the day was spent. The thought of the usual taxi-driver chat about the state of the economy or the cricket scores was enough to make her brain snap, so she slid into the back seat where she could quietly lick her wounds and think.

On any other morning Freya would have been at Café Nero for the office coffee order. Skinny flat whites all round. James would have been answering emails at his desk. Vann would have been on a teleconference in her private office instead of *en route* to a Party meeting in town. The tables would have been turned.

That bomb was meant for her. Of that, she was sure.

Why would Steptoe want to kill her? Granted he was as unpredictable as a cut snake but he wasn't a psychopath. Was he acting as someone's puppet? Someone who wanted her dead.

The taxi wove along Gympie Road, dodging buses and road works that never seemed to end. Lightning flashed like strobe lights, rendering the neon signs of the shopping strip dim. Her head throbbed, her eyes stung. Her handbag was stuffed with dozens of soggy tissues and one blood-stained hanky.

Maybe she should take Lance's advice and called it quits before the election. Retirement might have its benefits. For one, long nights of carefree sleep.

The cab dropped her at a modest weatherboard house with striped metal awnings. A coach lamp on the wall lit up the foliage of a blossoming Murraya bush. Its cloying sweet perfume triggered a rush of sneezes.

An icy gust propelled her through the gate. Hard rain smashed onto the path. Holding her handbag like an umbrella, she raced to the porch. The sounds of grief spilled through the doorway. Inside, human shadows moved about slowly.

She knocked.

A middle-aged woman came. Big breasts, fair hair, upturned nose. An exact replica of Freya, only older.

'Mrs Ekeberg?' said Vann.

'No. I'm Hanna, her cousin. Poor Hilda's in a bad way. Losing an only daughter like that. So horribly utterly dreadful …'

She howled for a moment, then mopped her face with a tea towel. 'Please excuse me, Ms Willis. I'm a bit upset. Do come in.'

Vann followed her into an old-fashioned living room where she met Freya's parents, two elderly aunts, and one dog. She sat in a floral armchair and listened through three cups of tea to stories about their beautiful girl. Inside, her heart was breaking, but she remained calm and strong for the sake of the family.

From its perch above the TV, a cuckoo clock announced the passage of an hour. Her head was as light as a balloon and her bladder was full of tea. When the taxi tooted, she hugged them all goodbye (even the dog) and promised to see them at the funeral.

The thunder storm had cleared, leaving the rich scent of moist earth. The city was washed clean. She inhaled, held the fresh air in her lungs like a drug, felt in its restorative powers a new sense of wellbeing. The cab rolled around the bends of Route 20 to Riverdale in the west.

Her tenth-floor apartment was exactly as she'd left it. Breakfast dishes in the sink, ironing in the basket, piles of papers on her desk. So cosy, so familiar. Yet, in that short space of time since this morning, her entire life had changed.

Vann poured herself a long-awaited Scotch and soda, turned off the lights, and sank into an easychair on the balcony. The first hit of alcohol took away her breath. She swallowed it like medicine, felt its warmth flow through her veins. As she nestled into the cushions, her eyes drifted across the nightscape. To the east was a forest of lights, sprinkled here and there with patches of dark foliage. To the west the suburbs petered out at the humped backbone of the ranges. Somewhere, in that vast twinkling curve, there must be an answer.

As she dozed in the chair, the kitchen light came on. She jumped up, the whisky glass rolled off her lap and broke on the tiles.

With her heart in her mouth she hissed, 'Who is it?'

'Only me.' Lance.

'You scared the shit out of me.'

'Thought you'd be in bed.'

She squatted and picked up the pieces of glass. The aftertaste of the Scotch was rough in her mouth.

He bent over as if to help but kissed her forehead instead.

'Ooow, that hurts.' She felt about the hairline and found a plum-sized lump where she'd hit her head on the taxi door. She leant in to him and breathed the heady scents of pasta sauce, garlic, and red wine that had seeped into his clothes.

'Sorry I didn't get home sooner. We were busy tonight.' He ambled to the kitchen and opened the pantry. 'A supremely shitty day all round.'

She wrapped the broken glass in newspaper and dumped it in the bin beneath the sink. The stink of last night's cabbage and pork bones reminded her to take the garbage out to the chute. By the time she came back, he'd made two cups of camomile tea with honey and lemon, and a toasted cheese sandwich.

'You want to talk?' he said.

Before she could stop herself, every sordid detail came tumbling out. 'I can't believe what happened. I saw it with my own eyes and I still can't believe it.'

'You were good on TV. Came across calm and sensible.'

'You know me. Always in control.' She gave a tight smile. 'Nevertheless, it should have been me in the morgue today.'

Lance squeezed her hand. 'I'm glad it isn't.'

Across the kitchen bench they embraced. Over the ten years they'd been together, their lives had become as comfy and sexless as old slippers.

Vann pulled away. 'I saw him from the taxi. I know who he was.'

'Did you tell the cops?'

She raked her fingers through her hair. 'What good would it do? Poor bastard's dead.'

'He tried to kill you and you're sorry for him?'

'Normally the man wouldn't hurt a fly.'

'So, who is this *harmless* murderer?'

'We knew him as Steptoe. You know, from the sixties TV comedy.'

'I lived out west, remember? No TV.'

'He collected old junk and castoffs but never sold a thing.'

'Why would this Steptoe fellow want to blow you up?'

She shook her head. 'I don't know but I intend to find out. He surely wouldn't have acted on his own. There must be another person behind it.'

'Then go to the police.'

'I will when I've worked it out. It could be some sort of political protest against our policies, or the budget cuts, or the job losses. Some people will stop at nothing to prove a point.'

Lance grasped her wrists and pulled her to him. He looked her straight in the eye. 'Are you sure you want to go through with this election? You don't have to. We have enough money. I don't want you to get hurt.'

'We've been over this many times. One more term. I can't let it go. There's too much to be done. The report from the Commission of Inquiry is due in a week.'

She gasped. 'Oh my God. That's it! Who's going to be exposed?'

Her mind was in overdrive, churning through the events and the individuals who'd come forward since the adoption inquiry first began. Nothing stood out, nothing made sense.

'What if you're wrong? What if it's a terrorist cell?' he said.

'You've been reading Jeffrey Archer novels again.' She flashed a wan smile.

He kneaded her shoulders. 'Your muscles are as tight as steel cables.'

Starting to relax, she turned to him.

He kissed her mouth, lifted her blouse, unclipped her bra, cupped her breasts in his warm hands.

It felt so good. She melted into him, sighed. It'd been a long time.

Then, like a lover in a trashy paperback novel, he scooped her into his arms and carried her to their bed.

*

If you enjoyed this sample of *Baby Farm* and would like to read more,
you can purchase a paperback edition or an eBook
from most online booksellers.

Check out my website *terranovapublications.com*
for more details.

www.ingramcontent.com/pod-product-compliance
Lightning Source LLC
Chambersburg PA
CBHW021013120726
47905CB00009B/2986